MURDER IN STYLE

MURDER IN STYLE

An Ellie Quicke Mystery

Veronica Heley

severn House

This first world edition published 2016
in Great Britain and the USA by
SEVERN HOUSE PUBLISHERS LTD of
19 Cedar Road, Sutton, Surrey, England, SM2 5DA.
Trade paperback edition first published
in Great Britain and the USA 2016 by
SEVERN HOUSE PUBLISHERS LTD

British Library Cataloguing in Publication Data
A CIP catalogue record for this title is available from the British Library.

ISBN-13: 978-0-7278-8630-9 (cased)
ISBN-13: 978-1-84751-735-7 (trade paper)
ISBN-13: 978-1-78010-799-8 (e-book)

All Severn House titles are printed on acid-free paper.

Severn House Publishers support the Forest Stewardship Council™ [FSC™],
the leading international forest certification organisation.
All our titles that are printed on FSC certified paper carry the FSC logo.

MIX
Paper from
responsible sources
FSC® C013056

Typeset by Palimpsest Book Production Ltd.,
Falkirk, Stirlingshire, Scotland.
Printed and bound in Great Britain by
TJ International, Padstow, Cornwall.

ONE

Thursday morning

Ellie's daughter was after money – again.

'Mother, it's the opportunity of a lifetime! I heard about it purely by chance, but we have to act quickly. I know you will want to support me—'

Ellie didn't know anything of the kind. What she did know was that when her difficult, demanding daughter rang it was either to ask for money, or to babysit young Evan. This time it was money. 'Sorry, Diana. Got to dash. You caught me just as I was leaving.'

'But Mother, this can't wait! Time is of the essence, and—'

Ellie looked at her watch. 'Diana, I'm on my way to the dentist. Ring me later?'

Diana started to object but Ellie crashed the phone down. Now, had she got her keys and did she need a jacket? It had looked like a nice morning, but . . .

The phone rang again. Almost, she let it ring. But didn't.

'Ellie, do you have a minute?' A tense, breathless voice.

'Not really.' It was her good friend from the police. 'Lesley? What's wrong?'

'Will you be in this afternoon, about three? There's someone I want you to meet.' Controlled panic in her voice?

'Is it serious?' Ellie glanced at the clock. 'I might. But—'

'Yes, it's murder. At least, I think it is. But then . . . Got to go. Speak later!'

Down went the phone and out of the door went Ellie, wondering how to juggle the errands she'd meant to run after she'd visited the dentist, who might be running late but – on the other hand – might be on time. It was only a routine appointment, and she didn't think anything needed to be done, but after that there was a whole lot of stuff she had to attend to: take a library book back, collect the dry cleaning, pop into the clock shop to see if that nice man could look at her watch which was losing time and . . . Where had she put her shopping list? She hadn't left it on the kitchen table, had she? Today of all days!

The doorbell rang. Three o'clock on the dot.

Ellie shucked off her gardening gloves, slipped out of her clogs and managed to ease her feet into her brogues on her way through the hall to the front door. It was a fine afternoon, if breezy, and she'd stolen a few minutes away to tie up some dahlias which the wind had torn away from their stakes.

She glanced at the clock. Very soon she ought to be in the kitchen, starting supper. Ellie and her husband didn't have people over for a meal very often and she wanted to do it properly. They did have a lodger in the flat upstairs who cooked for them occasionally, but this was not one of her nights, and Ellie was responsible for putting food on the table. She'd allowed herself enough time to prepare a steak and kidney pudding and set the table in the dining room . . . if all went well.

Bother Lesley! Didn't she know better than to inflict visitors on Ellie at short notice?

'Mrs Quicke? We're not intruding, I hope?' A sixtyish couple, prosperous, silver haired, well padded and half out of their minds with worry. They weren't too sure of their welcome, either.

'I'm Ellie Quicke. Do come in.' Ellie was also sixtyish, prosperous, silver haired and well padded. She understood these people. He would be a self-made businessman. A glance at the car parked in her drive confirmed that he wasn't short of a bob or two. His wife – presumably they'd been married a long time; they had that air of presenting a united front – was well groomed and expensively upholstered, but some trick of the light caused Ellie to imagine her in a comfortable wrap-around pinny, with her hair in a bun. A farmer's wife, perhaps?

The man held out his hand. A gold ring flashed. 'Cordover, Gerald. Builders. The wife, Marika. Good of you to see us at such short notice.' No smile. He was too worried for social niceties.

Mrs Cordover – Marika – said, 'We appreciate it.'

A slight sibilance? English was, perhaps, not her first language? Polish?

Ellie said, 'May I offer you tea or coffee?'

They shook their heads, so she led the way into her pleasant, high-ceilinged sitting room. They didn't glance around them but seated themselves on the settee with their eyes on Ellie.

The man said, 'I don't know that there's anything you can do. The policewoman said you might be able to think of something, but now we're here, I don't see what anyone can do.'

Ellie prompted them. 'My friend Lesley Milburn suggested . . .?'

'The thing is,' he said, giving every word its weight, 'it's all my fault.'

'That is not true!' Marika pressed his arm.

He said, 'I thought I was doing the right thing.'

'You were,' said Marika, comforting him. 'All these years, it has worked.'

Ellie understood that this wasn't the first time they'd had this discussion. He threw up his hands. 'I swear he killed her, though I can't prove it, and the police won't act.'

Marika turned her eyes back to Ellie. 'The police say there is nothing to prove she was murdered. But when the will is read, when he finds out he's killed her for nothing . . . what will he do then? His temper is very bad.'

Ellie decided she needed a drink, even if they didn't. 'Look, I've been working in the garden and I need a cup of tea. So, will you join me? If you'd like to wait here, I'll just put the kettle on—'

'The kitchen?' Marika was on her feet. 'We will be happy to have a cup of tea with you in the kitchen. Right, Gerald?'

Yes, they had the appearance of people who had started life with very little, who had worked hard all their lives, and who would feel at home in the kitchen. And, perhaps, an informal atmosphere would help them to explain their problem?

Ellie led the way back across the hall into the kitchen quarters.

Midge, their marauding ginger cat, was asleep on top of the fridge. He opened one eye a fraction, inspected the newcomers and closed it again. Midge was supposed to be a good judge of character, so Ellie took heart. If Midge liked her guests, so would she. Probably.

They sat round the old-fashioned table, and drank tea strong enough to stand a spoon up in, while Ellie passed the biscuit tin round. She glanced at the clock, calculating that if her visitors were to leave within the next half-hour, she'd still have time to make a steak and kidney pudding and follow it with an apple crumble. Rib-sticking fare for a chilly autumn evening. As this was a special occasion, she'd planned that they'd eat in the dining room, which was rarely used nowadays . . .

'Good biscuits,' said Marika, who would know a homemade biscuit when she saw one. 'You bake?'

'Our lodger is a student of cookery. These are some of hers.'

Almost, a smile from Marika, but her anxious attention never strayed far from her husband.

Rain rattled against the window, reminding them that the year was turning from summer into autumn. The central heating clicked on.

Gerald started, bringing his thoughts back from some dark place. 'We shouldn't have come. I don't see how you can help.'

Marika pressed his arm again. 'Start at the beginning.'

He ran his fingers back through well-cut but thinning hair. 'How far back should I go?' He addressed Ellie direct. 'My first wife died, you see. She'd come over from Poland to improve her English and found work as a cleaner. I serviced the boiler in the house where she was staying, and we hit it off. We got married and had the twins, both girls. Life was hard, but it was good. Then one day she was walking down the street with the girls in their pushchair and a lorry mounted the pavement and . . . that was it. She lived for nearly six weeks. Eventually we had to switch the support systems off. And there were my two little moppets, three years old, without a mother.'

Marika took over. 'She was my younger sister. I came over from Poland to look after the little ones.'

'So we comforted the girls, and one another.'

The glance they gave one another proved that theirs had been a good marriage.

He said, 'I've always worked hard, and I won't deny it helped that I got some compensation from the lorry company. I took better premises, employed staff. Marika did the books. So we upsized twice, no skimping, good schools for the girls, we gave them whatever they asked for within reason.'

'We did our best to teach them the value of money. They had an allowance but if they overspent—'

'Which they did.'

'—then they had to wait till the next month.'

Both nodded. Gerald picked up the story. 'When they left school, we paid for their driving lessons and we bought them a small car each and we encouraged them to go on to college. Poppy – she's the one who could add up without a calculator—'

They both smiled, proudly. Remembering.

Gerald continued, 'Poppy took a business course. And Juno – she's the artistic one – she got a place at art school.' Another proud smile. 'Of course they went out partying, particularly Poppy. They were in a great crowd, most of them we liked, and if some of them weren't quite what we wanted for our girls, well, it was better they worked that out for themselves. Maybe it was a mistake for us to keep open house because their friends could see we had money, what with the swimming pool and the cinema and all. But we couldn't have foreseen . . . we never dreamed . . .' He faded out, looking miserable.

Marika took a deep breath. 'They both got pregnant at eighteen. The men had both been going out with them for some time. They said they'd marry the girls if we helped them to buy a house each. It left a nasty taste, as if we had to pay them to marry our girls. If we'd picked husbands for them, we wouldn't have chosen those two.'

'It cost us an arm and a leg,' said Gerald. 'Identical town houses out in the suburbs, and they didn't come cheap even then. A big, double wedding. That cost, too. One boy was training to be a solicitor and the other was working in his father's garage, but I could see them thinking they were marrying money, that they'd be in clover for life.

'Marika and I, we talked it over. We've both seen marriages where the women have given up their careers to stay at home and look after the children. And then, when their women are past their best, the husbands go off with someone younger, leaving their untrained, stay-at-home wives on short commons. We didn't fancy that for our girls. So the first thing I did was to make them sign pre-nups, and I put the houses in the girls' names.'

'Sensible,' said Ellie.

A deep sigh. 'But then what did I do? I had the bright idea of setting the girls up in business together so that they wouldn't have to rely on their husbands for every penny. I bought them the lease on a shop and made them a loan so that they could open a boutique for classy clothing.'

Marika said, 'They pooled their childcare and worked hard. Juno bought the stock, Poppy did the accounts, and they both worked in the shop. It's called The Magpie, and it was a hit from the first day.'

'There was an unexpected bonus,' said Gerald. 'The lease included a flat above the shop. I advised the girls to fix it up and rent it out. I promised them that if they did well, I'd turn my starter loan into a gift. They took to it like ducks to water. At the end of the second year I wrote off the loan, plus I gave them the deeds to a couple of run-down terraced houses nearby, which I'd come by in a business deal and didn't want. I said that now they'd got the shop going, they could afford to take on some help, and could diversify into the buy-to-let business. I suggested that Juno could choose new kitchens, bathrooms, furniture and decor, while Poppy sourced materials and acted as project manager. It worked like a charm. Within a few years they turned the flat over the shop into an office, and later on they extended both the shop and flat out into the yard at the back.'

'So what went wrong?' said Ellie.

'Nothing. I got them to make wills in one another's favour, and to take out insurance on one other in case of accidents. The girls saw the point of that, didn't they?'

Marika sighed. 'Two years into their marriages, they understood they'd picked losers for husbands but, to give them their due, they kept going.'

'Chips off the old block. They enjoy work. But,' gloomy face, 'I hadn't liked the men when they'd first appeared on the scene, and I got to like them even less as time went on.'

Ellie looked a query.

Gerald said, 'Here's where I went wrong. I said to the girls that they should keep quiet about their buy-to-let business. The men knew about the shop, of course, and that it was doing well. They complained like mad that the girls had to spend such long hours at The Magpie, but they enjoyed having the extra money to spend, did they not! The girls agreed with me that it was best their menfolk didn't know exactly how well their wives were doing, in case the husbands gave up trying to earn their own livings altogether. Which, unfortunately, is what happened anyway.'

Marika looked as if she wanted to say something, but he raised his hand and shook his head. 'No, I know what you mean, we couldn't have anticipated the accident, but it's no excuse for his giving up work altogether. For this reason and that, Mrs Quicke, the men gradually let the girls take over all the household bills, fork out for holidays and cars and whatnot.'

'Meanwhile,' Marika said, 'we told our sons-in-law that Gerald and I were downsizing to pay for their houses. We didn't want them thinking we would be a purse without a bottom for them to draw on. Gerry's business was doing well, and we could have stayed on in the big house, but we did not need five bedrooms once the girls had left home, so we sold up and moved to a smaller property. Gerry hopes to work till the day he drops dead. I retired from doing the books for him some time ago, but I work for a charity three days a week. We are comfortable with what we have. We live quietly without any desire for foreign holidays or yachts or diamonds.'

Gerald said, 'The twins tried to be strict with their daughters – they had one each. Poppy and Juno didn't want the girls growing up to think that money grew on trees, but they could see that even though the men weren't pulling their weight, there was always plenty of money in the kitty. Trixie in particular thinks she can carry on spending regardless – no matter what her mother says.' He corrected himself. 'What her mother *said*. Trixie thinks she was born to shop. I believe her.'

'Clemmie's not like that.' Marika's mouth closed in a thin line.

'True,' said Gerald, but he didn't seem to like thinking about Clemmie, either.

Ellie refreshed the teapot, and pushed the biscuit tin round again. She shot another glance at the clock. She was going to have to cook the steak in the microwave before making the suet-based pastry. There wasn't going to be time to do the usual slow cook, was there? Perhaps she'd better abandon her plan to open up the dining room tonight. 'So, what went wrong?'

Marika dabbed at her right eye, and then her left. 'Ray – that's Poppy's husband who runs the garage on the ring road – he's always placed the odd bet but as the years went on, he spent more and more time and money on what he called "his little hobby". Poppy used to cover his debts, because he always promised never to . . . but of course he didn't keep his promises and it got worse and worse. She couldn't bear the thought of divorce, but she was starting to think she might have to go down that road when he found out through a wrongly addressed bill that The Magpie wasn't just the shop, but that there were a number of other properties involved. That did it! He said she was a treacherous, lying so-and-so, and how dare she try to conceal her business affairs from him, her husband who had never looked at another woman, not once in all the time they'd been married. He threatened to divorce her and take half of everything she owned.'

Gerald said, 'To make matters worse, he told Trixie that Poppy had been hiding a small fortune from them. So then Trixie started up, wanting her mother to finance her going into films! Can you believe it?'

'What!' Ellie choked on the biscuit she was eating.

Her guests both nodded. Ellie hadn't misheard.

Marika said, 'Trixie said it wasn't going to be a porn film. She thought that made it all right. She said she had friends who can operate a video and they'd hire in lighting and pay for studio time and . . . she has no idea of the costs involved, none! There was a family meeting at our house which went from bad to worse, and later that night Poppy fell down the stairs at The Magpie, and broke her neck. She's been up and down those stairs almost every day for twenty years with never a slip. She wasn't wearing high heels, and she wasn't carrying anything.'

'Accidents will happen,' said Ellie, trying not to look at the clock again. If they ate in the dining room, that would mean buffing up the best silver. She was running out of time. 'What makes you suspect foul play?'

Silence.

Ellie looked from one to the other. 'You think Ray or Trixie tumbled her down the stairs?'

'We're sure Ray did it but—' he made a gesture of frustration – 'there's no proof. Unbreakable alibi and no forensics, the police said. The detective inspector. He said our "feelings" weren't evidence. But I *know*, I just know that she was murdered. That woman police officer, she knows it too. That's why she said we should talk to you, Mrs Quicke, to see what you could do about it.'

Ellie spread her hands. 'I don't see what I can do.'

Marika said, 'I think you can help us if you wish, Mrs Quicke. That policewoman was telling us how you get people to talk to you, and how you have no fear of anybody, and have solved some nasty cases.'

'I'm just a housewife who happens to have inherited some money, which I've put in a trust fund to . . . ah!' She saw their expressions sharpen.

'That's it!' Gerald thumped the table. 'We could introduce you to the family, saying that you have a fund which Trixie might be able to tap into for her career. Then you could keep your eyes open, couldn't you? See if you can spot how he killed her?'

'But it's a charitable trust which would never, ever—'

'No, of course they wouldn't,' said Marika, 'but you can make it an excuse to get to know them? Gerry's right about one thing. The family's like a, what do you call it? A pressure cooker at the moment. There's grief; oh yes, there's deep grief with some. It tears my heart to see them suffer. But Poppy's husband and daughter . . . Well!' She threw up her hands in frustration and, yes, perhaps some anger as well. 'I do not deny there is some shock, and perhaps later on there will be sorrow, but of all the selfish, self-centred . . .! I see them smiling, talking about silver linings and I can't bear it. And tomorrow . . . oh dear!'

Gerald said, 'You see, Ray and Trixie think they'll inherit Poppy's share of The Magpie. He's already been on the phone to his pals, boasting how he can pay off his debts and sail away into the sunset . . . by which he means getting back to the gaming tables. And she's texting her mates, planning how to use the money for her venture into films—'

'What they don't realize is that Poppy only ever made one will, and that's the one leaving everything to Juno. I checked with the solicitor. Zilch. I checked with Juno; she hasn't made another will, either. They did talk about it recently because of Poppy having come to the end of her patience with Ray, but neither of them had done anything about it. I dread to think how they will react when the truth comes out.'

Marika added, 'Ray and Trixie know there is some other property, but they don't know how much. It's true the girls started with two small terraced houses—'

'But they've worked hard and reinvested. Now they have ten! Whatever's going to happen when the will is read? There's going to be such an explosion! And Juno, poor Juno, she's devastated. How she's holding it together, I do not know. To tell the truth, I'm worried sick what might happen. When Ray realizes the money all goes to Juno, won't he try again?'

Marika reached out to take Ellie's hand. 'We want you to come to the funeral and on to the house afterwards.'

'My poor Poppy. My brave little girl,' said Gerald, on the verge of breaking up.

Marika said, 'Mrs Quicke; when there is screaming and shouting, people are not always careful what they say, and sometimes the truth will come out. So, will you help us find out who killed our little girl?'

'No, no. I really don't think—'

Gerald got to his feet, leaning on the table. 'No, Marika. She won't. I said, didn't I? I said, "Why should she help us?"'

'Because,' said Marika, 'a great wrong has been done. I know we may never have proof that Ray killed our daughter, but perhaps we can stop his destroying our granddaughters as well. I have prayed about it and I know Mrs Quicke will help.'

Ellie understood that Marika was a good woman, strong and

sturdy, and that she would survive this and keep her husband on an even keel. Perhaps she would even save the remaining members of their family . . . with help.

Dear Lord, what do you want me to do?

Ellie knew. Of course. Her mind raced ahead to the forthcoming week, and she realized without any sense of surprise that she was comparatively free of engagements. Had God prepared the way for her? Possibly. Though, if He wanted her to get involved, it wouldn't have mattered how many coffee mornings and meetings and evening events she was supposed to attend. But as it was . . .

'Come to the funeral, midday tomorrow.' He produced a card, wrote on the back. 'Here's the details. Contact me at any time. Day or night.'

Ellie closed the front door behind her visitors, her mind racing ahead. How was she to rescue her plans for supper? It was too late to serve anything which required a long, slow cooking time, which meant . . . and she hadn't set the table in the dining room and . . .

The phone rang. Pulling a face at the interruption, Ellie lifted the receiver. She might have known! It was her police friend Lesley ringing back. 'Ellie? Did they come?'

'The Cordovers? Yes. Lesley, I honestly don't know that I can do anything—'

'I know, I know.' Annoyed. 'Poppy fell down the stairs of her own accord, right? Let's put it down to suicide or an accident, and tidy it away, shall we?' Sarcasm unlimited. Lesley really was wound up over this, wasn't she?

Ellie tried to keep calm. 'Was there any reason for her to commit suicide?'

'No. Added to which, throwing yourself down a flight of stairs is not exactly a sure-fire way to kill yourself, is it? You might get a broken bone or two, but as an efficient way of committing hari-kari it's a no-no.'

'There was some mention of divorce?'

'The husband, Ray, is a right whatsit! Scum of the earth, that one. Yes, she might have had to pay him off, but good riddance, if you ask me!'

'Look, Lesley; I've got people coming for supper and I'm way behind with—'

'It stinks, Ellie. Believe me. There's something seriously unpleasant going on there. I agree that the fall down the stairs might have been an accident, but there's something wrong. I can smell it. Even my boss got a whiff of it, and you know he couldn't smell rotten fish if it leaped up and smacked him on the nose. But he's stuck, as I am, because there is no evidence to prove she was murdered. Yet I *know* . . .! Well, all right, I can't *know!* But how else to describe how I feel about it? I *believe* that it would be a miscarriage of justice if nobody looked into it any further. I've been yanked off on to another case, and I'm up to my eyeballs with the wedding and stuff . . .'

Lesley and her live-in boyfriend were getting married in a fortnight's time, so it was understandable that she felt stressed.

'. . . so please, Ellie! Will you please look into it for me?'

'If I poke around a bit and find nothing, you'll let me off the hook?'

'Yes. I trust your instinct.'

Ellie looked at her watch. It was running slow. She hoped. She hadn't had time to take it into the clock repair man in the Avenue. She must try again tomorrow. 'Look, Lesley, I've got to go and start the supper. We have guests tonight, so—'

'One of your friends who lives locally? Might they have some gossip about the Cordover family?'

'It's Vera, who used to be our lodger and part-time house-keeper, the one who's now married to her old sweetheart, and Vera's teenage son – you remember him? Mikey? In and out of mischief, bright as a button, bless him. I had planned a big meal, but I'm running late—'

'Vera's pregnant, isn't she? And married to that teacher . . . what is he, deputy head at the high school? He might have known the Cordover grandchildren. They're all local. You could ask him.'

'Lesley! Shut up and let me get off the phone! It'll be bread and cheese for supper if I can't get on with it.' She put the phone down on Lesley, who was still talking, and raced through to the kitchen, glancing distractedly at the grandfather clock, which must surely be running fast. It couldn't possibly be that late, could it?

The phone rang again. Ellie knew, she just knew it would be Diana. Well, let it ring. Diana had married a much older man, a wealthy estate agent, but she was always looking out for a chance to make more money. Diana's schemes usually went awry and there was no way Ellie was going to put money into her daughter's latest crackpot idea, whatever it might be. Yes, she could hear Diana's sharp voice on the answerphone, ordering her mother to ring her . . . Now! Immediately! Urgent!

Well, tough. Now, how long before her guests arrived?

TWO

Thomas arrived home five minutes before their guests were due, to find Ellie in something of a panic. Racing from stove to fridge, she apologized for the shortcomings of the meal and for not having managed to set the table in the dining room. Half laughing and half serious, she said it was all Lesley's fault for trying to embroil her in some local family dispute!

Whereupon Thomas, who had long recognized that his wife had unusual gifts when dealing with people who'd got themselves into difficulties, gave her a hug and a kiss. 'My dear, if you've been called to arms again, then all I can say is, "What can I do to help?" Shall I dish up? Find some beer for Dan to drink? Take it from me, Vera and Dan won't be wondering why we haven't got the best silver out for them, and Mikey certainly won't notice.'

Upon which Ellie calmed down, and even managed to feed the cat before their guests arrived.

Instead of the steak-and-kidney pudding which Ellie had planned to make, she produced a pie. Even so, she'd had to take a number of short cuts to get the meal on the table on time. She'd pre-cooked the meat in the microwave, and used a packet of flaky pastry to go on top of the pie instead of fiddling with flour and shortening herself. But the top had browned nicely in the oven and the pie had tasted all right, praise be.

She'd made mashed potatoes to go with the pie, plus a small mountain of carrots and cauliflower sprigs. The real, genuine, home-cooked apple crumble afterwards had gone down a treat. All right, the apples had been rescued from the freezer, but nobody cared and everyone had seconds.

Once they'd scraped the last mouthful of apple crumble off their plates, Ellie relaxed and remembered to ask Dan if he recalled the Cordover grandchildren. 'They wouldn't be called

Cordover, of course. Their mothers were twins called Poppy and Juno and I haven't a clue what their married names were, so really I have no business bothering you with this, as they must have left school long before you became a teacher. Their children are the next generation down, and I suppose they'll have left school maybe a year, maybe two years ago? There's . . . let me think,' Ellie rubbed her forehead. 'Trixie, who was born to shop and . . . Clemmie . . . is that right? They'd be cousins. I'm burbling because, come to think of it, they would probably have gone to private schools.'

Mikey, the teenager, took no notice of the conversation. He was sprawled across the table, teasing Midge, who pretended to be annoyed but was actually enjoying the attention. Those two had always got on well.

Mikey's stepfather passed his plate down the table for Thomas to put in the dishwasher, saying, 'That's an unusual combination of names. Trixie and Clemmie. No, I don't remember any girls of that name at school, but . . . Trixie? Trixie?' He turned to his wife, 'Didn't you mention a Trixie, or Trixibelle recently? Could it be the same one?'

Vera had been working in Reception at the big hotel nearby until the previous weekend when she'd gone on maternity leave. 'Way back, when I was a wage earner?' Vera patted her bump. 'That's right. I did tell you about her, didn't I? The thing is, Ellie, that a local photographer has been running a competition in the local paper, and invited the prizewinners to the hotel for the prize-giving ceremony. Bouncing Babies, Beautiful Teens, Glorious Grannies, that sort of thing. The babies squalled, the teens tossed their hair around, and the Grannies tried to talk one another down. Chaos!'

'You think a girl called Trixie was involved?'

Vera nodded. 'If it's the same one, she was something else! Her bright red lipstick matched the bandeau round her hair, which matched the red polka-dot dress she was wearing. Very fifties, I thought . . . Not that I was born then. She wasn't the most beautiful girl there and she was, if I remember rightly, a little older than the rest – perhaps nineteen? – but she had a certain something. I could see why they didn't give her first prize – which went to a stunning Indian girl – but I could also

see why they couldn't overlook her. She was the runner-up. I
can't remember her second name. I suppose it was in the
paper.'

'Newspapers! Do you still keep them for recycling?' Mikey
sprang up from the table and darted across the room to scrabble
among the old newspapers which Ellie had put aside for recycling but which hadn't got any further than the ledge by the
back door. Mikey riffled through the top ones and brought a
selection back to the table. 'If it was in the local paper, it should
be here, right?'

'Not now, Mikey,' said Vera. He ignored her to deal out
papers round the table.

Thomas was amused, rather than annoyed. 'Let me have
the rest of the dirty plates, Ellie, will you?'

Mikey said, 'Would she be a Page Three girl?'

Vera said, 'Not in the *Gazette*. Family fare. The girls I saw
were fully dressed. Got it! Two weeks ago.' Vera folded the
paper over, and held a page up for them to see. Three pictures
of babies, three of pretty girls, and three of glamorous grannies.
'The middle one. Trixie something . . . Cordover?'

'Builders. Cordovers, the builders,' said Dan, turning pages
on another edition. 'They built our new sports hall. Did a good
job. You see their signs everywhere.'

Ellie peered over Vera's shoulder. 'Pretty girl. Unusual, as
you say. What we used to call "speaking eyes".'

'She's a tart,' said Mikey, also looking over Vera's shoulder.
'Bedroom eyes.'

'Mikey!'

'Do you prefer "slag"?' Mikey tried to look innocent.

His mother tapped him with the paper. 'She's probably a
very nice girl.'

Mikey grinned. 'Doesn't look it.'

Dan held up his hand. 'Cordover again. In last week's paper.
Listen to this. "Tragic accident at The Magpie. Poppy Cordover
was found at the foot of the stairs at her upmarket boutique on
Tuesday morning . . ." Blah, blah. "Her family are devastated.
Her husband, Ray Cocks . . ."' He suspended his reading to
remark, 'Cocks. There's a Cocks's Garage in Acton, isn't there?
Now, what do I know about them?'

Thomas was about to put the kettle on when the phone rang. He said, 'I'll take it,' and disappeared into the hall.

Ellie took over making tea. 'Builders' tea all round?'

'Let me help,' said Vera, trying to get to her feet and failing.

'Sit down, woman!' thundered Dan.

Vera said, 'Yes, sir!' in an unusually meek tone, and everyone laughed.

Thomas returned, looking annoyed. 'It's Diana. I said you had guests. She said she'd drop in to see you late tomorrow morning. Now, what were we talking about? Cocks's Garage? I know them by repute. Dicey.' Thomas never said anything bad about anyone, so this was tantamount to accusing the garage of committing all seven of the deadly sins.

'Really?' said Dan. 'Not that I use them.'

'I spoke out of turn. I might be wrong. Someone told me a long story about being overcharged. Take no notice. They're probably as pure as snowflakes.'

Dan looked thoughtful but resumed his reading. 'Well, I suppose you can understand why mother and daughter kept the Cordover name rather than using "Cocks". In the paper here they say how much the family will miss their lovely, caring wife and mother, who died on the premises of the boutique to which she had devoted her life. They say, "She is always in our thoughts." There's an announcement of the death and funeral on the opposite page. Mm . . . they say . . . crematorium at noon, immediate family and friends only. "No flowers by request." That's a pretty terse send-off. Nothing about going on somewhere afterwards. I wonder why not? Nice-looking woman, I must say.' He passed the paper over for Ellie to see.

Ellie looked, and saw a heart-shaped face with a high, thin nose and long neck; flaxen hair in a pixie haircut, discreet make-up, diamond stud earrings, a fashionable dress that hadn't come out of Primark.

If she'd met this woman in the street, what would she have thought of her? A successful businesswoman? Someone you'd think you could touch for charitable purposes? She had a generous mouth.

What was it her father had said about her? Poppy, who didn't need a calculator to add up. Poppy, who acted as accountant for The Magpie concern, and was the project manager for their buy-to-let properties. Mm. Yes. This woman would have been formidable in her own way. Sharply beautiful, sure of herself . . . perhaps the fact that she had her own successful business gave her a poise beyond her years? She must be, what, knocking forty? But looked younger.

Ellie asked, 'Vera, have you ever shopped at The Magpie?'

'I've heard of it. I have friends who haunt the place. It's a bit out of the way for me.'

Mikey was still scanning the photos. 'I don't half fancy the girl who won the teenaged section. And phew! Look at that one! She can't be a granny, can she? Mrs Quicke, you ought to have entered for the Glamorous Grannies competition. I'd have voted for you.'

Everyone laughed at that because if there was one thing Ellie did not do, it was spend time and money on her appearance. Her skin was lovely and her silvery hair curled prettily, but she paid very little attention to what she wore and had been known to leave the house with a button missing from her coat, or wearing the clogs she'd slipped on while working in the garden.

'Well,' she said, 'tomorrow I have to go to the funeral, so I'd better smarten myself up for the occasion.' Also, it would be a good excuse to be out when Diana called.

Friday morning

Before she left next morning, Ellie managed to catch Thomas before he went into his study. 'I don't know if I'll be back for lunch or not. I have to go to the Cordover funeral at noon.'

Thomas gave her a hug. 'I'll be thinking of you, and praying. God bless.'

She phoned for a cab.

Crematoriums – or should it be crematoria? – seemed a bit other-worldly to Ellie. She imagined she could feel strong emotions lingering in the air from those who had occupied the pews before her. On the other hand, she'd attended one or two funerals which had attracted hardly any mourners. Ellie looked around her and gave a gentle sigh.

At some funerals the very air seemed dark with grief. And

at others, people were looking at their watches even as they arrived, anxious to shuffle off the deceased to . . . wherever . . . and to get on with life. This one was a nice mix of irritation and sorrow.

Ellie wore her best midnight-blue dress and jacket. She had no black clothes in her wardrobe, and she didn't possess a suitable hat. It occurred to her that she ought to patronize The Magpie boutique, so that she might have something in her wardrobe suitable for formal occasions.

She had arrived early and taken a seat at the back. The minister – robed, Church of England? – wandered in and set some taped music going. Nothing which you could immediately put a name to. Something in a minor key by Bach?

The senior Cordovers arrived and plodded up to the front pew, looking neither to the right nor the left. Both were in black. They looked as if they hadn't slept for a week.

Ellie remembered their proud smiles when they'd talked about the twins. Had Poppy been their favourite? The girls had not been identical, and it was possible that one had been favoured over the other.

Ellie also wondered about the arrangements for today. If she hadn't read the details in the *Gazette*, she'd have imagined that people like Gerald and Marika would have gone for a church service, with organ and choir and bells and smells and a slap-up buffet lunch afterwards. Especially since she thought it likely that Marika might have been brought up a Roman Catholic, and would have taken the rituals of passing seriously.

This felt stingy.

A middle-aged couple came in. He would be a successful businessman, not flamboyant but quietly sure of himself, in a good, grey suit. She was slender, with a tiny black toque on well-cut short grey hair. Well dressed by The Magpie? Were they neighbours of the deceased? They didn't attempt to speak to the senior Cordovers, but took seats at the back opposite Ellie.

Three women followed, also looking unsure of themselves. Two were fortyish, but the third looked as if she'd only just left school. Businesswomen? Office workers? They exchanged greetings with the couple who'd immediately preceded them

– they knew one another well? – and filed into the pew directly in front of them. Perhaps that whole group were people from The Magpie shop and agency?

Another good suit arrived. A greyish man in a grey suit and an expensive haircut. A solicitor? He had the air of one who was accustomed to going to funerals and who didn't allow the hushed air of the crematorium to faze him. He took a seat behind the Cordovers. They nodded to him, and he to them. Yes, they knew one another.

A stir outside. Two more women arrived, middle-aged, not in black but in dark clothes, looking flustered. Neighbours? Close friends of the deceased? They took seats halfway down, looking around them, perhaps for faces they recognized? They didn't seem to know the people at the back or the elder Cordovers at the front.

A creaking. A wheelchair was pushed down the aisle to the front pew on the right, a pew reserved for family. The occupant of the wheelchair was a middle-aged, slender man in black. A man who would have been tall if he'd stood up. A triangular face topped by smooth dark hair with streaks of grey at the temples. Black eyebrows in straight lines over pale grey eyes. His face was paper-white and lined. There was no kindness in his face. Pain could do that to you, of course. Or, Ellie wondered, was he something of a control freak? Now, why had she thought that? A man in a wheelchair couldn't be a control freak, could he?

The pusher was a girl with a coffee and cream complexion: latte rather than cappuccino. Young. In black. A quiet face, with strong planes. Emotionless, hiding . . . what? Was this Clemmie, the grandchild whom Gerald hadn't wanted to talk about?

Beside them and with them came Grief.

Grief was all in black. Grief was one of the most beautiful women Ellie had ever seen. Fair, well-brushed hair in a chignon under a tiny hat. She was high of cheekbone, blue-grey of eye, commanding of demeanour. Tall, well built. Sleepwalking.

The twin sister: Juno? The man in the wheelchair would be her husband?

On their heels, in a stir of air, came the clip-clop of high heels on the tiled floor. A dark-haired girl wearing a black silk coat and a black satin bandanna round her hair. Bright red lipstick. Would this be Trixie?

At the girl's side came a fortyish, dapper man with slicked-back hair and an easy smile. Charming? Yes, but it was surface charm. Ellie disliked him on sight. She remembered Thomas saying that Cocks's Garage was dicey. No, that's not exactly what Thomas had said. He'd heard *someone else* say that it was dicey.

Would this be Poppy's bereaved husband? His head turned this way and that, eyes snapping, checking on who was there and who was not. He followed the dark-haired girl into the front pew on the left, moving the senior Cordovers along. Yes, this must be Ray Cocks, widower. His daughter tried to hand him a service book. He flicked a dismissive hand at her, and a large gold watch slid down his wrist into view. No obvious signs of grief.

Ellie told herself she could understand why Gerald Cordover had been worried on seeing his daughter marry this man, who was loose of lip and roving of eye. Then she told herself that she ought not to jump to conclusions. Ray must have some good qualities, even if they were not immediately apparent.

The coffin arrived. Plain. Cheap?

And some latecomers. A middle-aged man with a lined, monkey face, wearing a black leather jacket of all things! Trixie and her father both turned round to see who the newcomers might be. The man in the leather jacket lifted his hand to Trixie and she winked, *actually winked* back! He slid into a pew directly behind her, and for an instant laid his hand on her shoulder . . . an attention which she did not seem to resent.

Leather Jacket would be someone who might help Trixie in her ambition to become a film star? An agent, possibly? Slightly seedy? Not out of the top drawer.

The other latecomer was a well-padded, well-dressed, middle-aged man with tiny, blackcurrant eyes. He nodded to Ray Cocks and plumped himself down in a pew by himself. Trixie turned her head to see who it was, and so did Ray. Evidently, they both knew him, for while Ray nodded at him, Trixie gave him a fleeting smile.

A businessman, known to the family? What a sharp nose he had!

Ellie thought, *The vultures are gathering* . . . and then wondered why she'd thought of birds of prey. Were the businessman and Leather Jacket here to feed on the corpse of the deceased? Ellie shuddered.

The muzak was turned off. The minister was one of those who aimed to get through the service in twenty minutes and have a fag before the next coffin arrived.

Ellie felt a surge of anger on behalf of Poppy, who was being tidied away in such a perfunctory fashion. She felt tears rise in her throat, and began to pray. She thought that, appearances to the contrary, someone else was also praying.

Marika? Yes, probably.

Also the grief-bound sister? Or, perhaps, the coffee-and-cream girl? The man in the wheelchair was white, so he couldn't be her father. But if he wasn't her father, then who was he?

Muzak, muzak. A few short sentences to sum up the life of a woman who had worked hard and been much loved by her father, stepmother, and sister.

The widower fidgeted.

The man in the wheelchair gazed ahead, as still as the Sphinx. He moved once, to hold out his hand for something. A bottle of water from a bag at the back of his wheelchair? The invalid's wife and the girl of mixed race ministered to him with clinical efficiency. Not tenderness. Just efficiency.

Gerald Cordover wept, and Marika put her arm around him as far as she could. Neither of them was particularly sylph-like. Ellie was glad to see that someone, at least, was grieving for the departed woman.

The coffin slid away into the wall and it was over. More muzak. A sigh of relief from someone.

Gerald and Marika subsided into their seats. Mopping up. Recovering. Getting ready to face the world again.

With a wide gesture, the man in the wheelchair indicated that he wished to depart. He seemed annoyed that his womenfolk didn't spring to do his bidding straight away. Their movements were slow. They were both worn out with grief. Ellie told herself he might well be grieving, too. Not everyone grieved in the same way. She must not jump to conclusions.

The widower and his daughter left their pew with a nod across the aisle to Juno, and a quick word with the neighbours a couple of pews back, the couple who hadn't known anyone else. Yes, undoubtedly neighbours. Ellie could hear them saying how sorry they were, they felt they had to come; they'd known Poppy for so many years.

The widower said the right things in a subdued, suitable-for-funerals voice. 'So glad you could come, Poppy would have been pleased. I'm sure you'll understand we're not having a public wake, just family back to the house . . .'

Which the neighbours didn't understand, no, not really. But they fluttered away. The widower frowned at Leather Jacket, who had attached himself to Trixie's side, and looked on the point of saying something sharp to him. The businessman thrust himself between them, saying he had his car outside, and could he give anyone a lift to the house? So the neighbours had not been invited back to the house, but the businessman had? Trixie was going in Leather Jacket's car, was that right?

Surely the funeral director would have provided at least one car for the mourners? And wasn't it supposed to be family only back at the house?

Juno, slowly pushing her husband in his wheelchair back down the aisle, spotted the group at the back, whom Ellie had guessed might work at The Magpie. Juno abandoned her husband in his wheelchair to greet them. She took their hands one by one and said how good it was of them to come, and she was so sorry but they were only having family back at the house. They all three said they quite understood, and they were so, so sorry . . . and disappeared.

Which left the middle-aged business couple in the back row.

Juno embraced the woman. 'Oh, Celine! I'm so glad you . . .' And broke off to blow her nose. Celine returned the hug. Celine had been crying, too. They had both cared for Poppy? Juno and Celine were close friends?

Juno held out her hand to the man. 'Thank you for coming. You understand, don't you? I can hardly take it in.' To which he responded with a firm pressure of both his hands around hers, and a pass at her cheek by way of a social, token kiss.

A harsh voice broke in. Not patiently. 'Juno! I don't like to hurry you, but . . .' The man in the wheelchair didn't like to be kept waiting, did he?

'Sorry, sorry!' Trying to smile through her tears, Juno took hold of the wheelchair again, saying to the woman in black, 'See you back at the house? You will come, won't you?'

'If you want me?' Celine didn't seem sure of her welcome. The man with her said something, making his excuses.

The girl of mixed race stepped up. 'Please come, Celine. My mother needs you.'

Celine – whoever she might be – gave in, saying, 'If you really want me? Charles has something else on.' And to the man, 'Can you drop me off? I'll get a taxi back, afterwards.'

They left in a huddle, arguing about who was going in which car.

Now there was no one left but Ellie, the solicitor, and the senior Cordovers. The solicitor was conferring with Gerald and Marika. He hadn't taken any notice of Ray, but he seemed to know the senior Cordovers well. He was their solicitor, and not Ray's?

Gerald looked around. A blind look, unfocused. He said, 'Ready for the fray? Do you have your car with you? You know that we're going back to Poppy's . . . to Poppy's.' His voice had broken on his daughter's name, but he kept going. Good for Gerald.

There was a stir outside, and a large woman came in, breathing heavily. She must have weighed twenty stone at least. 'Are we the first?'

Another funeral service was about to begin. Ellie hoped it would be more meaningful than the one she'd just attended.

The Cordovers walked slowly back down the aisle, looking strained and unhappy but resolute. The solicitor kept pace with them. He glanced at Ellie, and glanced away. She meant nothing to him.

Marika spotted Ellie and held out her hand. 'So glad you are here. Come in the car with us?'

Hadn't any cars been ordered for the mourners? The senior

Cordovers apologized to the solicitor, and to Ellie. 'It appears there are no cars. So embarrassing. An oversight, of course.'

The solicitor said, 'I have my own car. I'll meet you at the house.'

Apologizing still, the senior Cordovers wafted Ellie into the back of their limousine, which purred off back to the heart of Ealing. Their way led along the Avenue, a pleasant shopping parade not far from the A40. Ellie spotted The Magpie boutique. Closed, and the blind drawn down. When would it open again? If ever?

The car turned into a busy road of large detached houses. Late Edwardian, red brick, a small turret perched on the top floor to one side, and a spacious forecourt on which several cars were already parked. Gerald eased the limo off the road, parked, turned off the ignition but seemed in no hurry to get out of the car.

Ellie looked the house up and down. She had a pretty good idea how much it would cost to run, having a similar if slightly larger house herself. She tried to keep the doubt out of her voice as she said, 'It's a big house for the three of them.'

Gerald sighed. 'Poppy never asked us for a penny, even at the beginning.'

Marika said, 'Unlike *him!*'

Ellie said, 'You mentioned gambling debts?'

'Poppy used to say that he ought to have sold the garage when he inherited it and gone into something else. She said working there didn't fulfil him. The truth is that he's lazy to the core and thinks hard work is for dummies and that he can gamble his way to a fortune. When they were first married, he only used to bet on the big races every year. He said everyone did that, and that you had to have a little flutter now and then to keep the old adrenaline going. Only, the occasional flutter turned into a weekly and then a daily occurrence. Sometimes he won, but not often. It wasn't an enormous problem until someone introduced him to a private gaming club, and told him he had a flair for playing poker. That was two years ago and I don't think he's thought about anything much else since.'

And that's how he'd run up debts? That businessman at the crematorium . . . was he holding the widower's IOUs? Had he come to the funeral to call in the debt? No, no. Surely debts to a gambling club were collected by large men with LOVE and HATE tattooed on their knuckles? Men with thick necks and a thirst for destruction?

Ellie counted the number of cars in the driveway. There were too many to be accounted for by the immediate family. The high, taxi-looking one would be for the man in the wheelchair and his family. The sleek model for Ray, the slightly beaten-up one for Trixie's leather-jacketed agent – if that is what he was. The solicitor's car was the discreet, expensive-looking one.

Celine had asked to be dropped off by Charles, so the limo with the tinted windows would belong to the businessman, whoever he might be.

Ellie said, 'Poppy was contemplating a divorce?'

Marika sighed. 'With sorrow, yes. We only knew something was wrong when she put off refitting her kitchen and down-sized on a holiday. We knew the business was all right, so we asked her what was going on. She said Ray kept promising to stop but couldn't, that it had become an addiction and that she wasn't sure how much longer she could continue to pay his debts. I don't know what she might have decided to do, but when Ray found out about the buy-to-let properties, it was like bursting the bubble . . .'

'The boil,' corrected Gerald. 'Like bursting a boil. Ray said that as she was worth so much more than him, she could well afford to pay for his "entertainment". He said that if she drove him to divorce her, he'd be entitled to half of everything she had.'

Marika said, 'We advised her to talk things over with Juno because a divorce settlement might affect The Magpie. She agreed. But then she died.' She put her hand on Gerald's arm. 'We ought to go in?'

Gerald said, 'I'd give a lot to turn tail and run for it, but yes; let's get it over with, shall we?'

THREE

The front door was ajar. Gerald pushed it open and walked in. Ellie followed, feeling awkward. She did not like gatecrashing a family 'do'.

The hall was square with a tiled floor. The walls were also tiled to dado height. It was an old fashioned way of doing things but suited the house. The Lincrusta wallpaper above the dado had been painted a dull green. It was so out of date it was stylish, but it made the place rather dark.

The girl Trixie was already there, communing with a mirror on the wall as she tarted up her lipstick. She had flung her black coat over a chair, and was now revealed to be wearing a little black dress, expensive, very. From elbow to wrist she tinkled with a dozen fine silver bracelets. Dangly silver filigree earrings. Heavy rings on the fingers of each hand. Leather Jacket was at her elbow, whispering in her ear.

Gerald made an effort. 'Trixie, love. How are you doing?'

Trixie stretched her scarlet mouth into and out of a smile. 'Hello, Gramps. Hello, Gran. I'm fine. You don't need to worry about me.' She walked off through a door at the back of the hall with Leather Jacket at her heels.

Marika and Gerald followed but Ellie hung back because she really needed to use the toilet. There was a door ajar on the left? Ah, yes. Thank goodness.

When she came out, the hall was empty but the murmur of conversation and the clink of glassware came from a room at the back of the house.

Ray appeared in the doorway, fidgeting with his gold watch. A very good watch, worth a few thousand pounds. 'Oh, there you are!' Speaking direct to Ellie. 'You're late! We've given everyone a drink, but they want their faces fed. The stuff's in the kitchen. Make sure the coffee's hot. I'll send Clemmie out to help you.' He turned back into the room.

Ellie realized she'd been taken for a waitress. She was not

affronted but amused. And, it gave her an idea. She hadn't liked the thought of being introduced as the head of a charitable trust on such a difficult occasion, but hardly anyone ever looked at a waitress's face and she was wearing midnight blue instead of the more usual mourners' black. If she adopted the role which had been given her, she'd be practically invisible at the forthcoming family reunion . . . a reunion which might well end in tempers being lost. When tempers are lost, truth sometimes pops out of hiding, and she'd be in the front row of the stalls to see it happen. Gerald and Marika knew her, but if she avoided meeting their eyes . . .?

The coffee and cream girl – Clemmie? – came out of the main room to give Ellie a fleeting, social smile. 'The kitchen's this way. Thanks for helping out.' Clemmie also wore a black dress, but it was neither very expensive or new. She wore one, rather old-fashioned, brooch. Pearls, set in gold. A gift from a relative? From Poppy, perhaps?

Clemmie continued to talk as she led the way. 'Uncle Ray says their usual cleaner laid everything out before she had to go on to another job. He did ask her to find someone else to help us out. Thank goodness you could come.'

A large, black and white kitchen, with a slightly tired look. Ellie remembered Poppy's plans to update it had been scotched by the need to pay Ray's debts. There were trays of sandwiches under clingfilm on the central unit together with thermoses marked 'Water', 'Coffee', and 'Tea'.

'Milk is in the fridge, I expect,' said Clemmie, foraging. 'Can you lay the sandwiches out on those big plates and take them round? There's some plastic gloves on the counter over there. My aunt was very keen on hygiene in the kitchen.' She stood still for a moment, swallowed hard, attempted a smile, and resumed. 'There should be a hostess trolley somewhere . . . ah, here it is. Are there plates and napkins . . .? Yes. I'll load up with the cups and saucers and thermos flasks and deal with the drinks, if you can cope with the sandwiches.'

She disappeared and Ellie set to work on the sandwiches, transferring them to large serving platters.

So the girl of mixed race was Clemmie, who was Poppy's niece and Juno's daughter . . . but not, presumably the daughter of Juno's husband . . . unless the man in the wheelchair was not Juno's husband?

Ellie thought that Clemmie was being treated like a servant. An au pair, perhaps? But not like a daughter of the family. Not like Trixie, who was obviously not going to lift a finger to help.

What was going on in this family?

Ellie finished filling one platter, and started on the next.

Clemmie returned. 'I forgot the sugar. How are you getting on?'

'Nearly done,' said Ellie, putting the last touches to the second platter. 'I'll follow you in, shall I?'

'Most of them want alcohol, not tea, but my mother doesn't touch alcohol and neither does Celine. If you come across any used plates and glasses, would you bring them out and stack them in the dishwasher?'

Ellie didn't think she'd be able to pass herself off as an agency waitress for very long, but she nodded and followed Clemmie through the hall and into a big sitting room at the back of the house. The room was large but seemed full of people; some were restlessly moving around, talking in low voices; others sat in silence, staring into space.

The fireplace was elaborate and probably authentic – more tiles here – but it was dwarfed by an enormous plasma television placed directly before it. In front of that matching settees, which probably faced the television on other days, had been angled to face into the room instead. Each one was attended by a glass-topped coffee table.

Gerald and Marika had seated themselves on one of the settees with the solicitor, whose face was giving nothing away. The senior Cordovers looked grey and drawn. Suffering. Gerald and Marika waved Ellie's offer of sandwiches away without looking at her. The solicitor also declined, with a shake of his head and a glance at his wristwatch. Did he have another funeral to go to? Or was he just anxious to get the reading of the will over and done with?

On the companion settee were Juno, and Celine from The Magpie, hands tightly clasping one another. Truly grief-stricken. Both wore gold wedding rings but no other jewellery.

Juno was wearing the very minimum of make-up but her

beauty was ageless. She outshone even her own daughter, who
was also beautiful in her own way. As Ellie offered sandwiches,
she was struck by the notion that Juno was unwell. Possibly
feverish? Or in pain?

Ellie wondered why she'd thought that.

Celine urged Juno to eat something. 'It will do you good.'
A slight smile. A shake of the head.

Ellie passed on to Juno's husband, who sat in his wheelchair
beside them, looking bony, bored but also . . . pleased with
himself? Hiding amusement? He had heavy-lidded, pale grey
eyes, which were constantly shifting, working the room. His
triangular face was pale, from a lack of fresh air? He was
wearing an expensive silk and mohair mixture suit, and a silk
tie. His hair had been cut by a master, his nails were mani-
cured and his shoes shone with glossy polish. He'd spent
money on himself. He took three sandwiches without looking
at Ellie.

Trixie, the daughter of the house, and Leather Jacket stood
close to one another in one of the windows. He was whispering
to her. Advice as to her future, or love talk? Both held cut-glass
tumblers, half full of . . . what? Whisky? Leather Jacket took
a stack of sandwiches, Trixie nibbled one.

Ray, the widower, had a cut-glass tumbler in his hand, whose
contents he drained as Ellie approached him. He handed her
his glass, asking her to fill it up again. She sniffed. Whisky,
neat. She thought he'd probably had enough to drink already
but there was a drinks cabinet open at the side so she located
the whisky bottle and did as he asked.

Ray was talking, partly to himself and partly to his friend
the businessman, saying how much he was going to miss his
darling wife. The businessman sat on his plump behind, a solid,
almost menacing, presence. He was listening to Ray but his
small, blackcurrant eyes roamed the room, lingering on Trixie,
who was apparently unaware of him. Or was she? If he were
a friend of the family then surely she should be making an
effort to talk to him? The businessman consulted his watch.
Time was money, et cetera. He took four sandwiches, which
disappeared into his fat-lipped little mouth, leaving not a crumb
behind.

Clemmie, dry-eyed, offered coffee or tea to everyone but Ray. Wise child.

Somewhere a clock chimed the hour, and Ray held up his glass. 'A toast! To my darling Poppy!'

Everyone drank, from glass, coffee or teacup . . . or mimed drinking from empty cups if they had nothing left to drink.

Ellie slid on to a high-backed chair in the shadow of the drinks cabinet, hoping no one would notice her. Which they didn't. From this vantage point she surveyed the room. Yes, it was clean and tidy, but already there was evidence that the mistress of the house had departed; a picture hung crookedly, there was a dead plant in a pot, a film of dust on the glass of the coffee tables and an untidy stack of old newspapers and magazines which ought to have been put in the recycling bin.

From where she sat, Ellie could see everything without being seen. She saw Ray take his daughter Trixie's elbow and say, 'Get that fellow of yours out of here. Family only for the reading of the will.'

Trixie smiled sweetly. 'He's my future. He stays.'

Ray reddened. He turned on Celine. 'Well, you're not family!'

Juno started. She said, in a tired voice, 'Oh, let it go, Ray. Hasn't Celine been part of our lives for years? Poppy would have wanted her to be here and I'd like her to stay.'

Ray didn't bother to ask the businessman to leave, but dragged a chair forward and seated himself, gesturing to the solicitor to proceed. 'So, let's have the good news, then!'

The grey man produced a folder tied up with pink tape, and opened it. 'This is the last will and testament . . .'

Ellie tuned him out. She knew what was coming. Who else knew? She scanned faces. The senior Cordovers knew but were giving nothing away.

Juno knew, but she seemed to have removed herself from the scene. Once again Ellie wondered if Juno were sick. She seemed uninvolved. Ellie wasn't even sure Juno was listening. Did she not know, or did she not care that this was the only will Poppy had ever made? Did she not realize everything came to her?

'I appoint as executor . . .' So Poppy had appointed the solicitor as sole executor? Not a bad decision. And the date was . . . 'On the twelfth day of May 1999—'

'What!' Ray, laughing. 'All that time ago? That can't be right!'

'On the occasion of the signing of the agreement for the partnership to be known as The Magpie—'

'You mean, she made this will when they first started up in business?'

The solicitor gave a stately nod. 'When the partnership was formed and the business was put on a formal footing, yes. Two years after they first started The Magpie. When two people enter into a partnership, it is common practice for them to make wills in one another's favour, so that the business may proceed if one partner is, er, lost.'

'You mean, she left the shop to her sister?'

'That is correct. Together with everything else she might possess at the time of her death. In the event of Juno predeceasing Poppy, then everything would have gone to Gerald Cordover, her father.'

Ray wasn't worried yet. He even looked slightly amused as he turned on his sister-in-law. 'Juno, did you know she was going to leave the shop to you?'

Juno roused herself. 'Well, yes. I suppose so. We signed identical wills, leaving everything to one another. Nineteen ninety-nine. Yes, that would be about right. I haven't done anything about updating my will. I know I ought to.'

The man in the wheelchair smiled, showing very white teeth. 'Yes, my dear. You really must.'

Ray looked uneasy for a moment, then grinned. 'Well, if Juno gets the shop, I suppose I get the houses and her portfolio of shares.'

'Er, no,' said the solicitor, unperturbed. 'This house is in her name, is it not? I have done the conveyancing for all the houses owned by the sisters, either for private or for business purposes. The deeds for the private houses have always been in the names of Poppy or Juno alone. This house is in Poppy's name.' He twitched a smile, signalling that he was about to make a joke of sorts. 'Mrs Cocks always made the excuse that you were having a minor problem with the bank at the time.' The smile faded. It wasn't much of a joke.

Ray's bonhomie began to fade at the edges. 'Well, yes. I suppose, sometimes there was that. But this house comes to me now, right?'

The solicitor returned his eyes to the will. '"Everything of which I die possessed." This house is in her name, and therefore passes to her sister.'

Ray shot to his feet. 'You mean that by some freak of the law, which was certainly not intended by my wife, Juno gets this house as well as the shop?'

The solicitor nodded. 'Together with all the other properties owned by The Magpie partnership.'

'But . . .!' Ray swayed on his feet, going red . . . and then the blood left his cheeks and he began to shake. 'You can't mean . . .! What about the houses she and Juno bought and did up to let? I was so angry when I found out about them! What sort of wife conceals her assets from her husband like that, eh? How deceitful is that! But now, it's payback time and I come into my rights. She didn't own those houses when the will was made, did she? So they must come to me.'

The very slightest of frowns marred the solicitor's brow. 'As a matter of fact, she and her sister did own two houses when the will was signed. Those houses, and however many more there are now, are covered by the wording of the will which includes all properties owned by the partnership. It doesn't matter whether there were two or ten properties at the time of her death.'

'I don't believe it!'

The solicitor didn't bother to repeat himself.

Ray was getting desperate. 'Look, she was pretty well fixed, always had plenty in the bank. I know she dabbled in the stock-market, because she had to sell some shares when she bought me my new car. She'll have left me her shares, at the very least.' Beads of sweat appeared on his forehead.

The solicitor was getting bored. 'I repeat, your sister-in-law is the residual legatee.'

Silence as this began to sink in.

It was as if the solicitor had chanted a spell and turned them all to stone.

The solicitor continued, 'You must remember that this will was made seventeen years ago at the start of the sisters' part-nership. At the time of her marriage, the testator owned nothing of her own except the small house which her father gave her on that occasion. You and she signed a pre-nuptial agreement to the effect that you would keep the garage in the event of the marriage breaking down, and that she would keep the house. Two years later, when the partnership agreement was signed and this will was drawn up, Mrs Cocks owned not only her house but also her half of The Magpie partnership, which by that time included the shop and two run-down terraced houses in parlous state. At that point in time you were doing well at the garage and in no need of extra funds, whereas Mrs Cocks knew that she and her sister were going to have to work very hard indeed to make The Magpie project work. This will was drawn up to protect her and her sister in case of accidents. There was also a hefty insurance policy, I believe, designed to cover them for all contingencies, payable also to her sister.'

'Yes, but . . . things have changed since then. My outgoings . . . she was happy to help me out when . . . if she'd made another will—'

'So far as I know, she didn't do so.'

'I don't believe it! I'll sue! No court in the land would deny me, her husband—'

Trixie pushed him aside. 'Oh, Dad! Shut up! You've had your turn! She gave you everything you asked for over the years, didn't she? She paid your debts and your holidays abroad and your cars. So now it's my turn. You!' She turned on the solicitor. 'What did she leave me? She wouldn't have cut *me* out!'

The solicitor said, 'You were a child of two years of age at the time she made her will. It never occurred to her at that time to leave you anything. I suppose she might well have made different provisions for her family if she had made another will. Unfortunately she died before she was able to do so.'

Ray dabbed at his forehead. His colour was poor. 'She must have made another will! Of course she did. She wouldn't leave me in the lurch like this.'

The solicitor said, 'If she did make another will, it was not drawn up by me. This is the will that I drew up for Poppy Cocks, née Cordover, signed on the occasion of the incorporation of her business with her sister, who made an identical will in her favour. In the absence of any later will, this one will be submitted to probate.'

All eyes turned to Juno, who seemed to be thinking of something else.

She's ill! She's going to be sick . . .? Can't they see how ill she is?

Ray said, hoarsely, 'Juno; tell them! Poppy never intended to leave me penniless.'

Juno brought her mind back from wherever it was. She touched a trembling hand to her mouth. 'We never thought of this. It just seemed . . . well, common sense. I never thought . . . from that day to this . . . we never dreamed that she'd die so soon . . .!'

Her grief was real.

So was his anger. 'You'll have to give me my share. Whatever she left should come to me! You aren't going to refuse me my rights, are you?'

Juno looked as if she were going to faint.

Why doesn't someone help her?

The solicitor rose to his feet. 'As I said before, unless you can produce a later will, this is the will which I, as sole executor, will be submitting for probate.'

The man in the wheelchair broke into a soundless laugh, which developed into a coughing fit. Clemmie rummaged in a bag at the back of his chair. She produced the bottle of water and tried to hand it to him. He struck her hand away and the bottle fell to the floor. Instead of rescuing it, Clemmie turned back to her duties at the tea trolley.

Trixie took centre stage, stepping forward to ally herself with her father. 'Dad, I'll help you challenge the will. I need money, too, remember.'

Ray chucked his almost empty glass away in a gesture of frustration. It missed Trixie but hit the window behind her. And broke it.

An indrawn breath. Everyone froze.

The solicitor shut his briefcase and stood up. 'If that is all, then I—'

Ray whirled round on the senior Cordovers. 'You knew! I see that you did! You should have made sure she updated her will. You knew how I was placed; that I needed to . . . I shall sue! The courts can't refuse to give me, her husband—'

'What about me?' wailed Trixie. 'I need, I've promised, I
have commitments . . .'

She turned on Leather Jacket. 'Don't worry! I'll get the money
somehow, I swear I will!'

Did Ellie imagine it? Did Trixie shoot a glance at the
businessman? She wasn't appealing for help, was she? No,
she was issuing what looked like a challenge. What was all
that about?

Ellie could feel someone's eyes on her.

Clemmie was looking at Ellie in considering fashion.
Suspiciously? Yes.

Ray had lost his cool. Trixie was in the process of doing so,
deliberately, enjoying herself. Hysteria loomed.

The businessman stood up. 'Ray, you'd better come and see
me, tomorrow.' It was a statement. An order. Understated but
real. And then, he walked out. Just. Like. That.

Ray screamed, 'Don't go! I swear to you—'

The solicitor held out the folder containing the will. 'I'll
leave you with a copy of—'

Ray snatched the folder, and tore it in pieces. 'That
for your—!'

'Enough!' Gerald Cordover, heaving himself to his feet, trying
to defuse the situation.

Clemmie collected a couple of dirty cups and saucers,
signalled to Ellie to follow her, and left the room. Ellie went
after her with the half-empty platter of sandwiches.

In the kitchen, Clemmie didn't even bother to open the
dishwasher. She said, 'Who are you? You aren't agency staff,
are you? You understood what was going on. You *knew* what
was going to happen, which was more than I did. So I'm asking,
who and what are you?'

'Ellie Quicke. I run a local charity. Your grandfather and
grandmother asked me to be present, because they were
desperately worried about the situation and wanted me to
help sort it out. As if I could! Your grandfather thought I
might be able to talk to Trixie about achieving her ambition
to be a film star—'

'Wait a minute. He wouldn't do that. He thinks it's a stupid
idea.'

'I agree. He thought he could use it as an excuse to introduce me to the family. I didn't think it was a good idea, either, but he was so unhappy . . . I'm sorry, I shouldn't have come. I apologize. I'll leave straight away.'

'And tittle-tattle about what you've heard?'

'Certainly not.' Ellie was beginning to like young Clemmie because she did seem capable of thinking of other people. 'I wouldn't dream of it. The fact is that your grandparents want me to look into your aunt's death.'

Clemmie shot Ellie a sideways look. And breathed out, very very slowly. 'Ah. So that's it. But Ray's got an alibi.'

'You aren't shocked by the idea that he might have caused your aunt's death?'

Clemmie lifted her hands and let them fall. 'I don't know. I can't think straight. We're all so tired, so worried. We don't . . . we daren't talk about . . . or even think it. End of.' She turned away to put some of the dirty cups into the dishwasher. She was not going to volunteer any more information.

The front door slammed shut. The businessman departing?

It opened again. Closed gently. The solicitor leaving, too?

Ellie could hear angry voices, trying to shout over one another. Trixie, heading fast into hysteria! Would she let rip with a scream or two? Mm, possibly.

Gerald's voice rose, angry.

Marika's softer voice, trying to diffuse the situation.

Juno's husband had a penetrating voice. 'All of you! Shut up!'

As if that would do any good. And now, yes, Trixie let go with a full-blooded scream. Perhaps she would do well in horror films.

A woman's voice, distressed. 'I think perhaps I should go.' Celine?

'Trixie, behave!' Marika trying to help?

Gerald's voice. 'Once Trixie starts . . .!'

The door to the back room slammed, and there was peace in the kitchen.

Clemmie was weeping. She didn't try to hide her tears as she stacked the dishwasher.

Ellie hesitated. Her instinct was to touch, to comfort, but she didn't know the girl well enough to know if it would be appreciated. She said, 'I'm so sorry. Your aunt was a lovely woman.'

'Yes. Please, would you go now!' A suggestion, not an order.

The door opened. Juno stood there, swaying, holding on to the lintel, looking as if she were going to pass out any second. Screams and shouts and crashes seeped into the kitchen from the room behind her. Juno ignored whatever was going on behind her. 'I wonder if . . . Clemmie, perhaps a glass of water?' Her eyes closed and she began to sway.

Clemmie caught her mother and eased her to the floor.

Ellie rushed to the sink, poured water. 'She's ill, isn't she? Shall I ring for an ambulance?'

Clemmie held her mother in her arms, closely, lovingly. 'She's worn out. She ought to be in bed. She insisted on coming.' She took the glass from Ellie, and held it to her mother's lips.

Juno sipped, opened her eyes and looked up at Clemmie. Tried to smile. 'Stupid me. Sorry. Didn't mean to—'

'Shut up!' Clemmie's voice was rough but loving.

Juno tried to get up. Failed. 'I'm quite all right. Gordon wants—'

'He can look after himself for once.' Not a kind tone of voice. So what was going on there?

Juno closed her eyes again. Relaxed in her daughter's arms. Seeing them both so close, Ellie could see the likeness. High cheekbones, broad forehead, generous mouth, beautifully arched eyebrows. Juno had blue eyes, didn't she?

Clemmie's were brown. The eyes of the man in the wheelchair were light grey. That was something to think about, later.

Celine appeared in the doorway. 'Has Juno gone? Oh!'

'I'm perfectly all right,' said Juno, trying to smile. 'I'll be all right in a minute. Gordon wants to be driven home but I'm so tired!'

Celine and Clemmie exchanged looks which meant, if Ellie were reading them aright, that neither of them had much time for Gordon . . . who would be Juno's husband?

Celine knelt down by her friend. Yes, Juno was her friend. There was love and trust between the two women.

'Juno!' The man in the wheelchair appeared in the doorway,

commanding, demanding. 'I said, I want to leave. What are you doing on the floor?'

Juno gasped, 'Oh dear!' and tried to get up. 'I'll be all right in a minute. I think maybe I'm going down with something.'

'Well, it's no good running to the doctor for antibiotics if you've got a cold. You know they have no effect. Pull yourself together. It's time I went home.'

'You bastard!' from the sitting room. And a scream. Trixie in fine voice.

Smash . . .! What was that? Another glass? Who was going to clear up the mess? Not Ellie. Nor, it seemed, was Clemmie rushing to the rescue.

Gerald appeared in the doorway with Marika at his shoulder. They took in the scene with one glance. Marika said, 'Juno shouldn't have come. She should be in bed. Shall we take her home with us, Gerald?'

'Certainly not,' said Gordon. 'I won't allow it. She'll be perfectly all right if she only makes an effort.'

Clemmie ignored Gordon to speak direct to her grandfather. 'Actually, Gramps, I think that's an excellent idea. Mum needs a good night's rest. Dad, I'm sure you can drive yourself home, and if you don't feel up to it, you can call a taxi. Let Mum have a little peace and quiet on her own for once.'

Gerald and Marika helped Juno to her feet, nodded to Celine and Clemmie. 'She'll be better off with us tonight.'

'No, you don't! Juno, come back here!'

Too late. She'd gone.

Gordon was furious. Red patches appeared on his thin white cheeks. 'How ridiculous! Gerald has no right to take Juno off like that. It's her duty to look after me. She's my wife, for heaven's sake!'

'She's worn out,' said Clemmie. 'She needs a rest.'

'And I need looking after, don't I? Well, I suppose, if she's back in the morning . . . Oh, yes! She'll be back. Or else! Now, who's going to help me out to the car? You know I can't manage the step without assistance.'

'I'll do it,' said Clemmie. She reached for the wheelchair and he struck her hand away – not pettishly, but with some force.

Ellie blinked. Clemmie's eyes went blank but she made no sound. Ellie had seen children who'd been hit react like that before. The scene conveyed a certain message, but for the moment she couldn't think what it was. Clemmie made as if to rub her arm, but refrained. She said, 'Celine, can you get home on your own?'

Celine rubbed her eyes. 'Yes, of course.' She sounded exhausted. 'I'll fetch my jacket. It's somewhere . . .' She looked around, vaguely.

Ellie got out her mobile and pressed buttons. 'Celine, I'm ordering a cab to take me home. I'll drop you off first, if I may?'

Celine nodded. She didn't seem very aware of what was going on. She plucked a jacket from a pile in the hall, saying, 'Juno gets ear infections when she's run down. Ever since I've known her, almost sixteen years. I manage the shop, you see.'

'Yes,' said Ellie. 'I do see. It's a mess, isn't it?' She walked with Celine to the front door. 'Would it help to talk it over with me?' Immediately, she wondered how she'd dared to issue such an invitation. She must be mad.

'No one can do anything,' said Celine. 'It is what it is. I'm opening the shop tomorrow. It's been closed for a week. Juno may not be up to it, but I have to open.'

Ellie nodded. Yes, she could see that. Well, she'd put in a spot of prayer about the situation, and see what happened.

FOUR

When her taxi came, Ellie gave Celine a lift, and dropped her off at an upmarket block of flats. As she'd never learned to drive, Ellie kept a monthly account with a local cab firm, and had fallen into the habit of praying when she was being transported from A to B. Now was a good opportunity.

Ellie was worried. Her policewoman friend, Lesley, had been right. Something was deeply, seriously wrong in the Cordover family, and yes, if the situation were not dealt with, Ellie believed that there could indeed be more violence.

Ellie's mind buzzed with questions. Clemmie: she couldn't be Gordon's child, could she? The colour of her skin, the colour of her eyes . . .

Her cousin Trixie: overindulged brat, who might possibly have talent, but . . . How did anyone break into films, anyway?

Ray, her father. Deep in debt. Threatened with divorce by his wife, Poppy. An unpleasant character, but if he did have an alibi then he couldn't have killed his wife.

Juno: heartsick. Grief-stricken. Query, sickening for something?

Gordon, her husband. An invalid; poor man, Ellie had to feel sorry for him, even if he were somewhat self-centred and not exactly her idea of a caring husband. Perhaps he couldn't be loving and caring, confined to a wheelchair.

It was all very well acknowledging that something was wrong, but what could Ellie do about it, except worry?

To be fair, Ellie Quicke could worry for England. She worried about her husband Thomas; though, if challenged, she had to admit that he could perfectly well take care of himself. She worried about being found inadequate as the chair of her charitable trust fund, even though other people thought she made an excellent job of it. She worried about finding herself in all sorts of situations, some imaginary and some real, even though she usually managed to worry through them somehow or other.

But not this affair. Surely, this one was nothing to do with her. She would ask God to look after the Cordovers, and get back to worrying about her everyday problems.

She let herself back into her house, called out, 'I'm back!' to whoever might be around, and found that her daughter Diana had left her an envelope marked 'Urgent' on the hall table.

Ellie grinned. So she'd missed another meeting with her daughter? Tough! She didn't bother to open the envelope but went into the kitchen to make herself a cuppa, only to find that Susan, their lodger and part-time housekeeper, was cleaning out the larder.

Now Susan was not normally a worrier. She'd been wished on Ellie and Thomas by her aunt Lesley who, yes, was the policewoman who had got Ellie involved in the Cordover case. Susan was in her final year as a full-time student of cookery at West London University and needed somewhere to stay in term-time. She was doing well in her course, and would have no trouble getting a job when she finished. She had fitted into the household as if she'd been brought up in it.

Susan adored having her own space in the flat at the top of Ellie's big house, even if it didn't have its own entrance due to some officious person at the Town Hall declaring that Ellie wasn't allowed to make a separate front door because that might mean someone bringing another car into the road, even though there was plenty of off-road parking.

Susan had a light hand with pastry and a sunny disposition. She only tackled Ellie's larder when she was in distress about something, which would be about twice a year. On those occasions she would move the chutneys which she'd made to the shelf which usually held her homemade marmalade and mincemeat, and vice versa. She would bang and sweep and sniff and turn her little radio up high, sending up flags of distress.

Ellie dithered. She didn't want to barge in on someone who was having a private scream to themselves which would soon be over. On the other hand, Ellie could make a pretty good guess as to what was causing Susan such distress, and ignoring the matter was not going to make it go away. Susan had been asked to be a bridesmaid at Lesley's wedding, and was dreading the event. Ellie could understand why.

So, steeling herself to interfere, Ellie knocked on the door to the larder, which was ajar. 'Susan, have you time for a cuppa?'

Ellie could only see Susan's behind from where she stood, as her head was under the bottom shelf.

'Go away. I'm all right.' A muffled voice, full of tears?

'Oh, Susan.' Ellie sighed. 'Come on out. We'll have a cuppa, and you can tell me all about it.'

Mumble, mumble. Which, being translated, meant Susan didn't have anything to tell.

'Come on,' said Ellie, surprising herself by being firm with the girl. 'I'll put the kettle on.' Which she did.

Susan duly extricated herself from under the shelf, blew her nose, whispered something about being an idiot, and seated herself at the kitchen table in front of the large mug which she preferred to any other. Ellie poured tea, pushed the box of tissues towards Susan and investigated the contents of the biscuit tin.

The official arrangement was that Ellie cooked for herself and Thomas, and Susan got her own meals in the small kitchen at the top of the house. However, Susan also liked to try out recipes in the big kitchen downstairs where there was more room to work and a bigger oven. Some of the resultant dishes would be popped into the freezer, and some she would leave out for the household to devour for their evening meals.

Occasionally Susan felt moved to make a batch of ginger-bread, shortbread or brownies and this was Hurray Time for the household. (Anything but coconut: Thomas didn't care for coconut for some reason.) Ellie didn't buy many biscuits now-adays. The Cordovers had pretty well cleaned out the tin yesterday, but apparently Susan had decided to bake some chocolate-chip cookies today. Hurray. Ellie took one and pushed the tin at Susan.

Investigating the biscuit tin had given Ellie time to consider how to approach the vexed question of the forthcoming wedding.

Lesley Milburn – Susan's aunt – was marrying a pleasant young man who taught at a local primary school. Bride and bridegroom had asked suitable members of the family on either side to act as bridesmaids. Susan had been invited, had tried to decline and been overruled. Susan was a solid-looking girl with capable hands and sandy, frizzy hair drawn up into a no-nonsense knot. She had a large bosom of which she was ashamed, and which she tried to disguise by wearing black T-shirts with silly slogans on them. Susan was not, and never had been, a size nought.

The bridegroom had a young sister, Angelica, who *was* a size nought, and who was glorying in the fact that, as bridesmaid, she would be in all the photographs and the centre of attention after the bride. Angelica had long blonde hair, long black eyelashes and a sylph-like figure.

The contrast between the two girls set one's teeth on edge and, to make matters worse, Angelica had been allowed to choose the bridesmaid's dresses, which were to be a floating chiffon overdress in peach, with the tightest of figure-hugging sheaths underneath. This revealing style could never in a thousand years look good on Susan.

Susan had refrained from murdering Angelica, but the iron had entered into her soul. Lesley, going straight from the Cordover affair into a sordid case of child abuse, and distracted by the last-minute hitches that can occur in the weeks before a wedding, was unapproachable.

Susan knew she had to put up and shut up, but the thought of being held up to view as a laughing stock was ever on her mind.

Susan munched a biscuit and said, indistinctly, 'I've been off my food lately. Perhaps I'm going down with something catching. Salmonella. Something like that. Then nobody would mind if I wasn't a bridesmaid.'

'Have you asked your mother for help?'

'Humph. She's making the most of the menopause. She says nobody ever thinks of her problems, which are far worse than anyone else's because she's still suffering from her hip replacement, which hasn't worked, and how she's to walk down the aisle she doesn't know and the young never realize what she has to put up with. Which is true, but doesn't help solve it for me. I'm definitely going down with something catching.'

Ellie munched a biscuit, too. Yum. She'd never been very interested in what she wore, but she had conscientiously tried to understand what was in fashion so that she didn't look completely out of date. It wasn't that she cared what other people thought of her, but she was the public face of the charitable trust, and that meant she had to be appropriately – if not fashionably – dressed on occasion.

She said, 'I know it's tradition, but I don't see why you and Angelica have to wear the same style. Why can't you choose a dress for yourself? In the same colour, perhaps? You wouldn't want to outshine the bride by wearing white, but something in blue? An Empire-line dress with a low cleavage would suit you to perfection.'

'Angelica was told she could choose what she liked to wear.'

'So the same must go for you, too?'

Susan slanted a look at Ellie, and managed a giggle. 'You mean, I should rot her up by choosing something that doesn't make me look like an overweight Jelly Baby? Go on! Where would I get something that wouldn't make me look like a freak, especially as Lesley is paying for the dress and she's not exactly made of money?'

Ellie knew. Oh yes. She'd prayed that there might be some solution found to the Cordover problem, never thinking that He would bung her straight back into it. Bother. Oh well.

'There's a really good boutique called The Magpie in the Avenue. It's run by a sympathetic woman. I'm just wondering if they might have something to suit you. Tomorrow's Saturday and you've no need to be in college, so shall we go shopping in the morning?'

Susan struggled with her better self, but shook her head. 'No, it's tempting, isn't it? I can't make waves just before the wedding. It was nice of Lesley to ask me and I should just put up with being laughed at, for her sake. It's not the end of the world.'

Upon which, the doorbell rang. Once. Sharply.

'Lesley?' said Ellie, round the last of the biscuit.

Susan shot off back to the larder. 'Don't tell her what I said! I've got to finish cleaning the larder.'

It was Lesley. Ellie let her in, trying to assess her friend's mood. 'I thought you were tied up with a particularly nasty case and wouldn't have time to visit.'

'A witness went AWOL and we got a confession. Surprised all of us. What happened at the Cordovers?'

'Would you like some tea, coffee?'

Lesley shook her head. 'You went to the funeral? I'd have liked to go, if I'd been free.'

Ellie led the way to the sitting room. 'Have a seat. The service at the crematorium was cheap, rushed, meaningless. The deceased's husband and daughter were anxious to get to the reading of the will, from which they expected great things . . . only to be disappointed. Poppy and Juno made their wills when they set up The Magpie partnership, leaving everything to one another, which means Juno cops the lot. Not that she's ecstatic about it. She's a pretty sick woman, and . . .' Ellie considered what else and added, somewhat to her own surprise, 'And, I think she's frightened.'

Lesley pounced. 'Of what?'

Ellie lifted her hands and let them fall. 'I don't understand what's going on. There's cross-currents everywhere. Gerald and Marika seem, on the surface, to be straightforward. They set the girls up in business and kept an eye on their progress. Their solicitor did all the girls' work. So why didn't they ensure the girls updated their wills? Did they just forget? No. Gerald's a good businessman. I bet he updates his own will every year or so. What's more, the solicitor inserted the usual clause to the effect that if both sisters die prematurely, the lot goes back to . . . guess whom? To the father, who doesn't need it.'

'Yes, they say he's worth a bit.'

'Has that been checked? I know he seems to have doted on the girls, but he could well have had some reverses which might make him eye the girls' fortunes? No? No. That's not right. He's genuinely fond of the girls. But I did happen to notice that Marika wasn't wearing a wedding ring. Did he ever make an honest woman of her? Is their wedding something they've overlooked as time went on?'

'She's Polish. They wear their wedding rings on the other hand.'

'Do they? Oh, well, that explains it.'

'You don't really think he could be a suspect?'

'No. Not really. Now: Trixie. Trixie seems to think more about going into films than about losing her mother. Although, to be honest, I think she might well have what it takes to go before the cameras, not as a clothes model, but . . . Oh, what do I know about such things?'

'And Clemmie?'

'She's treated as a servant. She's not Gordon's daughter, is she? So whose daughter is she and how . . .? Oh, this whole thing is making my head ache.'

'Why should it make your head ache?' Lesley really wanted to know.

Ellie stared at her friend, not knowing how to answer.

Lesley paced up and down. Impatient.

Ellie tried to think clearly. 'Juno is afraid. Clemmie is, too. The senior Cordovers certainly are. I can smell it, almost taste it.'

'Smell? Taste? How about evidence?'

'Celine, the manageress of the shop. She's afraid, too, but she says there's nothing to be done. Why? It seems to me that the situation is fluid but that it could be sorted out with a redistribution of money. If Juno pays off Ray and Trixie, which she could well do . . .'

'Would that be what Poppy wanted?'

Ellie took a deep breath. 'No. You're right. It wouldn't. That's why Poppy didn't update her will, isn't it? She was going to divorce Ray. About time too, if you ask me, though normally I really don't think divorce is the right way to go. But, in this case, because Poppy was protecting herself from an addict . . .? Oh, I really don't know. As for sending Trixie to drama school, well, that might not be what that brat wants, but I suspect Poppy could have managed it if she didn't have Ray acting as an open drain on her purse.'

Ellie tried to think. 'In a way, Poppy keeping her will that way actually protected her from her greedy family. At least,' she qualified, 'it would have done if they'd known about it. Then again, we're supposed to believe they didn't know, that they had no idea that she hadn't made a recent will, but . . . suppose they did know?'

She drew her hand across her eyes. 'Cancel that. Neither of

them knew. Take it from me, it came as an unpleasant surprise to both of them.'

'But if they didn't know, then both had a motive.'

'Mm. Clemmie and the senior Cordovers both think, and even go so far as to say, that Ray did it. But they then add that he's got an alibi, so he couldn't have.'

'It's true. He does have an alibi. What a mess!' Lesley flung herself into a chair. 'I'd like to bang their heads together and leave them to it, but I can't because my instinct tells me that whatever poison brought Poppy to her death is still there, and still working away in the background. Everything about the way they behave rings alarm bells. I'm convinced that if nothing is done, there'll be another death. You say Juno is frightened? She didn't strike me as fearful when I interviewed her. Shocked, yes. Frightened for her life? No. Does she think she's next for the chop?'

Ellie argued, 'Why should she be? Who would benefit? If Juno died and her existing will was sent for probate, what would happen? Her father would get the lot. No, that's not the answer.'

'Then what is?'

Ellie wondered, 'It's over a week since her sister died and Juno, of all people, was in her sister's confidence. She knew what Poppy's will contained because they'd made identical ones. I'm beginning to wonder . . . What's the betting that she's already done something about hers? Those two women worked hard, expanded their business. Neither of them was a fool. Juno must have thought about changing her will and, if she hasn't done so, then there'll have been a very good reason why not. Is she protecting herself from her husband? He's not my idea of a caring, thoughtful spouse, but who knows what happens in a house when the front door is shut on the world? Maybe they're still devoted lovebirds. And yet . . . No, he twitted her on not having changed her will so . . . I have absolutely no idea what's going on there.'

Lesley tapped her teeth. 'I can't see where the threat is coming from. If Ray were to kill Juno, it wouldn't ease his finances, would it? And Clemmie's not the type . . . though, in my experience, anyone can be driven to kill.'

Ellie inspected her fingernails. They were pretty clean at the moment, considering the amount of time she spent in the garden, but they could do with some attention. 'Lesley, to change the subject, at least partly . . . what I'm about to say could be taken as blackmail—'

'What?' Lesley burst into laughter. 'You!'

'Yes. Hear me out. I know a way to find out more about the family—'

'Then take it. You don't need my permission.'

'Well, I do, really. You see, I'm very fond of Susan.'

'So am I.' Impatient. 'So what?'

'You very kindly asked her to be a bridesmaid with your future sister-in-law, who has, I understand, a beautifully slim figure.'

'Angelica, yes. She's something of a brat but it's family, you know how it is.'

'Indeed I do. Angelica told Susan she was asked to choose the bridesmaids' dresses and she has done so. Now I'm sure she was only thinking of how well she'd look in the dress she's chosen, but the style doesn't exactly flatter Susan . . .'

Lesley frowned, but didn't interrupt.

'So I said to Susan that perhaps we could find something in the same colour but a more suitable style for her at The Magpie boutique tomorrow morning, when they reopen. Susan refused, because she doesn't want to upset you.'

Lesley's face was a study.

Ellie stiffened her back. 'Neither of us wants to cause you any aggro.'

Lesley laughed. 'Liar! You are going to take her, anyway, aren't you?'

'No, no! Not unless you feel you can tell her to choose her own dress, which might cause some problem for you with Angelica, who is, after all, going to be family from now on.'

Lesley looked annoyed. 'Angelica is accustomed to having her own way. She's been spoilt from the word go. She is a brat and I suspect she may well have thought it amusing to choose a style which would make Susan look a fright in comparison with her. She's a size eight, isn't she? And Susan is probably a twenty-four.' A shrug. 'So, all right. Let Susan choose something for herself.'

Ellie shook her head. 'It's not that easily fixed, Lesley, and you know it. Yes, it's tempting to say that Susan should go ahead and find something to suit her, but if Angelica has always been indulged and her brother is fond of her, then perhaps it's not a good idea. For a start, it's the bride's family who usually pay for the bridesmaids' dresses, isn't it? So did your fiancé ask your permission to let Angelica make her own choice?'

Silence. Lesley grimaced. 'He's very fond of her.'

'That's not really an excuse, is it? Angelica chose a dress which you will have to pay for, right? She didn't ask you what you wanted her to wear, did she?'

'Well, in general terms no, I suppose she didn't. I was supposed to go with her to see a dress she'd found, but then I got swept up in this last case so—'

'So she got the dress by herself, and told Susan to go to the same shop and get the same dress in a larger size, right? An expensive shop?'

Lesley fiddled with a button on her jacket, not meeting Ellie's eye.

Ellie said, 'Which means you're presented with a *fait accompli*. Your fiancé is probably relieved that he doesn't even have to think about it. He certainly wouldn't worry about the dress being suitable for Susan, and neither would his family. Your parents are no longer with us, and your sister has her own problems. She won't stand up for Susan. And it might be best for you not to raise any objections, either. Because, if you question Angelica's taste, I fear that her family will come down on you like a ton of bricks. And the last thing you need, just now, is to start a row in the family. Right?'

Lesley frowned and shrugged. Then shrugged again.

'I'm serious, Lesley,' said Ellie. 'A feud of this sort can carry on for years, with one side carrying a grudge against the other. If you do want to intervene for Susan's sake, well and good. But I don't see how could you do it, without seeming to criticize Angelica and, by extension, your fiancé. I suppose you could just have a quiet word with him to warn him you won't put up with Angelica's wanting her own way all the time once you're married. You could say that you think Angelica has slightly overstepped the mark, but Susan is being very brave and will put up with whatever Angelica has decided. Tell him that you'll pay the bill without quibbling, but say you hope the girl will be more tactful in future? But, if you'd rather not interfere – and Angelica will take it as interference, believe me – then Susan will cope and all will be peace and quiet.'

Lesley pulled at her button. It came off in her hands. 'So I am to start my marriage by giving in to my husband, even though I believe he's in the wrong?'

'It's a small thing. A little diplomacy now would calm the troubled waters.'

Lesley considered the loose button. 'I'm fond of Susan. She's a great girl who's had a lot to put up with. My sister is much older than me and we haven't much in common. She never really wanted a child, especially after her husband walked out on the two of them. And now she's got the menopause and her hip replacement has gone wrong and goodness knows what else and everyone's walking on eggshells around her. Poor Susan. I daresay she would put up with wearing something which makes her look a fright, but now that I know about it I'll always be aware that Angelica's made her look a figure of fun. And don't tell me Angelica will spare her feelings on the day, because she won't. Angelica is not kind. She will make remarks about pink elephants and the like. Such things can hurt most terribly. I'll have a word with Sir about this and I'll tell Susan, myself, that she should get herself something she'd like to wear.'

'Go carefully, Lesley. I'm older than you, and have seen what family upsets can do. Sisters not speaking for twenty years, that sort of thing. If you have a word with your fiancé and he sees the point, then that's fine: Susan gets her own dress. But it might be a good idea to ask his permission before you tell Susan to go ahead.'

'Ask his permission, indeed!' Lesley put the button on her pocket. 'I can do without this! Who's paying for the wedding, anyway? I am. On his salary we'd have prosecco instead of champagne, and a tatty buffet in a pub rather than a sit-down meal.'

'Yes, I know. But tempers can get frayed so easily just before a wedding. I'm beginning to wish I hadn't mentioned it. Susan is very mature for her age, and for your sake she'll play along. It's only for one day, after all.'

'She might not find anything suitable at The Magpie boutique.'

'True.'

'You'll take her there tomorrow morning? Juno won't be there, will she? Did you say she was ill?'

'Celine knows where the bodies are hidden, and I think she might open up to me, with a bit of luck.' And, Ellie would be out of the house again if Diana called round. Idly, Ellie wondered how much money her daughter wanted this time.

Lesley got to her feet. 'I must go. The florist we'd chosen has broken her wrist and dropped out, so we've got to find someone else at short notice. You do realize that the person with the best motive for killing Poppy is her sister?'

'Yes. But I don't believe it.'

'It might have been an accident.'

'Juno would have come straight out and said so, if it had been an accident. But I'll bear what you say in mind.'

FIVE

Ellie wasn't at all sure she was doing the right thing by taking Susan to The Magpie boutique but, having got Lesley's permission to do so and, let's face it, because she was curious about the Cardover family, she went through with it.

Susan was ambivalent. 'What if they don't have my size in anything?'

'We'll know straight away whether or not they've got something suitable. If not, there's no great harm done and we'll treat ourselves to a coffee instead.'

The shops in the Avenue appeared to be thriving. There were two charity shops and three estate agents, but there was a butcher, and a baker and a . . . no, not a candlestick maker, but a bookshop and a library and dance studios and a fair number of good coffee shops.

The Magpie boutique was situated towards the middle. It looked prosperous, with gleaming paintwork and glass. It must be open, for the blind was up and a woman was going in as Ellie and Susan arrived. In the window were three outfits in white, grey and black, with vivid scarves thrown over their shoulders. Attractive. Some scarlet and green T-shirts were cleverly displayed on the rungs of a stepladder. Tasty.

Susan reared back, like a frightened horse. 'It's meant for teenagers.'

Ellie pointed to a tailored suit on a model just inside the door. 'For the Mother of the Bride?'

'I couldn't wear that.'

Ellie pushed the door open and coaxed Susan inside.

Racks of clothes lined the walls, all colours of the rainbow and of different lengths. A wedding dress, complete with train, hung from a high rail, and next to it there was a flower girl's outfit. To one side there was a stand of elaborately decorated hats, and above that shelves of matching handbags and shoes. Next to the hats there stood a cabinet full of costume jewellery and even, gasp! A tiara!

Several small chairs had been dotted here and there for respite purposes, and for partners waiting for their loved ones to decide on purchases. A large notice at the back advertised 'Fitting Room', and 'Evening & Bridal Wear'. A heavy curtain concealed an entrance to what must be an extension to the shop. They were cramming rather a lot into a smallish space, weren't they?

Two women were already in the shop, pawing through the rails of clothes, attended by Celine.

'Can I help you, or would you like to look around by yourselves?'

Ellie knew that voice. Yes. It was Clemmie, who had recognized Ellie but was going to pretend that she hadn't. Clemmie was wearing the same simple black dress that she'd had on the previous day, but without the brooch.

Ellie said, 'Susan here has been invited to be a bridesmaid, wearing some sort of peach-coloured outfit. Have you anything to suit?'

Clemmie transferred her attention to Susan, assessed her and nodded. 'Come this way. We keep the evening and bridal wear through here.'

Susan would have protested, but Ellie took her arm and they followed Clemmie through the heavy curtain into the back room, the walls of which were lined with mirrored cupboards. A stick-thin woman was already there, trying on a skimpy outfit. Evidently this was a communal changing room as well as a display floor.

Clemmie said to the customer, 'Would you like me to pin up the hem for you? We have someone who can do the alteration if you decide on that dress.'

'No, it's not quite right.' The customer proceeded to disrobe.

Clemmie was not fazed. She turned back to Ellie and Susan, gesturing to some chairs. 'Would you like to take a seat?' She pushed doors open to reveal evening wear on rails, each item encased in a plastic cover. 'Peach?' Clemmie ran a hand along the merchandise. 'Mm, too orange for you. That's too pale. Mm, no: too big for you. You'll want a nice low neckline, perhaps with an underwired bra. You can get them at Marks & Spencer's. Just make sure they fit you properly.'

Susan gulped. If Ellie hadn't been between her and the exit, she'd have made a run for it.

'Ah.' Clemmie extracted two dresses from the rail, and held them up for Susan to see. Both were peach in colour. One had a sweetheart neckline, and the other a very low-cut bodice which would show off a pretty bust to perfection.

Susan gibbered.

Clemmie glimmered a smile at her. Clemmie had a delightful, catlike smile. 'What I say is, "If you've got it, flaunt it. All you need to be a knockout is a better bra. Now, we might have to take this one in a trifle, for a snug fit. Don't bother to look at anything else. Do you mind trying the dresses on in here? We're a bit short of space, you see.'

Susan shot an imploring look at Ellie, who sent her a reassuring smile in return. 'I'll have a look at the rails outside, shall I?' And to Clemmie. 'Thank you.'

'My pleasure.' Polite. Frosty. Professional.

The skinny woman left, leaving the discarded dress on the floor. Clemmie picked it up without comment. A large woman entered, carrying a pile of dresses, followed by a sulky-looking young teenager, who clearly didn't trust her mother's idea of what was fashionable.

Clemmie didn't even blink. 'Let me help you with those. Is it a birthday party your daughter is going to? I might have just the thing for someone with such lovely long legs . . .? Do you have any particular colour in mind?'

Ellie drifted back into the main shop, drawn by the sounds of altercation.

Yes, there was the widower, Ray, in meltdown. Screaming at Celine. 'So where is she, the bitch?'

There were three other women in the shop looking horrified but, at the same time, fascinated. Clemmie ignored Ray. She went straight to one of the racks, hung up the dress that the skinny woman had discarded, picked out a couple of other outfits and retired to the back room with them.

Celine said, 'Please, Ray. She's not here and—'

Ray was not going to be hushed. 'She's in the back? Tell her to get out here, now!'

A nasty draught announced that someone was holding the door to the Avenue open.

'Can someone help me in? I can't get over the step without help.' An authoritative voice. It must be . . .! Yes, it was. Juno's wheelchair-bound husband.

Celine said, 'Ray, you can't just—'

Ray poked his finger at Celine. 'What have you done with her?'

The man in the wheelchair was getting impatient. 'Come on! Help me in, someone!'

Celine cast a despairing glance around the shop. 'Please, Ray; she's not going to be in for a few days. You saw she wasn't well. She went home with her parents, who are going to put her to bed and look after her.'

'Liar! She's not there. They haven't a clue where she is!'

'If you please! Somebody! Help me up over the step!'

Celine, desperately, 'Look, Ray, I've got customers who—'

'Your customers can—'

Ellie knew the words which a man like Ray would use on such occasions, of course she did. But in this context they seemed more shocking than usual.

'Really! Such language!' A heavyset matron with a slight moustache.

'Do . . . You . . . Mind!' A youngish businesswoman, objecting to Ray's language. She took a tailored red suit from a rack, and held it up against herself.

'Eff to you, too!' Ray shot back. He seized Celine by the forearm. 'Tell her to get the eff out here. Now!'

Celine tried to free herself. 'Ray, I swear she's not here.'

'She's not with her parents, so she must have gone home with you!'

'The last I saw of her, she was getting into her parents' car. Mrs Quicke gave me a lift home. Ask her.'

Ray let go of Celine to swing round, searching for Ellie, who was half hidden by a rack of clothes. 'You! What the eff are you doing here? Turn over a stone, and there you are. So, what have you done with her, eh?'

'Nothing to do with me,' said Ellie. Her eyes were on Clemmie, who had come back into the shop and was engaged in picking out another couple of garments for her teenaged customer. Ellie wondered if Clemmie knew what had happened to her mother? How could she? Now there's an interesting question . . .

The man in the wheelchair wasn't giving up. 'If you can just help me over the step . . . can't you see that I can't . . . thank you!'

Ray shouted, 'Don't you care what's happened to her?'

Celine rubbed her arm, trying to keep calm, worried that this fracas might upset her customers. 'Ray, I really don't know where she is. She said she needed some peace and quiet, and that I understand. Now, if you don't leave, I shall have to call the police.' And to the customers, 'I'm so sorry. I must apologize. My friend is grieving and—'

Ray wasn't giving up. 'I went upstairs to the office. The Monkey says he hasn't seen hair nor hide of her, so she must be here. If you don't get her out here, I'll have to go in and look for her.'

He made as if to go through the curtain into the back room. Clemmie, who had just been going to take a new selection of garments into the back room, cried out in alarm.

Celine was quicker. 'You can't go in there! There's people changing—'

'What!' From within came the voice of the mother of the teenage girl, outraged. 'Tell him he can't come in here!'

Clemmie said, 'Shall I call the police?'

'No, no! Oh, I don't know! Ray, calm down! She's not here!'

'I don't believe you! Let me see for myself!' Ray thrust past Clemmie to get to the back room.

Gordon had managed to get a newcomer to manoeuvre him in his wheelchair over the step into the shop. 'About time, too! Couldn't you see that the step was too much for me? I needed to get in to find my wife, who has unaccountably gone missing!'

Celine held out her arms, blocking Ray's entry to the changing room. 'Are you mad?'

Ray did indeed look demented, with his thinning hair uncombed and the middle button of his shirt undone. He yanked Celine aside. She stumbled and was caught by Ellie, who steadied her on her feet.

'Now!' Ray reached to part the curtains.

Clemmie tried to stop him, and was backhanded aside.

There was a shriek from within. 'Mum!' No young teen likes being caught in mid-strip.

Gordon tried to force his wheelchair through a knot of fascinated customers. 'If you'll kindly let me pass!' Angrily.

One of the customers took out her phone, to take pictures rather than call the police. Clemmie was on her knees on the floor.

A second shriek of horror from the back room, and then . . .

. . . slowly, step by step, Ray reappeared, walking backwards, arms in the air.

After him came the very picture of an avenging fury in peach satin, incredible, magnificent bosom heaving – yes, there was no other word for it, Susan's bosom was heaving sufficiently to cause an earthquake in Saigon. Her red hair was loose about her face, her strong arms were steady and the expression on her face was that of a gladiator readying for the kill . . .

. . . with a chair.

One of the legs of the chair was actually touching Ray's throat.

He had no choice. He had to reverse or be impaled.

'How . . . Dare . . . You!' The avenging angel kept pace with the retreating man.

'Shall I call the police now?' A customer to the businesswoman.

Celine choked back a laugh. Hysteria? 'Somehow, I don't think that will be necessary.'

Ray backed into the wheelchair.

Gordon squawked, 'Watch it, you fool!' He struck out at Ray. And missed.

Susan's voice grated. 'Enough? Yes? Then, get down on your knees and apologize to all these ladies.' Her eyes were blue as the sky. Her chin said that she wouldn't hesitate to drive the chairleg home. Perhaps she would have made a good police-woman if she hadn't decided to be a chef.

Ray couldn't seem to get the words out. He held up his hands, appealing for mercy. He slumped to his knees. And gobbled something.

Susan abruptly drew back the chair. She looked at it as if she wondered why she was holding it, turned on her heel and took it back through the curtain into the rear of the shop.

Clemmie got to her feet and brushed herself down.

Someone clapped.

The atmosphere broke up into relief and joy. 'How about that!' someone said.

'Brill!'

'Did you get it on your phone?'

Celine attempted to rescue the situation. 'Ladies! I'm so sorry. Please forgive. My friend is grieving. His wife, so recent . . . But Ray, Gordon . . . I honestly don't know what . . . but this is not the place to . . . why don't you ask at the office upstairs?'

'Been there, done that,' said Ray, slicking back his hair, checking his shirt was tucked into his trousers.

Gordon ground out, 'You know perfectly well that I can't manage the stairs!'

Susan's arm came out from the back room through the curtain, holding the peach dress. 'I'll take this. How much?'

Celine attempted a smile. 'That's on the house.'

The dress shook. 'Nonsense,' said Susan's voice. 'I pay my way.'

The businesswoman put down the red suit long enough to reach into her handbag. 'I'll throw a fiver into the kitty for you!'

The matron with the moustache did likewise. 'Worth it, for the entertainment. I haven't got a fiver. Take a tenner, will you?'

'Fifty p,' piped up the young teenager from within. 'That's all right, isn't it, Mum?'

Ellie delved into her own bag. She couldn't stop grinning. 'Here's twenty from me.'

'And another five,' said the businesswoman. 'Now, Celine . . .' holding up the red suit, 'I'll try this on.'

Celine made a good recovery. 'Ladies, thank you for being so forbearing. Might I offer you all a cup of coffee and a biscuit to compensate for the delay in attending to you?'

Clemmie said smoothly, 'I'll make the coffee.'

Ray produced a smile for the ladies, probably hoping it would charm them into forgiving his bad behaviour. Perhaps in his youth he'd been something of a ladies' man. From the stony expressions of the ladies present, he seemed to have lost the knack. But he tried. 'That's all very well, but I've got to find her. She's the only one who can help me now.'

Gordon flushed. 'You think she's going to bail you out yet again? In your dreams! I agree she had no right to take off like that, but . . .' He seemed to rethink what he was about to say, and tempered his tone. 'Well, if she really is ill, ill enough to have the doctor, then naturally I will make allowances. She'll be back, of course. She knows what will happen if she doesn't!' His voice had risen. Again, he brought it back down. 'In the meantime, you must see that I have to think of myself. I need someone to look after me. Now. I need another prescription filled. And, who's going to make my lunch?'

Celine was soothing. 'Well, Gordon, while Juno's recovering, perhaps you can ring the agency which looked after you when she had flu last winter. Ladies, do you all take milk in your coffee, or would you prefer a cup of tea? And do find yourselves a seat. If there's not enough chairs, we can bring some more in from the changing room.'

Ray selected the matron with the moustache to be his confidante. 'It's my sister-in-law, you see. The only one of the family worth tuppence. She went home with her parents last night because she was in distress after the funeral. At least, that's what she said she was going to do. But she's not there! They say they were only halfway home when she told them to stop and let her out as she felt she ought to go back to look after Gordon—'

'What!' Gordon was not amused. 'I tell you, she never returned. I spent a miserable evening worrying about what might have happened to her. Finally, when I got through to her parents and learned she'd walked out on them too, well, I had to ring round the hospitals, didn't I? Not a sign of her there, either. How selfish can she be! I had to take double my usual dose to get to sleep and when I woke up this morning, expecting her to have returned to get my breakfast, she still wasn't there and I had to get myself up and into the chair to let the cleaner in without having had a cup of tea or anyone to help me dress. Not a bite have I had—'

Celine said, 'Look, Gordon, this is really not the time or the place to—'

Ray pointed his finger at Celine. 'Aren't you worried? She might be lying dead somewhere, the victim of a mugger. Or had an accident, been run over by a car.'

'No, of course she isn't!' Celine wrung her hands. 'I'm so sorry, ladies. It seems that my boss – who's married to the gentleman in the wheelchair – is not well and has gone away for a few days!'

Ray said, 'She got out of her parents' car by Ealing Broadway tube station. She told them she'd take a taxi back home from there. But she hasn't. She's disappeared into thin air. Celine, you really don't know where she is?'

'No, I really don't.'

Ellie, in the background, was spellbound, as were the customers. They watched avidly, as if they were sitting in the front stalls at the theatre.

Clemmie put her head round the curtain. 'How many coffees? Anyone prefer tea?'

Ellie decided to become a maid-of-all-work again. 'I'll take the order, shall I? How many for coffee? Black or white?' She made a note in her diary of who wanted what, and traipsed back through the curtain, past Susan and the teenage girl who were in different stages of undress. At the back of the changing room there was an unobtrusive door marked 'Toilet', and another which was ajar, giving a glimpse of a small kitchen and a fire door which would give access to the outside world.

Shops of this kind usually had some kind of yard at the back, but it seemed that The Magpie had built out to take in every inch of space it could. The fire door must give on to whatever remained of the yard, but it couldn't be used as a fire escape for the shop unless . . . Ellie pushed on to the bar which held the door in place, and caught a glimpse of a small yard space beyond, bounded by a high door in a fence. And yes, cast-iron stairs climbed up from the ground floor to, presumably, the flat or office space above? There was a substantial door in the outer fence, locked and bolted. That would give on to a passageway leading out to the street? It wouldn't be easy to burgle the shop.

Ellie turned her attention to her duties as maid-of-all-work. She sang out, 'Five coffees, three with milk, two black. One tea, preferably peppermint.'

Clemmie had a kettle coming to the boil and was rapidly assembling mugs, milk and sugar on to a tray. 'Ta,' said Clemmie, not looking at Ellie.

Ellie considered Clemmie's actions that day. The girl was calm. Unflustered by all the goings-on with Ray and Gordon. Yesterday she'd been calm enough, but with an undercurrent of grief and concern for her mother. She'd been distressed then, barely keeping worry at bay.

Today she was hard at work. Focused on the job in hand. She hadn't jumped up and down and screamed when Ray arrived with the news that Juno had gone missing, nor when Gordon chipped in with his demands. In fact, she'd treated Gordon as if she'd never met him before in her life.

Why?

It seemed to Ellie that Clemmie was not particularly upset by the news of her mother's disappearance . . . if that is what it was.

Ditto Celine, come to think of it. Yesterday Celine had locked hands with Juno, had fussed over her, tried to get her to eat . . . had suggested Juno go home with her to be looked after. Today, she'd exhibited no surprise at all when Ray said Juno had disappeared.

The kettle boiled, and Clemmie's flying fingers made coffee and tea. She found a tin half full of biscuits and handed that to Ellie with a brief, 'Follow me, will you?'

Back they processed through the changing room, in which Susan was now almost fully dressed in her usual clothes and the teenage girl was wriggling out of a glittering tunic. The businesswoman was also there now, frowning at her image in the mirror as she tugged at the lapels of the red suit.

Clemmie and Ellie went through the curtain into the shop, into which two more customers arrived. The 'old' customers were now sitting or standing around, on their phones or talking to Ray and Gordon.

Someone's phone rang. All the customers dived into bags, and one of them – the moustached matron – answered hers with a sharp, 'What now!'

Susan came out from the back, wearing her usual outsize T-shirt and wrinkled jeans, with the peach dress over her arm. 'I'll go straight to Marks and get myself a new bra. Here's a twenty. Put that towards it, and I'll get the rest to you in the week.'

Celine said, 'I'm not taking your money. I'm giving you a discount, and my lovely customers have paid the rest.'

'Don't give it another thought, Susan,' said Ellie, watching Clemmie dispense her mugs of coffee and tea and take orders from the newcomers. 'If there's anything left to pay, I'll stump up for it. Worth it. Every penny.'

'Well, thanks, Mrs Quicke.' Grudgingly. Susan didn't like being beholden to anyone, did she? 'I'll get some money out of the nearest cash machine and go straight on to Marks's now. That is, if you don't need me for anything else?'

'You've done enough. Have fun.'

Ray was trying to explain his problem to the moustached matron, while avoiding the words 'debt' and 'gambling'. 'What I want to know is, how long do I wait before ringing the police? Juno wouldn't abandon her family. She knows how much we all rely on her.'

Gordon said, 'She'll be back tonight, see if she isn't!' He banged on the arm of his wheelchair. 'Talk about inconsiderate! If she has to go away on business for a weekend, she knows very well that she has to fix up with somebody to come in and take care of me. She wouldn't dare to abandon me. Something must have happened to her.'

Clemmie retreated into the back, presumably to fetch more refreshments.

'No. Wait!' Celine called out, 'Clemmie!'

Clemmie put her head back through the curtain.

'Clemmie,' said Celine, 'you must tell them. I know you promised your mother not to say anything, but we can't keep the secret any longer.' Facing the shop, she said, 'Clemmie was rung by her mother last night to say that she was taking some time out, and wouldn't be in for a few days. She said not to worry about her as she was going to be well looked after. She wouldn't tell Clemmie where she was going, but we think she's booked herself into a spa hotel for some peace and quiet.'

Ah-ha! thought Ellie. Now that makes sense.

Clemmie ducked her head. 'Two more coffees coming up.'

Ray swung round on her. 'What time did she ring? Why didn't you tell us? Where's this place she's gone to? What's the phone number?'

Clemmie stonewalled that. 'She didn't want to say. She said not to worry, and that she'd ring me again soon.'

'Well, ring her back, now! I've got to speak to her!'

Gordon was angry. 'She had no right to ring you instead of me!'

Eyelids lowered, Clemmie said in a soft voice, 'But you always take a sleeping pill at night.'

'Well, ring her back, now!'

'She said she was turning her phone off. No business, no worries. She said not to contact her. Actually, I did try this morning because I wanted to ask her about a stock delivery, but her phone was off. Coffee coming up.'

Gordon appealed to the room, 'How dare she not ring me! She's no right to behave like this. When she gets back . . .' He choked on his next words, caught himself up, and turned down the volume. 'She must have realized I would need to speak to her.'

No one answered that. There was, perhaps, a feeling that if they'd been Juno, they might have wanted to avoid speaking to him, too.

'I'll get her, now!' Ray got out his own phone, and pressed buttons. Trying to raise Juno? They could all hear that the phone at the other end was not taking calls. He chewed his lip.

Clemmie moved smoothly round the room, offering more coffee. She didn't raise her eyes from her tray until she got to Ellie, when she lifted them in one long, searching glance.

Clemmie was trying to tell Ellie something?

Ellie nodded. Perhaps they'd talk later?

The matron with the moustache said, comfortable in the knowledge that her own world was still intact, 'Well, there it is. Your wife will come home when she's had a little time to herself. When my husband was alive, I wouldn't have minded being pampered in a spa hotel every now and then.'

The businesswoman came in from the back with the red suit. 'I'll take this, thanks. And I'd like to look at that red handbag up there, as well.'

Mother and teenage girl also emerged from the back. The mother said, 'That outfit you've found for her is just right. Here's my card.' And, to her daughter, 'You'll be quite the belle of the ball, won't you? Though I still say that dress is on the short side.'

Predictably, the girl blushed and said, 'Oh, Mum!'

Once one of the customers had stirred themselves to depart, others either got down to business, or left. The businesswoman frowned over the handbag she'd thought might go with the suit she was buying. The woman with the moustache took another phone call, and left without making a purchase. Clemmie removed coffee and tea things, and then began to replace discarded items on the rails. Ellie took a seat in a corner, and watched Ray and Gordon trying to decide what to do next.

Brothers-in-law. Without anything much in common.

Ray got on the phone again. This time to his father-in-law. 'Look, Gerald; I've got to see you. I'll be round in, what, half an hour? . . . Trixie? I've no idea where she . . . She's been with you? Only just left? Why . . .? Well, that's one of the stupidest . . .! No, of course I don't think it's a good idea. I'll be round in . . . No, I know you said Juno wasn't with you, but she phoned Clemmie and I don't understand why she didn't phone you as well . . . She did! Well, of all the . . . I can understand why she wouldn't want to go home . . . yes, Gordon's here . . . Where are we? At the shop, of course. Where else would we . . .?'

His eyes switched to and fro. He listened, frowning. Pacing up and down.

Gordon grabbed his elbow. 'She must have given them her phone number. Tell them she's to ring me, straight away.'

Ray shook his hand off, continuing to listen. 'Yes, but . . . You don't understand. Unless I come up with some sort of plan . . .' He drew the back of his hand across his forehead. 'I'll come clean. I need to . . . Look, I'll be with you in half an hour, because the sooner . . .'

Still talking, he left the shop. Ellie could see him getting into a badly parked car outside, just as a traffic warden was about to tape a parking fine notice on the windshield.

'That'll cost him,' said the businesswoman, with a cat-like smile. 'I'm not sure about the handbag. I need to think about that. But I'll definitely take the suit.' She went out to her own car, which was properly parked on the other side of the road, and drove off.

Ellie felt someone at her elbow. Clemmie, watching Ray's humiliation as he tried to tear the notice off his car, even as the parking attendant took photographs recording the event.

'I wonder if Ray will try to hit him,' said Celine, also watching and also amused.

Two more customers came in, talking on their phones. One was pushing a baby buggy.

Celine said, 'A busy day,' and went to attend to them.

Gordon caught Clemmie's arm. 'Well, there's nothing for it. You'll have to step in to look after me till she gets back.'

'No,' said Clemmie, in her usual quiet way. 'I'm working, remember? Ring the local cab firm. They'll get you home.'

'You forget yourself, girl!'

'I don't think so.' Clemmie moved away, looking wooden, and disappeared into the back room.

Ellie saw Celine glance at Gordon, and glance away. Celine didn't call Clemmie back.

What on earth was going on there?

SIX

The door opened and in stalked Trixie in a low-cut blue-and-red sundress with a red bandana round her hair. She looked stunning . . . a fact of which she was perfectly aware.

Naturally Trixie would come, thought Ellie. She was the missing member of the family. She needed money for her film career and would want to track her aunt down. She would have tried her grandparents first, and then come on to the shop.

Oops! Gordon wasn't pleased to see her. 'Trixie, what are you doing here? Though I suppose I can guess.'

'I might say the same for you. Only thinking of yourself, as usual. If you ask me, it's more than time my aunt had a rest from your moaning.'

Lips whitening, Gordon struck back. 'I haven't noticed your paying any attention to her in the past, but now you want something—'

Trixie brushed him aside to concentrate on Celine, who was trying to avoid her eye while serving a customer. 'Well, where is she? You of all people must know where she's hiding.'

Celine said, 'Please, Trixie; we're very busy this morning. And no, I don't know where she is. She doesn't want us to know, apparently. She'll be back when she's had a rest.'

Gordon pulled Trixie's arm. 'Have you tried the office upstairs? I can't get up there, but Ray said he went up and the Monkey wouldn't give him the time of day.'

'Her office? I tried that first. She's not there. Where's Clemmie?'

Gordon gestured. 'Out back. But you won't get anything out of her.'

'Watch me!' Trixie swung through the shop, full skirts rustling.

Ellie stepped back into the shadows, thinking that there was a lot to be said for small waists and full skirts if you had the basic equipment to carry them off. Which Trixie did.

Clemmie appeared from the back room, her arms full of discarded clothing, which she started to hang on a rail. Had she heard Trixie's voice and come out to confront her? Yes.

Trixie put her hands on her hips. 'There you are! Where is she?'

Clemmie said, 'She's not here, Trixie.' She then ignored her cousin to speak directly to Celine. 'It's nearly twelve, Celine, and I'm due upstairs. Is the new girl coming to help you this afternoon?'

'Thankfully, yes. Off you go.'

Trixie grabbed Clemmie's shoulder. 'Where are you going?'

'You know very well I work in the shop on Saturday mornings, and in the office upstairs in the afternoon.' Patiently. Then, provocatively, 'Celine's busy. Perhaps *you'd* like to help her here in the shop for a change?'

'Come on! I'm no shop girl.'

'Well, I am. I have to work for my living, remember?' There was no animosity in this exchange. The cousins weren't at one another's throats, but there was a sense that each was testing the other.

'Fortunately,' said Trixie, almost to herself, 'I don't have to.'

Clemmie nodded, twisted away from Trixie and withdrew into the back room.

Trixie stamped her foot. 'Oh!' She swung on her heel and stormed out of the shop, just as Gordon was trying to leave in his wheelchair. They collided in the doorway, did some ritual shouting at one another, and exited.

Peace and quiet. Stares from customers. A sigh of relief and more apologies from Celine.

Ellie went through the back room into the kitchenette. The fire door was open on to the tiny yard. A tall, grey-haired, well-dressed man was standing at the base of the fire escape, talking to Clemmie. It was the same man who'd accompanied Celine to the funeral. Ellie had put him down as married to Celine. But was that right?

When he saw Ellie watching, the man turned away and went up the stairs.

Clemmie made as if to follow him, but changed her mind and returned to the kitchen, saying to Ellie, 'I'm off in a minute.'

'Is that the man Ray and Gordon call "The Monkey"?'

'I don't know why they call him that, but they were all at school together, so . . .' A shrug. 'His name is Mr Mornay and he's helping out at the agency for the time being.'

'He's Celine's husband?'

'What? Oh, no. Celine's a widow.'

'He was at the funeral with her.'

'He came to the funeral because he's a family friend and because he's been helping us out recently, but he didn't want to get involved in the reading of the will. He was just checking that I'd be able to work upstairs this afternoon, which I can. The office has been closed for a week and there's a pile of stuff to deal with. I'm going out to get some lunch for us all, and then I'm on duty upstairs.'

Ellie said, in a conversational tone, 'I hate to be a nuisance, but either you start talking to me, or I tell my policewoman friend that Juno has gone missing in mysterious circumstances. The police will put out an APB for her, and start questioning the family all over again.'

Clemmie produced her tiny, pussycat smile. 'Yes, I thought that's what you'd say. Give me half an hour, then ring the bell on the door next to the shop, and I'll let you in.'

'I'll do better than that. Tell me what you want to eat for lunch, and I'll get it for all three of us.'

'There's four of us upstairs. The first café along the Avenue knows what we like. Two sausage baguettes, two egg and cress sandwiches, two lattes with sugar, one Ribena, one chocolate milkshake. Collect the money from us on your return.'

Returning to The Magpie, Ellie looked for and found an unobtrusive door immediately to the left of the shop. A discreet plaque advertised the presence of the PJ agency. P for Poppy, J for Juno? That was easy to interpret. It was amazing they'd kept their activities secret for so long . . . or had they? Who – apart from the senior Cardovers and Celine – had known about the agency's success? Clemmie? Mm, yes. But who else?

There was a query in Ellie's mind about how much the husbands had known. Ray certainly hadn't realized how extensive The Magpie's activities had grown to be until he'd opened

some wrongly addressed mail. An eruption comparable to
Vesuvius blowing its top had ensued. Words such as 'treachery'
had been chucked around.

How much had Gordon known?

Ellie pressed the button on the speaker system, gave her name
and was buzzed in to a tiny lobby. Clemmie's voice floated
down from above. 'I'm on the phone. Come straight up.'

Steep stairs rose ahead of Ellie, ending in a small landing
off which a door led to the right.

It was down these stairs that Poppy had fallen to her death.

Ellie was not in darkness, as some light came from a transom
window above the front door behind her, and more came from
the open door at the top of the stairs. Also, there were timed
buttons at top and bottom of the flight to operate a light in the
ceiling. Ellie tested the nearest switch with her elbow and
the light came on.

There were handrails on both sides of the staircase, which
was carpeted in a coffee-coloured hardwearing material.
The walls had been painted magnolia, and decorated with sepia
photographs showing how the shops in the Avenue used to look
years ago. The decor was in restrained good taste. Perhaps
it was slightly dull, like an old-fashioned bank? But that wasn't
a bad impression to give if you were aiming to present yourself
as reliable and creditworthy.

There was no obvious reason why anyone should fall
down the stairs or – if they did stumble and lose their footing
– why they had ended up in the morgue.

Ellie put down the food she was carrying to brush the carpet
on the bottom steps with her hand. They were dry. There was
no sign of bloodstains. If there had been blood, it had been
cleaned away most efficiently, but the sort of deep cleaning
which removed blood would have left the carpet on the bottom
steps looking a shade lighter than the rest. There was no sign
of that.

Had the carpet been replaced? No. A new carpet fluffs up.
This one hadn't been disturbed for some time. Possibly not
for years. Was the bit on which she stood a shade darker than
the rest? Possibly. It was hard to tell. No, she'd probably
imagined it.

Ellie scanned the walls on either side. If someone tripped and fell, they'd probably have bashed themselves against the walls on either side on their way down, leaving marks on the plaster, even bloodstains or gouges. Nothing.

Did the pictures cover telltale bloodstains? Ellie left her packages at the bottom of the stairs and walked up them, twitching the pictures aside as she went. The walls were clean. The pictures were not hiding signs of someone who'd bounced off the walls in falling.

So, Poppy had fallen from top to bottom without leaving a trace behind.

Or, her neck had been broken at the top or at the bottom of the stairs, and her body left just inside the door to the street?

Ellie retrieved her packages and climbed the stairs as Clemmie appeared on the landing. 'Sorry about that. I should have come down to give you a hand, but . . . the phone. Mother arranged for all the incoming calls to be rerouted to Laura's home phone while the office was closed, and she's managed to deal with most of them, but there's a backlog, not surprisingly. No one else has been in, so the post has mounted up, too!'

Ellie looked to see where the pad controlling the speaker-and-entry system was located. It was on the landing next to the timer switch for the light. Not a very good idea. When someone rang the bell at the door downstairs, one of the office workers would have to get up from her desk and walk over to the landing before they could press the button to hear who was calling, and only then would they release the doorcatch to let them in. Which was what Clemmie had just done, interrupting her phone call in the middle.

Ellie handed over her packages and followed Clemmie into a large open office overlooking the street. Here the theme was also cream and cocoa, but now they were in the twenty-first century. Modernity ruled. Desks, computers, printers, maps, ranks of books, samples of carpeting and tiles . . . everything was neat and orderly. Even a mountain of opened post had been sorted into piles marked: Urgent, Pending and Junk.

Ellie recognized the two women in the office. They'd both been at the funeral. The nearest one had longish, grey hair

caught back with a comb, and was packing a briefcase while
checking her smartphone. She wore a business suit, discreetly
expensive. Forty-ish, efficient, intelligent. No wedding ring.

She gave Ellie a cursory glance, but didn't wait to be introduced. 'Clemmie, I'll take my lunch with me. Got a viewing
in half an hour. Then I'm checking on number nine. There's
a complaint about the work that new decorator's done. Should
be back about four. The paperwork from this morning's visits
is on your desk.'

Clemmie handed her some food, and she was off.

'That was Ruth,' said Clemmie. 'She does most of the
viewings and inspections. Over by the window is Laura, our
office manageress.'

Laura was the other middle-aged woman who'd been at the
funeral and who had sat with Ruth and a young girl. Perhaps
the young girl was the 'new' one, who was taking over from
Clemmie in the shop this afternoon?

Laura was talking on the phone, frowning, listening, pulling
on longish brown hair, and didn't stop when Clemmie placed
her food on her desk. Laura wore a wedding ring, and was casu-
ally, expensively dressed. She had a pleasant voice, reassuring
someone on the phone that a carpenter would be with the caller
on Monday morning. Like her fellow worker Ruth, she wasn't
interested in Ellie. Perhaps because both Ruth and Laura assumed
Ellie was a customer and that Clemmie was looking after her?
A reasonable assumption.

Clemmie led the way to the back of the room where a couple
of desks were unattended. 'Laura is the first port of call on the
telephone. She gets the enquiry, logs it, passes it to my mother
or to Aunt Poppy, and they deal with it or delegate to one of
us. I'm the dogsbody, dealing with a bit of everything. I answer
the phone if Laura's engaged; I do the filing; I log everything
on to the computer. I liaise with the team for repairs and for
refurbishing the houses when tenants leave or we acquire another
property. Electricians, plasterers, plumbers, decorators.'

'And enjoy it?'

Clemmie looked surprised at the question, then smiled. 'Yes.
I enjoy it.'

'Exactly where does Mr Mornay come into this?'

Her expression closed up again. In a flat voice, she said, 'Mr Mornay is our accountant, as well as a family friend. A couple of weeks ago, Aunt Poppy and Mother asked Mr Mornay to give them an overview of where the company should be going. The business has grown, you see. They thought perhaps we could combine some jobs or, if we're doing well enough – which is what we are hoping – we might afford to take on another person.'

She looked away, and said in a small voice. 'I don't mean someone to replace Aunt Poppy.' She swallowed. 'I suppose we'll need someone with a business head to try to replace her. But even before she died, we were running round like mad things trying to get everything done, and we never had time to stop and think about where we're going. When Mum gets back, I suppose they'll have a meeting and sort it out. He's said he'll stay on for the time being.'

'You don't like him?'

A compression of the lips. 'Of course I do. I've known him for ever, sort of.'

'He's a friend of your father's?'

'They were all at school together, Mum and Aunt Poppy and Mr Mornay and Uncle Ray. When I was little, I called Mr Mornay "Uncle Charles", but he says it's inappropriate now he's here at the office as, sort of, my boss.'

Ellie frowned. If Clemmie had always called him 'Uncle' before, why did he have to be so formal now?

'I'm not complaining,' said Clemmie, looking self-conscious. 'Because, if that's the way he wants it . . . sorry! I shouldn't gossip. I don't know why I'm telling you all this.'

'Because you're caught up in a horrible situation, and you're worried sick about what's going to happen. Because I'm here to help if I can.'

'Yes.' Another of her considering stares, almost accusatory. 'You're very easy to talk to.'

Ellie felt herself blush. 'I'm interested in people. I think that's why they talk to me.'

'You want to talk to Mr Mornay?' Clemmie gestured to the back of the office. 'He's working in the inner sanctum for the time being. I'll introduce you.' She led Ellie past a

toilet and a kitchenette, through a door into another sunny
room, one which must have been built out over the back room
downstairs.

Ellie looked around with interest. She believed you could
tell a lot about people by the way they 'nested' in an office.
Here there was evidence of two different personalities. Identical
desks faced one another across the room: one each for Poppy
and Juno. Twin computers and telephones, yes. The computers
and telephones on one desk were decorated with stickers; the
other set was plain.

One desk overflowed with catalogues and samples. A fuchsia-
pink cardigan hung over the back of the chair. A tumble of
glittery pens had fallen out of a china mug which lacked a
handle. A laptop lay in its case against the back wall. Poppy's?

On the other desk, a stark black mug, complete with handle,
held a selection of ballpoint pens in plain black. A dark grey
pashmina had been folded up and left over that chair. The desk
was severely clear. Juno's. No laptop in sight.

In the centre of the room there was a large table at which
Mr Mornay was sitting, talking on the phone and taking notes.
His computer was up and running in front of him, and there
were ledgers and bills around him. Real ledgers, real stacks of
bills. So this wasn't a paper-free office? Not that Ellie had ever
had any faith in such. Ellie was suspicious of how safe online
banking could be, and what happened to credit card details
when given over the phone. She knew this put her in the
dinosaur class, and she didn't care.

Mr Mornay looked up, sharp eyes noting that Clemmie had
brought Ellie into his office. He nodded. No smile. He said,
'Not now, Clemmie,' and concentrated on his caller. 'Yes, I do
understand. No, what I'm referring to is . . .'

Clemmie deposited some of the food on his desk and retreated
to the main office, taking Ellie with her. She said, 'I'll introduce
you when he's off the phone. Shall we eat at my desk?'

'How long have you been working here?'

'Nearly two years now.'

'I heard you say you were a working girl.'

Clemmie laid out the food, took the lid off her coffee to add
sugar, and stirred it. 'I support myself.'

Her cousin Trixie didn't? Perhaps Trixie would have to start now her mother, who'd been the moneymaker in the family, had departed?

Ellie bit into her egg sandwich. Luscious. Yum. 'So, tell me why I shouldn't inform the police that your mother is missing.'

'She's not missing.'

'Mislaid?'

Almost, a smile. A pretty, catlike smile that transformed her face. Clemmie had beauty and brains, but also charm. 'She needs to be quiet for a while, that's all.' But there was a hint of restraint there, and the smile quickly disappeared.

'May I venture to suggest that she has not booked herself into a spa hotel as you claimed?'

A shrug. A sip of coffee. 'Your guess is as good as mine.'

'I don't think so. I think you know all the secrets in your family.'

'Not all.' A note of pain?

'Tell me.'

Another shrug. Silence.

Ellie hadn't had any Ribena for ever. She opened the container with difficulty . . . all that cellophane wrapping! Was it still called cellophane nowadays? Perhaps it was called by another name? Clingfilm? No, not that. Ellie tackled the wrapping around the bent straw and pulled it straight. Eureka! Success! She forced the straw into the carton and sucked. Bliss.

Then she felt guilty. Did the drink contain more sugar than she ought to be consuming in twenty-four hours, or was it supposed to be healthy and to do you good?

She decided she didn't care. She was enjoying it. She said, 'Tell me about Gordon.'

'He's not my father.'

'No, I realize that. Blue eyes, brown eyes. And so on. You are very like your mother. She loves you dearly, and you love her. But you don't love Gordon, and I think . . . have you moved out of the family home?'

A nod. 'Gordon doesn't care for me. But then, why should he? If I'd been blue-eyed and blonde without two ideas in my head, he'd probably have been able to accept me. But I don't look like him, I was born asking "why", and I make up my own mind about things.'

'What things?'

'Oh, what's important and what's not. Table manners. Lights out at ten o'clock. Answering back. Not being a willing slave.'

Ellie slurped Ribena. It really did taste good! How many years was it since she'd had some? 'You answered back?'

'In spades.' A rueful laugh. 'Mum tried to tell me how to manage him. "Yes, sir. No, sir. Three bags full, sir." That sort of thing. But I couldn't. I did try. Sometimes. But perhaps not very hard.' She smiled and a dimple creased her cheek. 'I was a brat.'

Ellie laughed. 'But, a worthwhile person.'

'I made mistakes.' She was beginning to talk more freely. 'Looking back, I can see I could have made things a lot easier for myself. With a bit of tact from me we could have got along much better. I do try now. Well, sometimes I try.' A shadow passed over her face. 'This week I've tried like mad! I didn't want to make things worse for Mum than they were, what with her missing Aunt Poppy and the funeral and all.'

Ellie replayed in her mind the moment when Gordon had lashed out at Clemmie. The girl had reached for the wheelchair. He'd not just brushed her away, but hit her with intent to hurt. Clemmie hadn't responded in any way. She'd frozen. Now Ellie remembered where she'd seen that reaction before. It was from a stoical child who had grown accustomed to being hit by her parents. Ellie's mind went back to her schooldays. Nobody had suspected abuse till one day the police had arrested a school friend's parents for murder. The parents had gone to jail.

So, was Clemmie used to being hit? Mm. Possibly.

The girl was still speaking. '. . . in the past, the rows we've had . . .! It used to upset Mum.'

Ellie said, 'People who don't make mistakes don't usually make anything else.'

Clemmie sighed. 'Yes. I made mistakes. One very big one. I suppose I'd better explain. I went Interrailing with a friend, someone neither Gordon nor my mum liked; someone that they'd warned me against. We landed up in a small town in Greece. I had the cramps and went to bed early while he went out to a bar, got drunk and trashed the place. He ended up in jail and was told to pay a large fine or face a prison sentence. I hadn't enough cash on me to get him out. It was a frightening amount. Far more than my allowance for the year. He begged me to get a loan from a payday company and get him out. So I did. The rate of interest was frightening, but he promised to repay me as soon as he was released.

'Wasn't I stupid to believe him? As soon as he was free I tried to talk to him about repayment, because I was in my first year at uni and on a student loan. He said I was just another rich girl, pretending to slum it when I had millions in the bank. I told him it wasn't like that, that I was on a strict budget. He didn't believe me. Or maybe he didn't want to believe me, to make himself feel better. He stormed off and didn't come back. I don't know where he spent that night, but next day he was all over another girl and wouldn't even look at me. He went off with her on the ferry that night, without so much as a goodbye to me. Leaving me with the hotel bill, too! I was furious and upset and so ashamed of myself. I came straight home and confessed what I'd done.'

'Your mother understood . . .?'

'Unfortunately, she'd gone away for a couple of days and I couldn't get in touch with her. Yes, she really does go to a spa several times a year. I confessed to Gordon and asked him to advise me about the debt. I was afraid he'd crow like mad and of course he did, but I could put up with that. I deserved it, didn't I? But then, he refused to help me sort out the money. He said I'd been a burden on him long enough, and that it was about time I stood on my own two feet, and moved out. He meant it. I had to move out that very day.'

'Your mother wouldn't have thrown you out if she'd been there.'

'No. But he was right, you know. It was about time I grew up and took responsibility for myself. Only, I couldn't think how. I went to Gramps and Gran and told them what had happened. They took me in, just as I was, all dirty and sweaty from the journey home. They made me eat the most enormous meal and have a long bath and a good sleep. In the morning they said the first thing I must do was to speak to the boy and make some arrangement for him to pay me back. And, what do you think happened? He said that I'd paid to get him out of jail because I was besotted with him, and there'd never been any agreement for him to pay me back.' The hurt in her voice said she was still feeling raw about it.

'Oh, dear!' said Ellie.

'Yes. So I was on my own. Finally I got through to my mother and told her what had happened and yes, she did understand. She said it was better I found out what the boy was like before things had gone too far. She said she'd pay off my debt, but I got on my high horse and refused. I said I'd made a mistake and would pay for it. She said maybe I was right, but that I must get my overdraft sorted out because the interest I was paying was horrendous and to ask Gramps how to do it.

'So I did ask. He offered to write off my debt, same as Mum had done, but I couldn't have that. So he arranged for me to re-finance with a different company at a reasonable rate of interest. My godfather came through with an extra spot of cash for my birthday, which was soon after, and my godmother sent me a hundred pounds, too. I suppose Mum told them what happened. I hardly ever see my godmother – she used to be Mr Mornay's wife but they don't get along – and my godfather lives abroad and I've never seen him, but he does send me lovely presents. They both helped, which gave me a nice warm feeling. It was then that I started to think what I really wanted out of life.

'I dropped out of uni in order to get a job. Gramps said he'd like me to stay on at uni and he'd pay my fees, but I didn't want that, either. I'd never really wanted go to uni anyway, couldn't see the point. I wanted to get a job, to show everyone that I could earn my own living. And that's what I've done.'

Pride. Did she mean that she'd wanted to show Gordon that she could? Mm, probably. 'Your grandparents found you somewhere to live?'

The catlike smile. 'That's when I found out about The Magpie houses to let. Mum and Aunt Poppy said I could have a tiny house which had just been vacated by some students. It was in a horrible mess; the plumbing was shot and so was the decor, but they said I could move in straight away if I didn't mind workmen tramping all over the place for a while. I didn't mind that; in fact it taught me a lot about what has to be done to these houses to make them fit to live in. I pay rent, mind. I insisted. I've kept myself and scrimped and saved and walked everywhere instead of taking taxis, and the only clothes I've bought have been hand-me-downs or from the charity shop . . . although, to be fair, Poppy has tried to give me lots of her things, but they're not really my style, if you see what I mean. I've learned how to cook frugal meals. Gran helped me there. She loves to cook and I've learned so much from her. The upshot is that I've paid off my debt, every single penny of it! I went round to tell Gramps and Gran and, what do you know, he brought out a bottle of champagne for us to celebrate! They said they were so proud of me.' A broad grin.

'I kept trying to tell Mum, but she was so worried about Aunt Poppy and Uncle Ray that she kept putting me off. I thought that it didn't matter if she didn't get the good news for a couple of days and then Aunt Poppy . . . Oh dear! I can't stop crying when I think . . .' She dived for a tissue and blew her nose.

'What do you plan to do now? Get a different job? Go back to uni?'

'Oh no. I love it here. I've learned so much and I'm sure there's more to come, but if they decide not to keep me on, I think I'll look for another job in housing management.'

'Not in another boutique? You're great with customers.'

'That's OK as far as it goes, but I prefer working up here. Now I'm free of debt, I'm refreshing my driving skills. I had a driving test booked when everything went wrong and of course I haven't been able to afford to buy a car since then, but I've had a couple of lessons recently and lots of practice in friends' cars and I'm booked to take another test next week. I'm terrified! What if I don't pass? The instructor says I'll be all right but . . . if I get nervous . . .? It would be really useful at work, to be able to drive here and there. I've jumped the gun a bit, been looking at second-hand cars. I've even taken one for a test drive with a friend by my side. How about that!'

'Double congratulations, my dear. I can see another bottle of champagne being broken open in the near future.' They

grinned at one another. Liking one another. Ellie said, 'What
about the boy who let you down so badly? Did you ever see
him again?'

A shrug. 'He dropped out of uni, too. I heard he's on
drugs now. I would never have put up with that. I saw him in
a bistro, once. I threw my coffee over him.' Part satisfaction,
part guilt.

Ellie tried not to smile, and didn't quite make it. 'Better
luck next time.'

'Definitely.'

'No particular boy in view?'

A slight frown. 'Maybe. He's one of those who used to hang
around Poppy but he seems to prefer my company for some
reason. He gives me driving lessons in return for a meal. I like
him. I think I can trust him, but I'm being a bit more careful
now. Taking my time.'

'How did your mother take your leaving home?'

A sigh. 'We had a bit of a weep. She was distressed that
Gordon had thrown me out, but she wasn't going to go against
his decision. She's often had to decide between us, you see.'
She raised her hands. 'I understand why she's always had to
back him up. For as long as I can remember, *she* has given me
love and *he* . . . well, if I get too close to him physically, he'll
swat me away. With his stick, sometimes. Unless, of course, he
needs me to do something for him – wheel him around or fetch
him something from the shops. He can walk short distances
with two sticks and he has a big motorized wheelchair for
getting around on flat surfaces, but he can't hoist that into his
car by himself, so mostly he uses a lighter chair that he can lift
by himself. I used to fantasize about Mum leaving him so that
we could live together. It was years before I realized that she
could never do so. She said she'd made her vows for life, and
that was that. He knows it.'

'She takes herself off now and then to a spa, for a respite?'

'Three or four times a year. She gets a nurse to move in to
look after him for the duration.' Eyes down. A restricted tone
of voice.

'You check that that's where she goes?'

A slight flush, high on her cheekbones. 'I don't spy on her

exactly, but . . . yes. I need to know I can talk to her if anything goes wrong.'

'As it did when Gordon threw you out?'

A nod. 'She turns off her mobile when she goes there to get some peace and quiet. I did ring her when I got back from Greece. The people on reception took a message and she got back to me that evening when I was at Gramps's house.'

'You checked this morning and the reception said she's not signed in there this time.'

A tightening of the lips. 'Apparently not. Gran and Gramps think that's where she is, but they won't ring her because they think she needs some time away. That's why they're not panicking.'

'You aren't panicking, either. So you must have a pretty good idea where she's gone.'

'She said she was trying a new place. She promised to be careful, and I'm sure she will be.' Clemmie busied herself disposing of the remains of their picnic meal.

Ellie said, 'You and your mother have worked it out that since she's inherited the lot, she's next for the chop.'

Clemmie's hands stilled. She hardly seemed to breathe.

Ellie said, 'Was it you who found your aunt dead?'

A face of stone, but a muscle moved in Clemmie's throat.

'Tell me, was there any blood?'

A tiny shake of the head. Clemmie threw the leftovers in the bin. 'I really must get on. Busy, busy. So much to do. I have to get started on these worksheets.'

'Were the pictures skewed on the walls of the staircase?'

Clemmie looked at Ellie. Horror was in her eyes. She didn't seem able to speak.

Ellie said, 'If the pictures weren't skewed, and there was no blood, how do you know she was killed by falling down the stairs?'

Clemmie shot to her feet, eyes closed, throat working. Was she going to be sick? Yes?

She stumbled out of her seat and made it to the toilet, just in time.

There was a movement in the doorway to the office at the

back. Mr Mornay was standing there, aligning some papers in his hand, watching Ellie.

Ellie watched him, in return.

Behind them, Laura could be heard on the phone, taking details of a would-be tenant.

Mr Mornay lifted the papers in his hand, gesturing to Ellie to follow him into his office. Mr Mornay, the mystery man, who was not Celine's husband. Who had been brought into the partnership by Poppy and Juno to give them an overview of the business. A school friend. Retired?

He didn't look like a retired anything. He looked like . . . a judge? An observer in life. An introvert. A government official? He didn't fit into the picture, which meant either that the picture was much bigger than had been described to Ellie, or that his relationship with Poppy might have been more than that of a friend?

Ellie thought it would be interesting to find out.

SEVEN

'Well!' Mr Mornay swung back into his chair without waiting for Ellie to take a seat. 'Quite the little old busybody, aren't you? I can't feel your presence is helpful at the moment, and I must ask you to leave the family to grieve in peace.'

Ellie blinked. *Little old busybody?* Those words hurt, as they were designed to do. In the old days, Ellie might have burst into tears at being attacked in such terms, or slunk out of the room, apologizing for her very existence. Well, she supposed she was both 'little' and 'a busybody'. But, by invitation, which made all the difference. Didn't it?

So, instead of running away, she took a chair at the table and tried to work out why he'd been so rude. Did she threaten him personally?

She looked him over. No wedding ring. A signet ring on his little finger. A man whose tie was knotted 'just so'. Perhaps a little pernickety? A professional man. An accountant?

Clemmie had said he'd been brought in to conduct an overview of the business. That sounded feasible. And now, with Poppy's removal from the scene, The Magpie would undoubtedly have to take on someone else to manage that side of the business and, perhaps, appoint another person in the office?

Promote Clemmie? Mm. A possibility. Clemmie was management material.

This man was not on The Magpie's payroll. So, why was he looking at the books which littered his desk? Books which, now Ellie came to look at them, did not fit with the image of the well-run, well-kept Magpie office. These books were all, to put it mildly, a bit scruffy. Perhaps he was auditing some other firm's work while holding the fort in Juno's absence?

He seemed to have made himself very much at home, which argued that he had Juno and Poppy's backing . . . or the backing of the senior Cordovers?

He repeated himself in a louder tone. 'Didn't you hear me? Your presence here is not helpful and I must ask you to leave.'

She had it! 'So you've found the leak?'

He stiffened. 'I'm not a plumber.'

'No. An accountant, called in for a special audit of the books. Let me get this straight. When the partnership was set up all those years ago, Gerald Cordover built in certain safe-guards. Naturally he made it a condition of his loan that the books were to be audited by someone he trusted, both to safeguard his investment and provide his daughters with advice in case they needed it. He got his daughters to appoint you as auditor. Over the years you will have seen the business grow, but you knew them socially as well. Right?'

A stiffened backbone. A raised eyebrow. He wasn't sure how to take this.

Ellie frowned, trying to work it out. 'The annual audit for The Magpie wasn't due, so a cover story about wanting an overview of staffing was produced to account for your presence. You were called in because the twins had found a discrepancy in the accounts? Money has gone missing and they couldn't account for it. I suppose they wondered at first if they themselves had made a mistake. Neither of them could bear to think it might be one of their staff, whom they've known for ever. They had good relationships with Celine, Ruth and Laura, and would have known if anything in their circumstances had changed, or if they were in need of extra cash. This was not so. The twins were sensible enough to realize they couldn't ignore a leak which might turn into a tsunami and bring the whole firm down, so they asked you in to do an audit. To their horror, you confirmed that there were discrepancies.'

A grimace which was meant to be a smile. 'Ridiculous. The partnership books are perfectly in order.' He took out a handkerchief and carefully dried the palms of his hands.

He'd lied.

Ellie concentrated on what she'd seen and heard. Who she'd talked to, and what about. 'I don't think it's Ray. He needs thousands – maybe hundreds of thousands – and a smallish amount wouldn't help him out of the hole he's dug himself into. I don't think the missing amount can be all that much . . .?'

He wasn't going to answer. Or, was he? Finally, he raised his eyebrows and nodded.

'The low hundreds, perhaps? Five hundred? A thousand?'

Another stiff nod. 'A little over that.'

'Fifteen hundred, maybe? How was it done? Was money taken out of the petty cash box? No, that can't be it. There'd never be enough in petty cash to cover that amount. Trixie's to blame, isn't she?'

He flicked his fingers, dismissing the idea. 'Trixie? No! Ridiculous! She has a more than adequate allowance, and she only has to ask for an increase to get it.'

'Trixie is an expensive little minx, and I wouldn't be at all surprised if she overspent on a regular basis. I expect she was warned several times to rein in her expenditure, but there! She saw her father exceeding his income all the time, so she probably took about as much notice of her mother's warnings as he did. Fifteen hundred in excess of her already generous income? Yes, that's about her style.'

He almost laughed. She'd guessed wrongly?

He got to his feet, went over to the door and made sure it was shut. Returned to his seat. 'This is strictly in confidence, you understand? It's not Trixie. If it were, I'm sure we would all have understood. But it's not. It's far, far worse.'

'You think it's Clemmie? Absurd!'

'I regret, there can be no doubt. You cannot conceive how deeply her betrayal wounded her mother and her aunt. They had taken her in, given her a second chance . . . it makes my blood boil to think of how she has repaid their generosity!' He exhibited real emotion.

Interesting.

Ellie recalled Juno sinking to the floor after the reading of the will, and Clemmie going to her aid. Juno had looked up at Clemmie, Clemmie had looked down at Juno, and there had been love and trust in that interchange. No suspicion. No blame.

Ellie said, 'Hang on. You can't honestly think that—'

'Talk about biting the hand that feeds them! As soon as I've finished my present task, I'm going to have to go back through the books, to see where else she's been stealing—'

'I can't believe I'm hearing this!'

'Gordon said—'

'Gordon? Ah, now I'm beginning to understand. You were all at school together, weren't you?'

A stare. 'Well, yes. But—'

'Ray Cocks, too?'

He nodded, but pinched in his lips. He didn't want to talk about Ray.

'When you qualified as an accountant, you joined a firm which included Gerald Cordover in their client list? And, knowing you'd been at school with the girls, he asked you to take over the books at The Magpie, which was and is doing well. You continued to have some social interaction with the family, yes? Tell me; how did Gordon come to be in a wheelchair?'

A pinching in of lips. Was he going to reply? But then, he decided to do so. 'A car accident. They said he'd never walk again, but he has gradually got back some sensation. On a good day he can walk a little but . . . What's that got to do with anything?'

'Who was Clemmie's father?'

Grimly. 'A gatecrasher at the girls' eighteenth birthday party, brought by someone unknown to the girls and never seen again. Gordon accepted Clemmie as his. His cross to bear. He's next door to a saint. Even when he's in pain, he struggles to get to the local day centre, where he helps rehabilitate others in the same position as him. He's endlessly concerned for their welfare; writes letters, speaks to politicians. An inspiration to us all. It hurts him to realize how Clemmie has responded to all his loving care of her.'

'Mm,' said Ellie, thinking that what little she'd noted of Gordon hadn't given her the impression of his being any kind of saint, and that his treatment of Clemmie was disgraceful. 'So he's put the boot in, has he?'

'I don't know what you mean.'

'Told you all about Clemmie's disastrous holiday and subsequent debts? About the payday loan which should have kept her in penury for years? Did he tell you that he threw her out of the house when she was on her knees asking for help?'

'Threw her out? What nonsense! She knew she'd over-stepped the mark, and walked out, just like that! He covered up for her then, but . . . now! This!' He spread his hands. 'He can't cover for her any longer. Oh, believe me, we've discussed it endlessly. The girls couldn't make up their minds what to do. It couldn't have happened at a worse time . . .'

He must mean that it had come just as Ray found out that The Magpie was doing better than he'd realized, that Poppy found herself facing his escalating debts and a divorce, and that Trixie had become fixated on a future in front of the camera.

Mr Mornay wiped his hands again, looking into the distant past and not liking what he saw. 'The night Poppy died, we had yet another meeting. Gordon spoke up for Clemmie, you know. He said he could understand her fall from grace when she was deep in debt and the temptation was right there, in front of her. He said it hurt him very much to say so, but he thought that, however harsh it might sound, they ought to prosecute, to ram home the lesson which the girl doesn't seem able to learn for herself. Poppy admitted she shouldn't have let the chequebook out of her sight, but . . .' He threw up his hands. 'You can't mend trust once it's broken. Poppy was coming round to the idea that yes, they must prosecute. Juno argued for a delay. I told them they had twenty-four hours to make up their minds, because I couldn't sign off the audit with a gaping hole in it.'

'Chequebook?'

He spread his hands. 'Cheques went missing from the firm's book. Ruth and Laura are not in need. The twins enquired, and they were not. It's common knowledge that Clemmie is deep in debt and spending way beyond her income. Driving lessons. Buying a car! On her salary! The sad thing is that she'd been doing so well here that Poppy and Juno were going to give her a raise.'

That was almost too much information. Ellie took a deep breath. 'Who told you Clemmie was buying a car? It's not true, by the way.'

A stare. 'Gordon did. He'd seen her on the ring road, driving a car. He wouldn't lie.'

'There's no love lost there.'

'I disagree. He's heartsick about what has happened.'

'Really? Does Clemmie know what she's been accused of doing?'

'No, of course not. Everything was left up in the air. Juno won an extra day to think about what to do, but that was the night Poppy died. I suppose, when Juno gets back, she'll tell the girl to go.'

Ellie thumped the desk. 'Where is your proof?'

'I told you that—'

'You're not thinking like an accountant. As an accountant, you are trained to be impartial, to weigh the evidence, but you seem to have forgotten that the same thing applies when you are dealing with people instead of figures.'

'What!' Real anger. He reddened, seemed about to explode in anger, but caught himself up and folded his mouth on the words he would have spoken. He even attempted a laugh. 'Well, well; Mrs Quicke. You are quite the . . . as you say, we are trained to be impartial, and I believe that I am. I go from client to client, spending a week here, a week there; checking this, balancing that. I've always had a feeling for accounts. Columns of figures dance for me. I can look at a set of figures and smell success or failure. And no, I never get involved.'

'Only now, you are.' Ellie wondered how fond he'd been of the twins. Both were married, but neither marriage was satisfactory. Which would he have favoured? Poppy or Juno? Poppy, probably. In which case, grief might well be influencing his thought processes.

'It sounds,' said Ellie, 'as if you have uncharacteristically allowed yourself to become involved in your clients' lives.'

'What! How dare you!' He bit back a couple more words. Had he really been going to use a profanity? He took a stride to the window. Thumped the glass, disturbing a pigeon outside. 'You had better apologize!'

Ellie decided to keep quiet and let him run out of steam.

Which he did. He sank back into his chair, and brought out his handkerchief to wipe the palms of his hands again. A long, long sigh. 'I suppose you're right. In a way. I have always been very fond of . . . so many years . . . But I insist, I am always professional in my work.'

Oh, yeah! She said, 'You've been listening to tittle-tattle from Gordon who, however much he likes to present himself as a loving father to another man's child, doesn't actually act like one. Have you ever seen him speak kindly to the girl?'

'Well, of course. I suppose. I don't often see her. She's not my generation.'

'If you'd ever talked to Clemmie, you'd realize she'd as soon bite off her own arm than steal from her family. What's more, she has absolutely no idea that she's supposed to have committed a crime.'

He primped his lips. 'The evidence is against her.'

'Evidence? What evidence? Some cheques go missing and you think it must be Clemmie, although other people in the office may well have had equal access to the chequebook. Your "evidence" is circumstantial, you must agree?'

'It's enough, with her background of debt. If her own father . . .'

Ellie choked back some hasty words. She reminded herself that somebody *had* been milking the firm's accounts. That was a given. Or was it? 'Tell me exactly what happened.'

'This is a waste of my time and yours.'

'Indulge me.'

'Why should I? You march in here and start—'

'Gerald and Marika Cordover came to see me the night before the funeral. They had been given my name by someone in the police force who was privately dissatisfied by the verdict of accidental death for Poppy. The Cordovers asked me to look into the situation and that's what I'm doing. So far I've not discovered anything which explains Poppy's death satisfactorily. I'm beginning to wonder if it was indeed murder. Officially, the police say it wasn't. Perhaps it was simply all these cross-currents, these secrets which weren't hidden well enough, these long-held resentments, that have caused people to doubt a verdict of accidental death. Was Trixie responsible? No. One doesn't kill one's Golden Goose mother for the sake of fourteen hundred pounds or thereabouts. Was it Clemmie? I very much doubt it, because she was not in debt.'

He opened his mouth to argue and she stopped him. 'No, she was not! I can prove it. She'd been trying to tell her mother exactly that when Poppy died and everything went awry. No, don't speak. Let me finish. At the time of Poppy's death, Clemmie was free of debt. She was thinking of buying a car, taking driving lessons, and looking forward to taking her test. So, now tell me what evidence you have against her.'

'Where did you get that tale from? Everyone knows she's deep in debt.'

'Everyone doesn't. I don't. Tell me why you think she did it.'

'Oh, very well.' He flapped his fingers. 'Laura, as office manager, keeps the partnership's chequebook in her desk. Both the twins' signatures are needed on each cheque. Poppy usually leaves a dozen or so cheques in the book already signed. Laura is responsible for checking the bills, making the cheques out, getting Juno to countersign, marrying them up with the paperwork and putting them in the post. Half a dozen cheques, already signed by Poppy, have gone missing from the book. The counterfoils have not been filled in. The bank statements show these cheques have covered a matching number of invoices. The total amount is over fourteen hundred pounds. I have asked to see the cancelled cheques. The second signature is enough like Juno's that a casual glance would pass it without remark.'

'And you haven't asked Laura about it, have you?'

'Of course not.'

Ellie pushed back her chair. 'Then I will.'

'You can't do that!'

'Watch me!'

Clemmie and Laura looked up when Ellie stalked back in, trailing Mr Mornay behind her. Both women were on the phone.

Ellie seated herself at Laura's desk, waiting for her to finish her phone call. Which Laura did. Puzzled, but not in any way alarmed. 'A problem?'

'Laura, I'm Ellie Quicke, and—'

'Yes.' A quick, warm smile. Uncomplicated. 'Clemmie's told me about you. We certainly can do with some advice at the moment. Now, how can I help?'

'How often do you see Trixie up here?'

She heard Mr Mornay exclaim something, but didn't look round. Of course the family would have known from the beginning that there was a twofold business going on at The Magpie.

The only 'secret' was the scale of the buy-to-let operation. Two small houses to let meant one thing; ten or more was another kettle of fish.

Laura was relaxed. 'Trixie? Oh, she comes up here every now and then. Sometimes for a cuppa, sometimes waiting for her mother. You know . . .?'

Ellie smiled back. 'Of course. And to collect something her mother might have left for her?'

A puzzled look. Then a quick understanding. 'Oh, you mean, when she needs topping up? Yes, of course.' An indulgent smile. 'She does love to shop. The stuff she buys, vintage dresses, you wouldn't believe! And the jewellery!'

'Does she bring it in to show you sometimes?'

'Mm. Sometimes. Such a tiny waist. Mine was never that small. She wants to go into films, you know.'

'She updates you on her career while she's waiting for her mother to write her a cheque?'

A reminiscent laugh. 'We had quite a joke about it last time. I was making out a cheque for the new boiler in number twenty-eight, and she said I could make one out for her at the same time, as her mother was giving her an extra couple of hundred that month; and I said "Wrong!" I said I couldn't do it from that chequebook as that was for the firm, but that if she could hang on, I'd pop in and ask Poppy to write her a cheque from her own, private book. Which I did. Trixie was wearing the prettiest little red skirt that day, with a black top. Red is her favourite colour. I can't wear red, I'm afraid.'

'No, I can't, either. Couldn't Clemmie have gone in to ask Poppy for a cheque, if you were so busy?'

A slight frown. 'No, I don't think Clemmie was here. Nor Ruth. Ruth's usually out and about. I remember now, Celine had rung up to ask if Clemmie could go down to help as they'd just had a delivery and she was by herself. It left us short-handed up here, of course, but that does happen sometimes.'

'I'm sure you coped beautifully. Can you remember how many cheques you made out that day?'

'Apart from the one for the boiler?' A slight frown. 'Just that one, I think. Poppy will know. Oh. Sorry. Of course. We can't ask . . . but there'll be a record on file. It was near the end of that book.' She opened a drawer and scrabbled around in it. 'I don't think I used that book again. I usually keep the stubs but . . . I expect Poppy took it.'

'Yes, I expect she did. Thanks, Laura. I don't suppose you've seen Trixie since then?'

A sigh. A shake of the head. Eyes filling with tears? 'At the funeral.' Indistinctly. Yes. A sniff. A hand reaching for a tissue.

Ellie pressed Laura's hand. 'Thank you.'

Clemmie had been on the phone while Ellie was talking to Laura. Charles Mornay had hovered, mouth down-turned. Now, Clemmie raised her hand to attract their attention. 'Mr Mornay, have you a moment? The plumber's on the phone. He says our usual supplier is out of stock of the tiles he needs for the job we're doing at number fourteen. We can either wait for another delivery, or switch to some which are slightly more expensive. I rang Ruth and asked her advice, and she says it's not her job to price tiles. Laura tells me the same thing but he, the plumber, is back on the phone, wanting an answer. The new tenant is supposed to move in next week, but he can't if we have any more delays.'

Mr Mornay shrugged. 'We'll let your mother decide when she gets back.'

Clemmie opened her mouth to say something, and closed it again.

Ellie saw an opportunity to help Clemmie. Or to interfere, if you liked to put it that way. 'What would you do, Clemmie?'

'Me?' A frown, a swift calculation. 'We're trying to go upmarket. If we do, we can charge a higher rent. The new tiles will be more expensive, but look better than the ones we've been using. We'd lose at least a week's rent if we can't get the tenant in on time. On balance, I'd say, "Go for it!"'

'You do that, Clemmie,' said Ellie. And, turning to Mr Mornay, 'Agreed?'

Mr Mornay was not pleased, but he managed to swallow his annoyance well enough to twitch a smile and a nod in Clemmie's direction. Then he turned on Ellie with what she could only describe as a snarl, and gestured her to follow him back into his office.

Ellie followed. Meekly. She said, 'I've seen Clemmie at work in the shop. She's brilliant. And now, look how quickly she solved a problem which you didn't want to tackle! She's definitely management material, isn't she?'

He shut the door with some force. 'That was disgraceful. You forced my hand, but it won't alter the facts. Clemmie will be out of that door as soon as Juno returns.'

'Oh, believe me, it was Trixie who took the money. Do you want me to question the girl? It wouldn't take long. Poppy and Juno were too close to Trixie – too involved – to do so, but I can. As for Gordon, he has always hated Clemmie and I think that when he saw a chance to badmouth the girl, he took it.'

He held up both his hands. 'Stop! Mrs Quicke, I understand that for some reason you have elected to be Clemmie's champion—'

'As you have chosen to be Trixie's?'

He opened and shut his mouth, like a goldfish. He sank back into his chair and brought out his handkerchief to wipe the palms of his hands again. For a moment she thought she'd got through to him, but then his mouth set in a thin line. 'I have to believe Gordon. It was Clemmie who took that money.'

'What proof does he have? The fact that Clemmie might have had access to the chequebook? But, so did Trixie.'

'Trixie is not in debt.'

'Want to bet? If I can prove to you that Clemmie was not in debt at the time of Poppy's death, will you give me your word to look at the evidence again?'

'How could you prove that?'

'Several ways. One: we could ask Gerald Cordover. He knows the state of Clemmie's finances.'

'Certainly not! I am not going to go to Gerald Cordover, whom I respect and admire, and for whom I have worked these many years, to ask him about his dealings with his granddaughter! He'd show me the door, and quite right, too.'

Ellie conceded that Charles might indeed find it awkward to question a man for whom he worked. 'Very well. There's another easy way to prove who took that money. You check which of the girls had accounts at the shops to which the money was paid.'

He blustered. 'I wouldn't dream of it.'

'If you don't know how to do it, I know someone who can.'
She was thinking of her teenage friend Mikey, who would love
to get his hands on such a project. But she wouldn't insult a
professional by suggesting an amateur could do better than him.
She said, 'Look, let me have the names of a couple of the shops
and I'll get them checked out for you. If Clemmie's name comes
up, then I'll step back. If Trixie's, then you must promise me
to look at the evidence again.'

'I can't do that! There's client confidentiality to—'

'If I get Clemmie in here and ask her to show us which store
cards she uses, do you think she'll object?'

'What . . .!'

'If she's innocent, she'll tell us which they are straight
away, and I'll guarantee she doesn't shop in the same places
as Trixie. Suppose we ask Trixie the same thing? What do
you think she'll say?'

'I refuse to let you do any such thing.' He could see the dark
hole which had opened up before him, just as she could.

She went to the door, opened it and called out, 'Clemmie,
there's a silly query come through from the bank. Which store
cards do you have? M&S? John Lewis?'

Clemmie sang back, without a pause, 'I don't have any at
the moment. It saves me from temptation. Either I pay cash, or
I don't buy it. Is there a problem?'

'I don't think so. Thanks.' Ellie looked at Charles, who had
sunk back into his chair and closed his eyes.

Ellie said, 'Let me guess. Trixie will have cards for Harrods
and Zara, for a start. I'm rather surprised she confined herself
to stealing fourteen hundred pounds.'

He pressed his handkerchief to his mouth. Mumbled something. Repeated the words more clearly. 'You just don't realize
what you're getting into. If it were only that . . .' He wiped his
brow with his handkerchief. 'Look, you don't know the half of
it. I can't tell you . . . I promised I wouldn't . . . Believe me,
I wish I didn't know that . . . But there is absolutely no doubt
that Clemmie is guilty. And I'm not just referring to her stealing
from the firm.'

He was in distress. He wasn't putting it on. He really believed
Clemmie was guilty. But, of what?

What was he not telling her? What did he think Clemmie had done? Not . . . No, he surely couldn't think Clemmie had been responsible for Poppy's death?

Why on earth would he think that?

She said, 'When Juno returns, I'm sure she'll sort it out.'

'We can't wait too long, Mrs Quicke. I promised Gordon I'd hold off till Monday morning, but if Juno isn't back and got things sorted by then, Gordon is going to the police with what he knows.' He got to his feet. 'So, don't make a fool of yourself by interfering in things you know nothing about.' He fished a card out of his wallet and handed it over to her. 'Please confine yourself to the telephone if you have any other queries. Now, if you please, I have work to do. Let me show you out.'

EIGHT

Ellie was whisked out of the office and down the stairs before she could object. In fact, she didn't want to object so much as to hit someone. Almost anyone would do, but she favoured Charles Mornay above all others.

He couldn't really believe Clemmie was guilty of theft, could he? In spite of the evidence? Of all the stupid, bone-headed, short-sighted, blinkered whatsits!

Could someone be both short-sighted and blinkered? Yes, they could, if their name was Charles Mornay.

Out on the pavement, Ellie stamped her foot. Which hurt. Ow! She stomped around in a circle, thinking it served her right for losing her cool.

She didn't often lose her temper, but every now and then . . . And this was one of those times . . . What she'd like to do was to smash his face in, and . . .

She found herself brought up short by a young mother towing a lad along on his scooter. She said, 'Sorry,' and sidestepped.

As they passed her, she heard the youngster say to his mum, in a piercing treble, 'What a funny lady!'

Indeed. Well, what was wrong with her? She'd gone in there firing from the hip, and been caught in the crossfire. Well, not actually crossfire. And not actually firing from the hip. Humph!

Suppose Charles really did have some evidence to prove that Clemmie had done something wrong? Ellie had been berating Charles for not having an open mind. Perhaps she ought to rethink her own approach to the matter as well?

No! No, and *No!* Clemmie was innocent of . . . whatever.

A taxi idled towards Ellie, and she hailed it. Somewhere she had the card which Gerald Cordover had given her. She'd transferred it from one pocket to another and . . . ah, with great good fortune, it had ended up in her change purse. On the front of the card were the details for his glass and steel office block

16

on the North Circular. She did not want to go there. Imagine presenting herself at the Reception desk and asking the master of all he surveyed to give five minutes of his time to a gossiping pensioner, who had nothing much to report! She'd be turned away, and quite right, too.

On the back of the card he'd written his home address, which was in a sixties-built estate not far away. Ellie knew it well. The estate was comprised of mixed housing: there were some terraced houses; two blocks of flats four storeys high; and some individual designed four-bedroom houses with well-groomed front gardens and double, if not treble garages attached.

Ellie gave the local address to the cab driver and got in the back, trying not to think of how badly she'd handled the recent interview with Charles Mornay, trying to think of the questions she needed to ask Marika Cordover. Trying to think.

While the taxi trundled along, Ellie got out her phone and accessed her messages. She was not one of those people who kept her phone switched on all the time. When she wanted to be in contact, she switched it on. When she didn't, then she didn't.

There were three voicemail messages from Diana and two texts. Ellie didn't read texts, on principle. If someone wanted to speak to her they could leave a voicemail message, but her eyesight didn't care for the challenge of reading texts. She deleted the lot. She'd get round to soothing Diana at some point, but not just at that moment. Talking to Marika was more important.

The Cordover house was one of the largest detached residences on the estate. Some downsizing! Ellie wondered what on earth their previous house had looked like, with its swimming pool and games room – or was it a cinema?

She rang the bell. It was another warm afternoon and there was not much activity in the road. A plane droned overhead. A lawnmower started up. A woman came out of a neighbouring house, got into a car and drove away.

Marika opened the door. She didn't look surprised to see Ellie, but said, 'Come on in. I've just put the kettle on.'

Ellie followed her hostess through a square hall with a highly

polished floor, into a spacious kitchen which boasted all the
latest gadgets. Everything sparkled. Floor-to-ceiling French
windows looked out on to a well-groomed lawn where a closed
parasol hung lifelessly over some garden furniture. No flowers,
but plenty of shrubs. A designer garden, low maintenance. 'Milk
or lemon?' said Marika.

'Milk, thank you. No sugar.'

'We won't sit outside. There's a wasps' nest somewhere
nearby.' Marika carried the tray of tea things through a second
door into a sitting room. This room faced south, and the blinds
had been lowered over the windows to keep the sun out. The
furniture was pleasantly old-fashioned and comfortable in
shades of cream and brown. A little uninspired, perhaps?

The chair into which Ellie lowered herself was the right
height for someone of her height and weight, and the small
table at her elbow was close enough that she didn't have to
reach across to pick up her tea.

There were some seascapes on the walls – Edwardian?
Rather good ones. There was a large television set but it was
not overwhelming. That day's newspapers had been read and
stacked in a pile nearby. A paperback book had been left,
open, on the arm of the biggest chair, with a footstool nearby.
Gerald's chair? Yes, the TV remote was on the other arm of
that chair. The master of the house controlled the telly.

There was no mantelpiece. The house would be heated and
cooled by some sort of duct system, or possibly by underfloor
heating? A number of Sympathy cards were in a pile on a coffee
table nearby.

Marika picked up some knitting. White, fluffy. Something
for a baby? She said, 'Do you knit, Mrs Quicke? I know you
can buy outfits for babies in the shops nowadays, but I like to
provide something hand-knitted for all the newborn babies in
the family.'

Of course, Marika probably had dozens of relations back
in Poland, all producing infants and being grateful for a
hand-knitted garment. Ellie said, 'No, I don't knit. I garden.'

Marika smiled, but didn't raise her eyes from her work.
Her lips moved as she counted along the row. 'Ah, I thought
I'd dropped a stitch, but all is well.'

Ellie leaned back in her chair and considered her hostess's behaviour.

Marika hadn't asked why she'd come.

Marika looked a lot better than she had done at the funeral. Tired, yes; but calmer, frowning a little as she consulted a pattern for the jacket, or whatever it was she was knitting. She wasn't in distress as she had been at the funeral and reading of the will only the day before. There was no tension in the air.

What a sea change was here! Something had happened to make Marika relax? Which same thing had happened to Celine and Clemmie . . . but not to Ray, Gordon or Trixie. Whatever could that be? The departure of Juno from the scene?

Marika lifted her eyes from her work. 'Yes, Mrs Quicke? You have something to tell me?'

Was the woman waiting for a report on what Ellie had been doing? Did she think Ellie had been hired, like a private investigator? Well, so be it. Ellie thought she'd do it with a twist. 'Was Mr Mornay in love with Poppy or Juno?'

If she'd hoped to upset Marika, Ellie had been mistaken. There was never a hint of discomfort as Marika replied, 'He could never make up his mind. Then he married someone else.'

'Mr Mornay thinks Clemmie stole from the firm. I tried to convince him otherwise. He refused to listen.'

Again, no surprise. Marika inclined her head. 'Twenty-four, twenty-six. It was Trixie, of course.'

'Of course.'

'So now you will concentrate on the men.' This was spoken in the same tone in which she'd asked Ellie if she wanted milk or lemon in her tea.

Ellie was intrigued. She tried to push the boundaries further. 'The family seem to have decided that the police will not be involved, no matter who was responsible for Poppy's death.'

'I wouldn't say that, exactly.' Marika pulled at her ball of wool. 'Some things are becoming clearer, while others remain to be decided.'

'Decided by Juno?'

An inclination of the head. 'And others.'

'You know where she is. And it's not at the spa she usually patronizes.'

Marika lifted the pattern closer to her eyes. 'I really must get my eyes checked some time. Thirty-two . . . or thirty-four?'

Ellie tried to work out what had been happening. 'Juno was not well. You got her in your car, with the intention of bringing her back here and putting her to bed. But she asked to be let out at the station. At least, that's what you told Ray. You and Gerald and Clemmie – probably Celine as well – all know where she is, but you're not telling. Very wise.'

'Yes, indeed. Clemmie is a dear, good girl.'

'What's Clemmie's new boyfriend like?'

Marika suspended her knitting to frown at the ceiling. 'The genes are good. She is in no hurry.'

'And Trixie?'

'Ah. Yes. Gerald and I thought you might like to go to the meeting she has called at her house to discuss the script for her film. She believes – and maybe she is right – that Juno will provide her with something towards the finance of such a film. I told her you might put in an appearance, as a trustee of your charity. Four o'clock at their house.'

'Why do you want me to get mixed up with Trixie's daft project? It can't be because you think her film will ever get made. You don't really think Trixie was responsible for her mother's death, do you? If so, it would have been an accident. She wouldn't kill the golden goose. Has she an alibi?'

'Of sorts. I am not convinced that her agent is a worthy enough person to provide anyone with an alibi. But you will judge for yourself.'

'And Ray?'

A shrug. 'I would not wish, myself, to be in his shoes.'

Thinking of the hard businessman who had attended the funeral and the reading of the will, Ellie could only agree. 'His fate is still to be decided?'

'I have no idea. And less interest.'

'What about Gordon?'

A moue of distaste, but no comment.

Ellie said, 'I saw him hit Clemmie. He demanded that she take him home and look after him. I nearly cheered when she refused.'

A half-smile. Marika held up her knitting to pull it into shape. 'He will survive, I suppose.'

'Charles Mornay says it's Gordon who wants to get Clemmie arrested for theft. I assume that you wouldn't want that. Shall I get proof that it was Trixie who stole the money?'

A slight inclination of the head. 'That would be a good idea.'

'You are not worried on Clemmie's account?'

'She is well protected.'

Ellie took a deep breath. Now for the big one. A guess, but it felt right. 'Juno has left Gordon.' Ellie made that a statement, not a question.

'Where on earth did you get that idea from?' Marika rolled up her knitting and put it in a padded bag. 'Look at the time! I promised my husband some of my special borscht soup tonight. Does your husband ask for favourite dishes in this hot weather?'

'Indeed he does.' Ellie felt colour rise in her face. She'd guessed wrongly. What on earth had led her to believe Juno had left her husband?

Marika got to her feet, smiling. 'I'll show you out.'

Ellie rose, too, but made no move to depart. 'Any minute now my friend in the police is going to ring me, to ask what I've discovered about Poppy's death. If I tell her that Juno has disappeared and that no one seems to know where she is, the police will put out an APB for her.'

'Then you won't tell the police anything. Juno needs rest and quiet.'

'Does she need to know how her sister died before she comes out of hiding?'

'What an imagination you have!'

'If I were in her position, I wouldn't know who to trust, either. Oh, she trusts you and Gerald and Clemmie . . . but not Gordon and certainly not Ray. Or Trixie. And I don't think she trusts Charles Mornay, either. I do hope her hiding place is a good one.'

'It is.'

Ellie wondered if Juno had been spirited abroad, to stay in the extended Polish family that Marika had come from. Ellie recalled that Juno's own mother had been Polish, which made Juno half-Polish herself. Yes, that made sense. She could tuck herself neatly away in Poland, surrounded by her extended family.

Ah, but would she have had her passport with her when the will had been read? Um, no. Not unless her flight had been planned. If it had been planned, then she could have gone straight to the airport from the reading of the will, and by nightfall be tucked up in bed with various aunts and cousins clucking over her.

But, if it hadn't been planned, would there have been time for her to go home and get her passport before she got on a plane to Warsaw? Possibly. Hm. It was something to think about.

Ellie said. 'How long can she remain in hiding? There are decisions to be made which affect the lives of all of you. Ray's debts, Trixie's ambitions, Gordon's living conditions . . . the houses, the business, the shop . . . so many people now depend on Juno.'

'She knows that. She needs time to think.'

'How much time?'

'We depend on you, Mrs Quicke, to help us decide.'

Ellie nodded. She'd suspected as much. 'It is not right to put it all on me.'

A slight smile. 'I know. I will pray. Every day, every hour since Poppy died, we have argued and worried and grieved about her death. One moment I would tell Gerald that it was an accident and we should accept it, while Gerald would say it was murder. The next moment, we would take the opposite sides, and so it would go on. The police refuse to believe it was murder, and maybe it was an accident. I don't know. No one knows. But, late at night, early in the morning, we couldn't leave the matter alone. We couldn't let it rest.

'We tried to talk to Juno, but all she would do is weep. She kept getting these flashbacks. Twins, you see. That special bond. As for Gordon . . . oh, Gordon! He's so dependent on her! But he couldn't leave well alone! Did he try to comfort Juno? No! Anyone would have thought Poppy had died to spite him. Then Ray and his debts . . . we knew about them, of course, though not in detail. They were a dark cloud hanging over us. We knew they would have to be dealt with, but how? Trixie and her fantasy . . . so inopportune! Couldn't she see that Juno wasn't able to cope . . .? And Charles, so stupid . . .

as if Clemmie would steal from us! How ridiculous was that! And, in the scheme of things, how unimportant. But Gordon insisted that she should be charged. It was all too much. No wonder Juno got ill.'

Ellie nodded. 'When the body's defences are lowered, it's easy to fall victim to a bad cold, or an infection. Is she on antibiotics?'

'She's being well looked after. Come this way . . .'

Ellie didn't move. 'In a way, I understand why Gordon is so difficult. It must be hard enough to be confined to a wheel-chair. Who was Clemmie's father?'

A shrug. 'A young man someone brought to the party that we hosted for the twins' eighteenth birthday. He went abroad the next day and we had no means of getting in touch with him. I'm sorry to say there was a lot of loose behaviour that night. Ray with his smart new sports car, everyone drinking far too much, with goings-on in every bedroom! Gordon had been seeing Juno for some months and was pressing her to get engaged. It seems he was a little rough with her that night; some personable young student consoled her and well, there it was. Both the girls found themselves pregnant, and of course Gordon thought, we all thought, that he was the father. The student went off back to Harvard or wherever it was that he came from and the girls had a double wedding. All as it should be.'

'Except that it wasn't all that it should be?'

'No one realized till the babies were born. Gordon said he'd stand by Juno and take the baby on as his own. Which he did. All legal.'

'It soured him?'

'Juno said they must have another baby straight away and they tried and tried, and went for tests, but it turned out he was infertile. Now that did sour him. So he went out, got drunk with some of his friends and they finished upside down in a ditch. No seat belts, of course. Young men don't believe in seat belts, do they? So you see, she can never leave him.'

Ellie wasn't so sure about that, but she understood that Marika's strong Christian faith might lead her to think that way. Perhaps she was right.

'You must go now,' said Marika, looking at her watch.
'Or you'll miss the meeting at Trixie's.'

'I need some telephone numbers. Clemmie's, for a start.
And Juno's, of course.'

'I'll give you Clemmie's, but I can't give you Juno's. She's
got a new phone. She rings us once a day but she withholds
her number. When she rings next, I'll ask her if she'll ring you,
and that's the best I can do.'

Exit Ellie. She felt as if she'd been thrown out, not once
but twice that day. First Charles and then Marika. She stumped
along the pavement feeling cross and anxious and, if the truth
were but known, rather inclined to tears.

She told herself to behave.

It wasn't her fault if people asked for help and then lied
to her.

They had all lied to her, hadn't they?

Well, not Clemmie. Ellie was pretty sure that Clemmie hadn't
lied to her.

Not even by omission?

Ellie stood still, and a young mum, pushing a baby in a
buggy while talking to someone on her phone, nearly bumped
into her.

'Sorry,' said Ellie.

Young mum gave Ellie 'A Look', and walked round her, still
talking on her phone.

Which made Ellie realize that she was in need of a good
sit-down and a long think, preferably accompanied by a strong
latte and, perhaps – oh frabjous joy – a piece of chocolate cake
from Cafe 786. Or some of their carrot cake?

She quickened her pace. It wasn't far to the Avenue.
The carrot cake at Cafe 786 was the best in the world. And,
with a good shot of proper coffee, she might feel able to face
the world again.

She found a seat in the window at the café and turned
her chair so that she could see what was happening in the
street outside – sometimes there were hilarious stand-offs
about parking, most amusing to watch – while she waited for
her coffee and cake. Feeling virtuous, she actually got out

her phone to see if there were any new messages on it. And there were.

First, her husband Thomas had left a voicemail message wanting to know where she was. She rang back and suggested he join her for a cuppa. With carrot cake? Carrot cake was not supposed to be on his diet, nor on hers, either.

'Yes, with carrot cake.'

'I'll be right there.'

Second: Young Mikey. 'You were asking about Cocks's Garage? One of my friends at school, his mother had a right old barney with them – had to miss a school trip or something because their car was in dock when it shouldn't have been. Would you like to talk to her? She runs Harrison's Deli in the Avenue, and said she was going to sue them because they'd ripped her off. Where are you? Shall I come over on my bike?'

She rang Mikey back. 'Yes, please. I'd really like to speak to anyone who knows something about the garage.'

Third: Lesley, her friend from the police. 'How are you getting on with the Cordovers?' And then, in a voice stiff with embarrassment and anger, 'By the way, the wedding's off!'

Ellie felt dreadful. She ought never to have interfered there. She had advised Lesley to be careful about talking to her fiancé about the bridesmaid's dresses, hadn't she? Ellie had foreseen it might be a ticklish subject. But Lesley had done just that, which had precipitated an argument and she'd actually called off the wedding? And it was all Ellie's fault!

Ellie told herself not to jump to conclusions. Lesley was suffering from pre-wedding nerves. Whatever it was that had upset her would soon blow over. Wouldn't it? Also, it was better to discover you were not compatible with a man before you married than after.

Ellie grinned to herself. The memory of her wonderful Susan in full sail, bosom to the fore, was heart-warming!

Coffee and cake arrived. Ellie tucked in. It was a day to forget about calories. In fact, she didn't want to think about anything worrying. Not anything! If people wanted to kill one another, to cheat on their income tax and steal money from their families, run away and hide, or lie about things . . . Well, let them!

They could all jolly well jump into the sea. Well, not necessarily the sea, since she lived a good few miles away, but they
could take their problems to an Agony Aunt, or a psychiatrist,
or a psychotherapist. Although, to be truthful, she'd never
been quite sure of the difference between one and the other,
while suspecting that the Agony Aunts probably spoke more
common sense than people who sat in a comfortable chair
waiting for their clients to unburden themselves about some
horrid scene from childhood which had probably never existed,
because there'd been a lot of bad publicity recently about
people retrieving memories which had never really happened,
hadn't there?

Ellie frowned. She was getting muddled up, wasn't she?

'Ellie, my dear.' Thomas sat down beside her, and placed
his warm, comforting hand over hers.

She felt her eyes fill with tears. 'Oh, Thomas, I've made
such a mess of things.'

NINE

Thomas patted her hand, while looking up at the menu on the board. 'I think I'll have one of their All-Day Breakfasts since we won't have time to cook properly tonight, will we?'

His reasoning was faulty. He was an excellent cook and so was Ellie. They could easily rustle up an evening meal between them. In any case it was a point of honour with Susan to keep the freezer fully stocked with her home-cooked dishes. All they had to do was select one and put it in the microwave to heat up. However, if Thomas felt like having an All-Day Breakfast, then he'd better have it and forget about his diet for once.

He said, 'Diana's been to the house twice, looking for you. She wouldn't tell me what it was about, except that it was urgent.'

'She wants money for something. Par for the course. I'm not playing.'

'She said she'd left an envelope of stuff for you a while back. She wanted me to explain why you hadn't attended to it.'

'Oh, poor Thomas. I'm sorry. You shouldn't have to put up with her nonsense.'

He grinned. 'I've a tough skin. And an empty tum. Now what sort of coffee shall I have with my meal? Or should it be tea?'

Outside the café, a man sitting in a wheelchair shouted, 'Watch it, you fool! You shouldn't be riding on the pavement!'

'Don't look,' said Thomas, hastily turning his chair away from the window.

Ellie looked. It was Mikey, of course. And no, he ought not to have been riding his precious bike on the pavement. The pensioner in the wheelchair was giving Mikey a right rollicking, and quite right, too. Like Thomas, Ellie turned her attention to the menu on the board. 'Shall I have another coffee?'

Mikey arrived at their table, his colour high. He knew that they'd seen what had happened. They knew that he knew that . . . but he'd been told off for it, and no more was going to be said.

He produced his most charming smile. 'Can I have an All-Day Breakfast? I had football this morning and it's ages since lunch and I'm ravenous.'

'*May* you . . .?' said Ellie. 'Not *can* you? Yes, you may.'

'I'll order,' said Thomas. 'Ellie, you'll like a camomile tea?'

She nodded. She felt out of sorts and the tea might calm her down. There would be no point in talking about her problems until the men had fed their faces. She began to relax, and even to smile as she thought of the horrid mess some families made of their lives, and of how extremely fortunate she had been with hers.

'Now . . .?' said Thomas, on his second cup of coffee.

Mikey slurped a Ribena. It was bad for his teeth and Vera wouldn't be pleased but it was all right for a special treat, wasn't it? Ellie's mind slid over the fact that she ought to have forbidden him to have a sugary drink. She couldn't say anything because she'd just had one herself, hadn't she?

Mikey said, 'My friend thinks you should speak to his mum who took their old banger into Cocks's Garage—'

'One thing at a time,' said Thomas. 'Now, Ellie?'

Mikey interrupted. 'But his mum's only going to be there till four and he's rung her and said you were going to call in to see her, so she's expecting you.'

Ellie sighed. 'Mikey, wouldn't it have been better if you'd asked me first?'

'No.' He sucked the last drop out of the container of Ribena, producing a horrible sucking noise. He let it fill with air, and squashed it flat with a slapping sound.

'Finished?' Thomas enquired, ladling more sugar into his coffee. 'Now, Ellie. Tell us what's been going on.'

So Ellie told. From the beginning. Once or twice she had to go back to explain this or that, but she didn't think she'd left anything out by the time she got to the end and looked at her watch. 'So if Juno doesn't surface – and it's very possible she's hiding out in Poland with her mother's relatives and won't get back in time – then Gordon's going to the police on Monday morning to accuse Clemmie of breaking all of the Ten Commandments, plus anything else he can think of. And, I don't see what I can do to stop him.' She looked at her watch again. 'I'm going to have to shift myself if I'm to get to Trixie's place in time – and what I'm supposed to do there, heaven only knows.'

'Hang on,' said Mikey. 'You've got to see my friend's mum first. At Harrison's.'

'Go back a bit, Ellie,' said Thomas. 'Did you say someone's been fiddling their taxes?'

'Did I?' She thought back. 'Oh, well, I didn't really mean that. I was exaggerating. I don't think anyone's said anything about taxes.' And yet where was something at the back of her mind . . .?

Mikey got to his feet, restless, aching to get on with the day. 'Harrison's. Car. Cocks's Garage. Remember?'

Thomas got out his wallet. 'I'll pay the bill here, Ellie. Then I'll take Mikey on to talk to his friend's mum at Harrison's. We know more about cars than you do.'

Did the men flick a conspiratorial glance at one another? Yes. Their combined air of innocence would have floated a battleship. Ellie could read them with ease. In spite of the fact that he'd just eaten an All-Day Breakfast, Mikey was slavering at the thought of the special pastries on sale at Harrison's, while Thomas was mentally selecting some of their finest cheeses and a portion of venison pâté for himself.

She ironed out a grin. 'Enjoy yourselves. You said something about taxes?' She started to worry about that as she got to her feet. 'Nobody has said anything about taxes, have they? And why would they? The Magpie's books are as clean as can be, except for the money which Trixie pinched. Charles Mornay wouldn't let The Magpie fiddle their taxes. He's far too upright. Perhaps a little unimaginative? I wonder if he's really top flight? Shouldn't the best accountants have some imagination, so that they can work out what fiddles their clients might be getting up to?'

'You don't usually assume the worst of people,' said Thomas, also getting to his feet.

Ellie sighed. 'I don't like having to be suspicious of everyone, but today is definitely one of those days.'

Ellie thought Poppy's house was beginning to look neglected already, or was it all in her mind? No, she was not imagining things. Some paper bags and a takeaway container had drifted into the forecourt, plus several cars. A superb white Lexus took pride of place, surrounded by an assortment of cars in descending order of value, finishing with a two-stroke bug-on-wheels which, judging by the number of dents in its bodywork, looked as if it had been in collision with a lamppost and several other immovable objects.

The front door was ajar. Again. Didn't they ever take precautions against opportunist burglars?

There was more neglect to be seen in the hall. A jacket lay on the floor, an empty mug on the table, some keys . . . What on earth were these people doing, leaving car keys out in the open like that? They deserved to be burgled.

Voices drifted through an open door from a room on the left. Someone laughed. A man. Trixie's voice, calling for order. A murmur of agreement. Was that where the meeting was being held?

Ellie hesitated, feeling not exactly shy but diffident about intruding on the meeting.

The door into the sitting room at the back – where the will had been read – was open, but no sounds came from it. Ellie wondered if anyone had bothered to replace the broken window.

Curiosity killed the cat? Well, never mind that. She walked in and sighed. Didn't anyone ever clear up after them in this household? The hostess trolley was still there, abandoned, festooned with all the glasses, cups and saucers and plates which had been lying around at the end of that apology for a wake. Added recently were a couple of pizza boxes, one with an uneaten slice still in it. And, no, the broken window had not been replaced, which made for a nasty draught.

'About time, too.' Ray Cocks walked in behind Ellie, shutting off his mobile phone. 'This place is a tip.'

Ellie blinked. Did Ray still think she was their substitute

cleaner? She could disillusion him, but her every instinct was to clear the place up. She couldn't bear mess. And, she'd learned a lot by playing the part of the cleaner the day before, so why not continue? Also, she didn't think she'd be very comfortable in a script conference for a film which was unlikely ever to be made.

So she put her handbag on the bottom tray of the trolley, and began to collect the dirty dishes.

Ray ignored her to take a picture off the wall, revealing the door of a safe. Containing . . . what? His wife's jewellery and valuables? Which he was fully aware now belonged to Juno?

He produced a small book from his pocket and began to leaf through it. Looking for the combination to the safe? Was that his wife's diary, or his?

He wasn't familiar enough with the combination to identify it, which meant he hadn't chosen it . . . Which meant that his wife had . . . Which meant that she had had control of whatever was placed in the safe. So what was Ray doing, getting into the safe?

Ellie collected the pizza boxes and piled them on top of the dirty dishes. Ought she to break into the meeting to tell Trixie what Ray was up to? But, wouldn't she look stupid if Trixie already knew? Perhaps the solicitor had suggested that Ray get the jewellery – if that was what was in the safe – valued for probate?

Ellie picked up a heavy glass which had rolled across the floor to come to rest by the window, risking a glance over her shoulder at Ray, who turned on her, saying, 'What the hell do you think you're doing?'

Ellie dithered. She could tell him who she was, which would entail having to confess that she had been spying on him in the guise of a cleaner. How embarrassing! Or, she could mumble an apology, red-faced, and get out of the room as quickly as possible. Which is what she did.

She was cross with herself. Hot and bothered. Undecided what to do.

The safe, once opened, had given her a glimpse of a stack of jewellery boxes and some bundles of paper. Share certificates? Bonds? Rolls of money?

What *was* she to do? She didn't *know* what Ray intended to do with the contents of the safe, though she suspected that . . . well, what? That he'd steal them? Yes, the word was *steal*. The contents of that safe did not belong to him. Of course, if they were his personal property . . .?

But, how was she to find out?

She pushed the trolley into the kitchen and started to put the dirty plates into the dishwasher, which contained only what Clemmie had put there the day before. Didn't Trixie realize you could easily run out of clean plates and cutlery if you didn't bother to wash up?

Laughter and a noisy babble came from the room in which Trixie's meeting was taking place.

Oh, dear Lord above; what am I supposed to do?

A burst of laughter from the meeting, a light-hearted cry of 'Tea break!' and Trixie rustled across the hall and into the kitchen. Yes, she rustled. She was wearing a taffeta petticoat under another of her full-skirted dresses. Good heavens! Ellie hadn't thought youngsters ever bothered about petticoats nowadays. But, well, Trixie was a one-off.

'Oh, you've come at last, have you? We'd like some tea, please. For six. Plus one coffee, black, no milk.'

Ellie stood up, easing her back. She'd asked God what she ought to do, and Trixie had arrived, prompt on cue. 'Sorry, Trixie. I'm Mrs Quicke, whom your grandma wanted to sit in on your meeting for some reason, but then your father mistook me for a cleaner, and there was quite a mess, so I started to clear up.'

'Well? What?' Trixie was annoyed. Discomposed, but annoyed. No one likes to be taken for a fool, do they?

Ellie stiffened a backbone which wanted to collapse. 'Your father – and it may be quite all right, I don't know, you must be the best judge of that – he's got the safe open and—'

The girl vanished. 'Father!'

Trixie had gone to see what was happening. Good.

Well, probably good.

Someone rang the doorbell. Hard and long. A tenor voice came from the front room, 'Trixie? Someone at the door.'

Ellie abandoned her task, but hadn't got as far as the

hall before a thick-set figure swept across her view and into the back room. The businessman. Now what exactly was his business with Ray? Ray owed him money, right?

'I thought we were supposed to meet at two.' The businessman, not pleased.

Ellie crept to the doorway, but didn't step into the room. Her eyes went to the safe. It had been hurriedly closed and the picture rehung in front of it, askew. Trixie was standing beside her father, looking flushed and anxious.

Ray looked at his watch. 'Is that the time?'

From where Ellie stood, she could see a bulging shopping bag . . . Tesco's? . . . on the floor behind Ray. It contained what? A fortune in cookies? The contents of the safe?

The businessman's eyes were everywhere, taking in the broken window, the absence of crockery, the look of guilt on Trixie's face. The bulging shopping bag. Ray's grin, which looked painful.

Trixie made a small, inviting movement towards him. And smiled. Again, it was a challenge, that smile. Not an invitation. Or was it? What was going on here?

The businessman replied to Ray, but looked at Trixie. He said, 'Do I have to remind you that I hold a number of your IOUs? You said you'd have something on account for me.'

Ray loosened his tie. 'You know what's happened, you were here yesterday, you heard. Everything belongs to Juno, and she's disappeared.'

'You've reported her disappearance to the police?'

'Well, no.'

'Then you will do so. I cannot wait.' He hadn't taken his eyes off Trixie, who returned his gaze steadily, watchfully. Not promising anything. Or was she?

Ray threw out his hands. 'You must understand that I can't touch anything that's hers. I rang the solicitor. He's adamant. Nothing can be sold or removed from the house till probate. Since the house is no longer mine, I can only stay here if Juno agrees, and we don't know where she is.'

The businessman didn't even bother to look at the shopping bag. Still his eyes were on Trixie, and hers on his. He said, 'You have the garage. Sign that over to me. That should reduce

your debt; maybe even leave you with a little credit.' Was
he speaking in code? Did he want Trixie in his bed, by way
of payment for Ray's debts? Would she play ball, to save
her father?

Ray was oblivious of this by-play. He said, 'The thing is, the
last time I asked Poppy for money, she made me sign over
the garage to her—'

'What!' from both Trixie and the businessman.

'The agreement was that she pay me to manage it. Only,
I haven't been there much lately, and she said—'

'She sacked you?' Trixie, horrified.

The businessman stood rock still. Feet slightly apart, head
forward. A bull about to charge. 'What about your personal
property?' His eyes flicked up to Trixie. Did he think of her as
Ray's private property?

'My watch!' With shaking hands, Ray fought to undo
the clasp of his gold watch, and held it out. 'Take it. It's worth
four, five thousand.'

'No, father! Wait! You can't—'

'My car. The Lexus. It's outside. Thirty thousand. It's mine.
Not leased. Take the keys.'

'Well?' The businessman said, to Trixie.

She turned her back on him, flushed. Trembling.

The businessman's eyes narrowed. Was he taking her reaction as a rejection? He snatched at the watch which Ray was
holding out to him. 'Add the contents of that bag on the floor,
and we'll call it quits.'

'No!' cried Trixie again. 'That's Mum's jewellery. It doesn't
belong to my father. You can't touch it!'

'Watch me!' He darted forward and whisked the bag up
from behind Ray's legs.

Ellie thought, Here I go again. 'No,' she said, stepping
into the room. 'Mister . . .? Sorry, I don't know your name, we
haven't been introduced, but Trixie is quite correct. Nothing
that belonged to the late Mrs Cocks can be removed from the
house till after probate.'

He swung round on her, bag in hand. 'And who may you
be?' His brain ticked over, and memory retrieved the sight of
Ellie serving sandwiches the day before. 'The cleaner? Hah!'

'Oh, quite,' said Ellie. 'But I'm also Mrs Ellie Quicke, of the Quicke Charitable Trust. If Mr Cocks wishes to pay his debt to you with his personal property, then he is certainly at liberty to do so, though I believe you should sign a receipt for the value of what you take and give him back his IOUs. But, my dear sir, you cannot remove property belonging to anyone else.'

'Try me!' Carrying the bag, he took a step towards her, clearly intending to thrust her aside.

Ellie stood her ground. 'I only have to raise my voice to summon Trixie's friends, who are conferring in the front room. Several very large men, I understand . . .' crossing her fingers that they were indeed large and of the male sex '. . . and several women who will have their smartphones to hand. They'd love to call the police to prevent a robbery taking place.'

His eyes swivelled, calculating odds.

Ellie's heartbeat was far too fast, but she managed to say, 'Trixie, find some paper and make out a receipt for the gentleman, in the amount of, shall we say, goods to the value of thirty-four thousand pounds? One watch, one car. And you, sir, kindly drop that bag.'

A stir in the doorway behind Ellie and a large young man appeared. Rugby player? Red hair. Lively blue eyes. He focused on Trixie. 'A problem?'

Trixie managed a smile, with difficulty. 'Sorry. No, not really. An unexpected visitor. I'll be with you in a tick. If anyone wants tea or coffee, could they get it themselves? You know where the kitchen is, don't you? I just have to . . .' She gazed blindly around her. 'Pen and paper. I need pen and paper.'

'I'll get some for you, shall I?' said the newcomer. 'We may not have any sensible ideas for a film script, but we do have pen and paper.' He disappeared.

Trixie said, 'Aidan. Junior doctor. Son of Councillor something. He writes comic verses for revues when he feels like it. His surname is . . . What's the matter with me? I do know it, don't I?' She rubbed her forehead.

Hang in there, Trixie.

Ray let himself down into a chair. Gazed into space. Opting out. Humph!

The businessman calculated the odds of pushing past Ellie and making his getaway. His shoulders bunched. He was going to make a run for it.

Ellie said, 'Of course, Ray could sue you, Mister whatever-your-name-is. There was a case in the papers a while ago where a man sued a club for letting him have credit when they knew he had no assets left. I don't know whether he won or not, but the publicity wouldn't do you much good, would it? I suggest you take the watch and the car and write the rest off.'

He weighed that up, and decided against it. Hefted the bag in his hand. She could see him thinking he would be able to push Ellie out of the way. How could she stop him? As well stop a charging bull.

'Pen and paper, all correct. Anything else?' Aidan returned, his eyes lively, taking in the situation, lingering on Trixie, switching to Ray and then back to the businessman . . . and finally to Ellie. His eyes narrowed. He was trying to 'read' her, wasn't he? No fool, this.

'I'm not signing anything,' said the businessman, 'and you will not prevent me from leaving with what is owed to me, or it will be the worse for you.'

'Oh!' Trixie turned away, hand to mouth. She'd turned to marshmallow, hadn't she?

We need Clemmie here, not Trixie. Clemmie wouldn't melt at the first sign of trouble.

Clemmie, Aidan . . . Aidan, Clemmie? Good genes. YES!

Well, hopefully.

'Threats?' said Ellie, her eyes on Aidan, who was reading the situation at the rate of knots. 'Two can play at that game. Aidan, this gentleman is going to sign a paper for us before he leaves. And, he leaves without that bag because it doesn't belong to him.'

'Do I call the police?' Aidan's eyes hardened, as did his chin. The genes were definitely good.

'Yes!' gasped Trixie.

'No!' said her father. 'I mean . . . if he would only . . .'

The businessman wasn't waiting. He lunged for the doorway. Ellie tried to step in front of him, and was thrust aside.

An immovable object prevented him. Thud! The businessman bounced off Aidan and staggered back, arms flailing.

Ellie plucked the bag from the uninvited guest's hand, and removed herself and it out of harm's way. 'Enough of fisticuffs. Aidan, could you bring the gentleman over here and sit him down so that we can complete our transaction? Ray, you need to make out a receipt.'

Ray seemed to have difficulty moving.

'Come along now!' said Ellie, becoming annoyed with him. 'How should we word the receipt? Something to the effect that this is in full quittance of all debts owing? How much do you owe, by the way? More than thirty-four thousand?'

'N-no. Probably not quite as . . .' Ray flapped his hands.

Ellie sighed. 'I suspect you probably owe a bit more than that, or the gentleman here wouldn't be so anxious to steal your wife's jewellery. Well, thirty-four thousand is a nice round sum, and probably more than he expected to get off you. Now, the wording. I don't particularly want to bring a solicitor into this, but it has to cover all eventualities. What do you think, Aidan?'

'Gambling debts?' Aidan nodded. 'I'd heard.' He picked the businessman up without apparent effort, propelled him to the table and dumped him on a chair, which he pushed right up to the board so that the man couldn't easily wriggle out from under.

Aidan picked up the pen and paper. 'Your name and address for starters.'

He was left-handed? Well, doctors' signatures were never legible, were they?

Ray tottered over to the table and, in a low voice, dictated the details which Aidan duly wrote down.

Ellie opened the bag of goodies long enough to see that the contents had been taken from the safe. 'Trixie, do you know the combination of the safe? I think it might be a good idea to put all this stuff back.'

'Um, yes.' Trixie pressed her hands to her eyes. 'Mum did tell me once, but I've forgotten. She's got it written it down in her diary.'

'Set a new one,' said Aidan, multitasking as he wrote to Ray's dictation.

Ellie took the picture off the wall. The safe door had not been shut properly, so she opened it up and stacked the goodies back where they'd come from.

'Under duress!' said the businessman. 'This is not legal.'

'Three witnesses to say that you signed of your own free will,' said Aidan, smiling. 'Or, of course, we could always call the police and give you in charge for attempted theft.'

The businessman almost shouted, 'That won't get you anywhere! I know the chief inspector of this division socially.'

Aidan retorted, 'The police inspector of this division is my uncle. I know him socially, too.'

Excellent genes! Now, should I use the combination which Poppy had listed in her diary, or think up a new one?

'Sign here,' said Aidan, pushing the paper towards Ray. 'No, no. Read it first. You're giving him your watch and your car in full payment, etc., etc.'

'I still have his IOUs,' said the businessman, perking up.

'This paper covers all IOUs up to and including today's date,' said Aidan. 'Of course, if you can entice him back after this and he plays and loses again, then that's your look-out, because you know he hasn't anything left to play with.'

'Never again.' Ray shuddered.

Ellie wasn't sure she believed him. Gamblers couldn't give up the addiction as easily as that. She said, 'Please note that his family won't be bailing him out again.'

'No, they won't,' said Trixie. 'Aunt Juno hates gambling and so do Gramps and Gran. No one else has any money in this family.'

Aidan gave his pen to the businessman. 'Sign, please.'

'Give me your car keys, and I will.' His eyes shifted this way and that, looking for a way out and not finding it.

They waited while Ray retrieved his bunch of keys from the hall, disentangled one and handed it over. The businessman signed. Next, Ray.

Then Trixie, and Aidan as witnesses. Finally, Ellie put her signature on the bottom.

Aidan retrieved his pen, and said, in a cheerful voice, 'Have you a photocopy machine in the house, Trixie? No? Right. Well, let's take piccies on our smartphones, shall we?

That way, we will all have a copy of what's been done. Me first.'

Ellie grimaced. She got out her phone. It wasn't an up-to-date one. It wasn't an 'I' or an 'E' or whatever it was they used nowadays. It certainly wasn't 'smart', being slightly chipped, and there was a smear on it which might be butter or possibly baked beans, from when she'd left it on the table while making lunch the other day. She held it out to Aidan. 'I'm not sure I've got a camera on this?'

To give him his due, he didn't even snigger. 'Not to worry. I've got it on mine. Now Trixie, your turn.'

Trixie stumbled over to the table and took a photo. She was ashen pale under her make-up. Her lipstick looked garish in contrast.

'Now, Ray. You'll want your own copy.'

Ray started. 'Oh. Yes. What have I done with . . .? He fumbled in his pockets and produced an up-to-the-minute phone. As he held it out to Aidan, the businessman snatched it out of Ray's hand, wriggled himself out of the chair, charged out of the room, across the hall, and was through the front door before anyone else could move.

Actually, Ellie thought that nobody had tried very hard to stop him. They heard a car start up outside.

'My car,' said Ray, anguished. 'He's taking my car. Stop him, somebody.'

Nobody moved.

'Splendid,' said Aidan, pocketing his pen. 'Who's going to keep that all-important paper receipt? Trixie?'

Trixie took the receipt from him. Her colour was improving. She even tried to smile. 'Now I know how to act fear. I did well, didn't I, Aidan?' She did the little-me-looking-up-at-big-strong-hero bit rather well.

'Sure,' said Aidan, smiling in amiable fashion, but not taking the bait. 'Now, what about our tea break?'

Trixie laid her hands on his arm, and pressed up against him in approved sex-kitten fashion. 'I was so frightened. I could do with a cuddle.'

Aidan freed himself with a smile. 'My inner man is screaming for food. I'm on nights, remember.'

'I'll see what I can do to rustle up some food,' said Ellie, thinking she might not be able to master an iPhone or whatever it was, but that she did know how to make a cup of tea. She wasn't particularly surprised when Aidan followed her out to the kitchen. She said, 'How many teas and how many coffees?' She put the kettle on.

'Aidan West,' he said, proffering his hand.

'Ellie Quicke.'

He nodded. 'I recognized you from the description I was given. LOL. It doesn't mean Laugh Out Loud, but Little Old Lady with diamond eyes.'

'Clemmie?' said Ellie, hoping against hope.

Aidan grinned. 'Quite something, isn't she?'

'You are her driving instructor?'

'Perish the thought. Though I have sat with her for practice sessions. She is an excellent driver and, unlike me – who had three goes at it – should pass the test first go.'

'I'm sure she will. You were Trixie's boyfriend at one time?'

'A friend dragged me along to one of her parties. I met Clemmie there and that was it. Hooked for life.' He seemed to mean it, too.

She said, slowly, not knowing how much he knew, 'Clemmie is in trouble.'

A frown. 'I know. She won't talk about it. She says everything will be all right when her mother returns.'

'I'm afraid that may be too late. Her father, Gordon. Er, you know about him, yes? Yes, of course you do. Not my idea of a cuddly daddy. Nor yours, either, I should think. Well, anyway, Gordon says he's going to the police on Monday morning to accuse her of theft and murder.'

He didn't even blink. 'Then she'll need all the help we can give her, won't she, Mrs Quicke?'

Ellie thought he was a lovely man. 'Let's feed the five thousand, and then be on our way, right?'

TEN

Aidan offered Ellie a lift in his car. She'd imagined him in something large and solid, like himself, but he handed her into the battered two-stroke. 'Apologies. My own car's in the garage. This is the one my mother uses when she's shopping locally. She has a "thing" about parking meters, she only has to see one to drive into it . . . but she's a brilliant surgeon.'

When he got in, the little car sagged. Ellie took a firm grip of the safety belt, and hoped for the best.

He glanced at his watch. 'Where are we going? I'm on night duty and have to eat first. Otherwise, I'm at your disposal.'

'Magpie's office. I've got Clemmie's phone number somewhere. I'll ring her, see if she's still there and will let us in. Otherwise, I'm hoping Celine at the shop has got a key. I need to check on something.' She managed to find the number, phoned and got hold of Clemmie, who said, 'Yes, I'm still here, but about to leave.'

'Can you hold on for five minutes and let me in?'

'Why?'

'Taxes,' said Ellie. 'Cheating on. Possibly a second set of books?'

'Ah-ha.' Clemmie clicked off.

'Taxes?' said Aidan, negotiating a roundabout at speed. 'None of those women at The Magpie would. You're after Ray?'

'Possibly.' Ellie used her phone again. 'Thomas? Yes, I'm on my way back to The Magpie. What did you discover at Harrison's?'

It sounded as if Thomas were walking home as he took the call. 'About what we'd been told. They ripped a customer off. She'd run an old banger into the ground, wasn't sure it was worth repairing, took it to them for an estimate. They said it would cost X. She told them to go ahead, but that if they found it was going to cost more, she wanted them to get her approval before they went ahead and did it. They didn't ask her approval but went ahead and did the work. The bill was double their estimate. She was furious, especially since the repair only lasted a fortnight. She gave me the name of a friend of hers with a similar story; estimate for X and charge double.'

Ellie said, 'Uh-huh. Did you buy some cheese?'

'A couple of . . . well, you know. A bit of this and a bit of that.'

They'd be eating cheese for a week. 'Is Mikey still with you?'

'He got a phone call from a friend, went off to play some game or other with him. On the computer. Chess, I think. He said something about a sleepover.'

'Can you check that Vera knows? Mikey might not remember to ask if he can stay the night away.' Translation: Mikey tried to get away with murder sometimes. Well, not actual murder, of course. 'You know what I mean,' said Ellie.

'I know what you mean. All right, I'll phone her.'

'He went off on his bike, riding on the pavement?'

Thomas laughed, and disconnected. Which meant that yes, Mikey had ridden off on the pavement. Ellie sent up an arrow prayer, *Please don't let Mikey knock anyone over or damage himself.*

Aidan drove with care and attention to detail, but rather faster than Ellie would have liked. Ellie could see the point of having a little runabout like this. He could zip in and out of traffic with ease, and parking would be a doddle. Unless you were his mother with a 'thing' about parking meters.

He drew up outside The Magpie and double-parked, with one eye on the clock. 'I can't stop here. I'll wait round the corner and give Clemmie a lift home if she's not going to be long. I'm on duty at seven.'

'I'll ask her to ring you.'

Ellie extricated herself from his car, straightened her skirt, and looked The Magpie over. There were still customers in the shop. A girl, probably late teens – the one who'd been at the funeral? – was taking a dress off one of the mannequins in the window, presumably to be tried on by a customer.

Ellie rang the bell for the office, and waited. She watched

Aidan manoeuvre out into the traffic, and turn into a side
road nearby. Smoothly. He'd done that before, hadn't he?
How long had he been hanging around Clemmie, and did
Trixie have mixed feelings about it?

The speakerphone clicked and Ellie announced her name.
Someone activated the lock on the door, Ellie pushed it open
and climbed the stairs.

Clemmie was waiting for her at the top. Clemmie did not
look pleased to see her.

Ellie got in first. 'You just wait till Aidan tells you what's
been happening back at the ranch! He's waiting for you round
the corner, if you can leave straight away. Give him a bell if
you can't make it.'

Clemmie gaped. Then frowned. Struggled with herself. Made
a sharp movement back to the stairs, contained herself. 'I don't
know what you want, but Mr Mornay is still here, and—'

'I hoped he might be. Thanks for letting me in, Clemmie.
You go off and have fun. It's Mr Mornay I came to see.'

'Yes, but—'

'Go, girl!'

'I'll have to tell him you're here first.'

'Tell him. And then, go.'

Clemmie darted into the inner office, where Ellie heard
her say, 'Mrs Quicke's come back. Is it all right if I leave you
to lock up?'

There was a mumble from within. Clemmie collected a
jacket and purse from her desk and, after sending a distracted
look in Ellie's direction, disappeared down the stairs.

The outer office was empty. Laura had already gone for the
day, as had Ruth.

Ellie walked into the inner office to find Mr Mornay sitting
back in his chair, his hands clasped and a frown on his face.
'Now what do you want?'

'Some answers.' Ellie took a chair, uninvited. 'The books that
you're working on at the moment. Those on the table. They're
not for The Magpie, are they? But they're relevant.'

'That is no business of yours.'

'The partnership books are all right, with the exception
of the money which Trixie took. But you don't only deal with

The Magpie, do you? You also do the books for Cordover's, the builders. And very likely also for Cocks's Garage. My money is on these books being from the garage.'

'You amaze me.' He steepled his fingers and looked at her over them. He was not going to admit anything but he wasn't throwing her out, either.

She continued in a conversational tone. 'You attended the funeral but absented yourself immediately afterwards, at a time when you knew Ray Cocks would be tied up with the reading of the will. Did you use that time to raid his office at the garage and remove his books?'

Her eyes switched to the heavy tomes on his desk. Old-fashioned methods. Transferring figures by hand at the end of every day. Not using modern technology. Her kind of bookkeeping, out of date but practical, leaving a paper trail and not subject to the vagaries of computer systems.

She said, 'I wonder if perhaps you were looking for two sets of books? One for the taxman and one for private consumption. I'd take a bet that Ray hasn't reported much of a profit in years, and yet I'm told the garage has been ripping people off left, right and centre. They give customers a low estimate, do some work and charge double. I suspect that the set of books currently residing on this table gives the real picture of how the garage is doing.'

'Now what makes you think that I would lift books from the garage?'

'Because Poppy had asked you to do an audit before she died. Some months ago she'd made Ray hand over the garage to her in exchange for bailing him out yet again. Perhaps she hoped this would stop the club giving him unlimited credit. To save his face and give him an income, she told him he could stay on as manager, but on his own admission he was hardly ever there. I'm told that Poppy wasn't happy about that. Was she working herself up to give him the sack?'

'Oh, surely not.' A twitch of a smile.

'Maybe. I'm not sure about that. What I am sure about is that, after he still didn't mend his ways, she finally gave up on him and was planning a divorce. A divorce would mean a division of assets, including her share in The Magpie partnership. This would have been painful but something she was prepared to consider. Her affairs at The Magpie were in order – apart from the vexed question of the missing cheques – but she was now also responsible for the garage and rumours were circulating in the community as to the conduct of affairs there. If the rumours were true then she, as the new owner, would be held responsible for any misconduct. If the garage was doing all right, well and good. But, if it were losing money or owing the taxman, it would be quite another matter.'

'Pure supposition!'

'Really? What if the police were going to get involved with the conduct of affairs at the garage? What if some disgruntled customers were to sue the garage for malpractice? She would be held responsible if Ray were still acting as manager, or if he'd become so lax in attendance that he'd let his staff get away with murder. Either way, she was having to face the fact that taking the garage off him had been a rotten decision, which was likely to cost her a great deal of money. She needed to know, urgently, where she stood. Hence her request to you for an audit.'

He spread his hands. 'Yes, she did ask me to do an audit. As Ray had asked her to keep it a secret that he'd let her have the garage, she thought the staff there might object if I simply walked in and asked to see the books, so she gave me a letter of authorization to take the books away and do an audit. She did this just before she died.'

'Exactly when?'

'I am a busy man. I'd have to look in my diary.'

'What nonsense. Shall I ring Gerald Cordover and tell him you've got Ray's books – or does he already know?'

'Yes, he . . . well, he . . . Look, it was the day before she died. She rang, asking me to meet for lunch. She told me things had gone from bad to worse with Ray and that she was considering a divorce. She told me he'd made the garage over to her, but some friends had rung her to complain about the way they'd been treated there. She and her sister have always been totally straight with their customers, and she found this complaint upsetting.

'She asked my advice. I suggested it might be a good idea

for her to have an audit of the garage's books, which in normal circumstances would not have been due for another four months, because I, too, had heard a rumour that the garage was over-charging. I pointed out to Poppy that if by any chance Ray wasn't up to date with his tax returns, she, as the new owner, would be held responsible. That was when she decided to act. The following day she sent me round a written instruction to remove the books from the garage and do an audit. That night she died and I really didn't know what to do for the best.'

'So you confided in Gerald Cordover and asked for his advice, which was . . . to do nothing until the police had proved Ray did or did not kill his wife?'

'Correct. So we waited. Everyone had a theory but none of them could be proved.'

'Gordon wanted it to be Clemmie. Gerald wanted it to be Ray. Ray was feeling guilty; he knew he hadn't killed her, but he thought his actions might have driven her to suicide, or caused her to be careless and tumble down the stairs to her death?'

'You read us well. And there was I, with Poppy's instructions to hand, beginning to wonder if there was something in Ray's books which gave him a motive for murder, even though Gordon had seen . . . To be frank, I didn't know what to think. Gerald hummed and hah'd and wrapped it up in so many words that it took me a while to understand what he meant, which was that it would be a good idea to whisk the books away from the garage before Ray could remove any incriminating evidence . . . always supposing that there was anything incriminating to be found. He didn't say so in so many words, of course.'

Ellie nodded. 'No, he wouldn't, would he? So you took a chance?'

'I did. Ray Cocks is a swindler, a thief, a gambler.' He gestured to the stack of books on the table. 'The proof is there.'

'Sufficient proof for him to kill his wife before she could confront him with his misdemeanours?'

'I believe so. But he had an alibi. The police checked.'

'What exactly did you discover when you looked at the books?'

'The garage is not doing well. Every week, money leaked

from the petty cash with no receipts to cover the loss. Also, Ray was withdrawing some three or four hundred pounds in cash from the bank every week for undisclosed reasons. That was bad enough, but a couple of months ago he seems to have stopped doing the books and let someone else take over. A woman. His foreman's wife, I believe. Since then –' he raised his hands – 'the books have been kept in a different hand. Only a little money is coming in, but costs keep rising. My interpretation is that Ray lost interest in anything but gambling.'

'You audited the books eight months ago?'

'Ray used a different accountant then.' He grimaced. 'That person is unknown to me and I cannot comment on what he did.'

He meant that the work had not been well done?

He continued, 'The tax bill for last year has not yet been paid. If Juno doesn't deal with it smartish, she'll be in real trouble with the Inland Revenue. As for what's been going on recently, she will have to decide whether or not to charge the foreman's wife with fraud. I rather suspect she will decide against doing so. If she puts in a decent manager straight away, perhaps he can pull the garage round and make it profitable again. Possibly her best bet would be to clear outstanding debts and sell the garage site off for whatever she can get for it. As to Ray, I have absolutely no idea what she will wish to do. I don't suppose she would want to prosecute him for fraud or to throw him out on to the street, but how do you treat a man with an addiction to gambling? Could he ever be trusted to hold a job handling money again?'

'Did Poppy know that Ray was skimming money off the garage?'

'She might have suspected, but I don't think she knew. I'm rather glad, in a way, that she died before she discovered what a scumbag he'd been. I know they say addicts can't help themselves, but the damage they do . . .!'

Ellie said, 'Do you, personally, believe Poppy's death was an accident?'

He shook his head. 'I keep telling myself it could have happened the way the police said, that she accidentally

tumbled down the stairs and broke her neck. But no, I still
don't believe it.'

'You don't believe it because you don't *want* to believe it,
or because you have heard something or seen something to
make you think it wasn't an accident?'

'I can't put my finger on anything. I'm not usually given to
feelings. I've been told I have very little imagination. I like
facts and figures. This equals that. Subtract so and so. The
answer is "x", incontrovertible, can be proved, will stand up in
court. And yet, I don't believe it was an accident.' He picked
up a pencil and began to fiddle with it. A sign of nerves?

'So, murder . . . by whom?'

A long sigh. 'I don't know. Poppy had taken over Ray's last
remaining asset, and even though she'd said he could stay on
as manager, his recent behaviour . . . well! And if she divorced
him . . .! As for Clemmie . . .'

He got up, and went to look out of the window, probably
without seeing the yard outside. He snapped the pencil in
two, looked at the pieces and threw them at the wastepaper
basket. For a man who didn't rile easily, he was flying flags
of distress. 'Well, if you must know: Clemmie had a confrontation with Poppy on the night she died. She was seen at the
door downstairs, trying to get in, hammering on the door,
pressing the bell.'

This was a facer. Or was it? 'Wait a minute, doesn't she have
her own key?'

'I suppose so.'

'Then why was she hammering on the door and pressing
the bell?'

'Panic, I assume. She'd just found out that her peculation
had been discovered, and that a meeting was being held that
very evening at The Magpie to discuss her future.'

'Who saw her?'

'Gordon. He was driving past. He has a specially adapted
car which he can use when he's feeling well enough. He had
come by to pick up Juno, who was working late. Juno had
already left, though he didn't know that. He parked and rang
her mobile to say he was outside. She answered his call to say
she'd already left and was in a taxi on her way home. He was

just about to drive away when he saw Clemmie arrive and try to get in. He didn't think anything of it at the time, but later on he understood that Clemmie must have got in and found Poppy there, and that there'd been a confrontation. I can hardly bear to think about it.'

'Why didn't he tell the police?'

'He didn't tell anyone for ages. He knew what it would do to Juno if Clemmie were arrested for murder, but he couldn't let the girl get away with it. He asked my advice and I said he should speak out. He promised he would. And that's exactly what he's going to do, even though it will cause Juno such anguish . . .! I don't suppose for a minute that Clemmie meant to throw Poppy down the stairs. I don't suppose she meant to kill her. I'm sure it was an accident, but you can see that your interference, though no doubt well meant, is . . .'

He didn't mean it was well meant. He meant it was unconscionable, but he'd been brought up to be polite on all occasions.

'. . . putting us under extra strain. But all will be made clear on Monday, when Gordon makes a statement to the police.' He patted his pockets, checking for keys and a smartphone. 'I'm about to leave. Can I give you a lift somewhere?'

'Thank you.'

Ellie thought over what he'd said as he showed her out to the staircase, and locked the door to the main office behind him. This left them in the shadows on the upper landing, with light only coming faintly through a transom over the doorway behind them. He hit the timer and the overhead light came on.

Ellie looked down the length of the stairs. Poppy had been standing on this very spot, the one where she, Ellie Quicke, was standing now. Had Poppy been about to leave? What was the weather like that evening? Did it require she take an umbrella? A jacket? If she was about to leave, she'd have needed her handbag. Where did they find her handbag?

Presumably she'd a bunch of keys in her hand as she was locking up to leave. If that is what she had done. Had the door into the office been locked or not?

If she had forgotten something, or the phone back in the office had rung and she'd turned back sharply to attend to it, she might well have lost her footing and been unable to prevent herself from falling. Yes, it could have been like that.

Only, no one in the family believed it.

Mr Mornay moved Ellie to one side, so that he could set an alarm on an unobtrusive alarm pad at the top of the stairs. 'After you.' The alarm set up a loud buzzing noise.

Ellie led the way down the stairs, holding on to the banister. Mr Mornay let them out into the street, and pulled the door shut behind him. The alarm stopped buzzing.

When Poppy died, had the alarm been set, or not?

Mr Mornay pointed to a sleek silver car nearby and clicked a key fob to unlock the door. 'May I drop you somewhere? I'm meeting my wife at the wine bar in Ealing Broadway. Perhaps you'd like to join us? To make sure I really do have a wife.'

She ignored the sarcasm. 'Thank you. Yes, I'd like that.'

He was a good, careful driver. The traffic was heavy for a Saturday early evening. She wondered how Thomas was getting on with his cheese mountain, and whether Mikey really was having a sleepover with a friend or was out . . . doing what? Perhaps it was better not to speculate about what Mikey might get up to. His imagination was more fertile than hers.

She said, 'Let's start from the beginning, Mr Mornay. Not this week, or last week. Right back to the beginning. The twins' eighteenth birthday party. The Cordover family were conspicuously wealthy. Rolling in it. The girls were coming on to the marriage market. They had a wide circle of friends, who were mostly young professionals, though they included some up-and-coming moneyed youngsters like Ray. You were there, too?'

His chin came out. 'What's that got to do with it?'

'I'm trying to work out how two hard-working, clever women ended up with losers for husbands.'

'Gordon wasn't—'

'Convince me. Were you yourself involved with either of the girls?'

A tinge of colour in his cheeks. 'No. Marge and I got married the following year. We've had our difficulties, but we're still good friends. She's in real estate, doing well.'

Real estate. Like the twins. Who did The Magpie company

buy their properties through? This Marge? That would make sense. Clemmie had mentioned a godmother who'd sent her some money when she was broke. Was that Marge?

He looked at his watch. 'Mustn't be late. We're going on a Caribbean cruise in the autumn. I was never romantically involved with the twins.'

So much for Marika's hints. Ellie was slightly annoyed with herself for having taken everything Marika said at face value. Or, was Mr Mornay sliding over the truth, too? 'But you were keen to help Poppy recently?'

'Well, yes. All friends, together. Long time. Naturally.'

'Back to the eighteenth birthday party. Was there lots to drink?'

He slowed down, coming to yet another red light. It was said there were too many red lights in the borough. Perhaps they were right. The alternatives seemed to be lots of round-abouts. Which was worse?

He said, 'Lavish. They had a mansion in those days, with a garden leading down into a wood, where we did tend to stray . . .' A self-conscious laugh. He'd been there, and done that, hadn't he? 'As for booze, yes: there was beer and soft drinks. The Cordovers didn't want spirits on their premises. There was also a fruit cup. Some people brought top-ups.' He twitched a smile as the lights changed and they drove on.

'Ah-ha,' said Ellie. 'Someone poured a bottle of vodka into the innocuous fruit punch when Marika's back was turned? Were the parents out for the evening?'

'Something like that.' A widening smile. 'Not that Poppy needed any encouragement to cut a caper. She was quite some goer in those days.'

'Unlike Juno?'

'Juno was the original Miss Prim. Gordon had to work hard to pull her off her pedestal. He was desperate to get a ring on her finger, but she kept putting him off. What a tease she was!'

Ellie swallowed bile. Yes, she'd known men like this before, who considered all women fair game. And yes, she had to admit that many of her generation of girls had been all too happy to lose their virginity at the first opportunity. Some, like Ellie, had waited. It sounded as if Juno at eighteen hadn't been any too keen to tie herself down to a life with Gordon.

Ellie remembered Clemmie saying that her mother didn't drink. A fruit cup at her birthday party must have seemed safe enough. Ellie said, 'Who spiked the fruit cup? Gordon?'

An amused laugh. 'No, no. Some gatecrasher, I believe. We were all on the sauce that night, Gordon, Ray, and I. We each took our girls down into the wood in turn for a bit of how's-your-father. Nothing wrong in that.' He swung into the roundabout and came out ahead of a car which had tried to cut in. 'I'll have to park in the multi-storey. All right by you?'

'Sure.'

'Someone, probably Ray, dared Poppy to dance on a table-top, and she did. We took turns lifting our girls up on to the tables. One overturned. I suppose it got a bit out of hand, but it was all in good fun.'

'Did Juno dance on the table, too?'

'Far too straight-laced. She was there later, though, when we were all smooching, dancing on the patio. We'd all paired off by then. Marge and I . . .' He laughed, shook his head. 'What a night that was!' They drew up at another red light.

Ellie was intrigued. 'Gordon and Juno ended up dancing cheek to cheek?'

'No, no. He'd passed out under one of the tables. At least, I think that was him. No, I lie. Didn't he tumble down the steps and . . .? No, that wasn't him. It was Ray's friend who threw up in the flower bed. Juno was dancing with some bloke who'd gatecrashed the party. Dunno who he'd come with. Some of us were too far gone to drive home, had to take taxis. Can't remember who gave Ray a lift. It was all a bit of a blur at the end. Marge lost one of her shoes and I had to carry her to my car, where she passed out. Happy days. Marge and I got engaged that night.' He swung into the ramp leading up to the multi-storey car park. 'We're meeting at a restaurant just off the Green, if that's all right with you.'

And that's when Ellie got it.

How stupid she'd been!

Real estate equals Marge. Real estate equals Ellie's ambitious daughter, Diana. They were both estate agents.

The ten houses owned by The Magpie partnership might now come on to the market, if Juno decided to sell.

Diana had known or had guessed that Poppy's houses might come on to the market. Did she want Ellie to advance the money to buy them? Yes, that would fit with Diana's preoccupation about making money. But, how could Diana have known about it?

Ellie thought back to the first conversation she'd had with Diana at the start of this business, when she, Ellie, had been about to leave the house for her dentist's appointment, and Diana had said something about it was a chance in a lifetime, something she'd only just heard about. Then Lesley had rung to introduce the Cordovers, and Ellie had been drawn into their family's affairs.

Diana had been trying to contact Ellie ever since, saying it was urgent. Actually, it wasn't urgent. Was it? Nothing could happen till probate had been granted, and there was no guarantee that Juno would want to sell up.

Ellie chided herself. She'd got hold of the wrong end of the stick. It wasn't common knowledge that Juno inherited Poppy's estate, so how could Diana have known about it?

Charles led Ellie into the lion's den, which looked like any other pleasant, middling good restaurant. He said, 'Do you often eat out in the Broadway?' Not expecting an answer.

Ellie thought that she must ring Thomas to say she was going to be late for supper . . . which would probably be cheese, cheese and more cheese. Possibly with some pâté in there somewhere.

'Let me introduce my wife, Marjorie. Marge, this is Mrs Quicke, the philanthropist.'

ELEVEN

Saturday early evening

Mr Mornay said, 'Marge, this is Mrs Quicke.'

'Delighted to meet you at last, Mrs Quicke.' The woman was already seated at the bar and didn't rise to greet them, but did extend her hand in welcome.

Ellie nodded and produced a social smile. They shook hands, all politeness, while taking stock of one another.

Marge was fair, fat, forty and gorgeous. She had curly ginger hair, pencilled-on eyebrows, bright red lipstick, brilliantly patterned floral clothes over a comfortable body, and a bandeau round her head with an artificial flower stuck into it. Ellie wondered whether Trixie had copied Marge, or vice versa.

Marge indicated a chair beside her. 'You'll join us for a bite to eat?'

'Just a coffee, if I may. I'm expected back home for supper.' She glanced at her watch, and decided to allow fifteen minutes' grace before she left.

'Charles will get you a cab when you're ready.' It was clear who wore the trousers in this household, wasn't it? No, wait a minute; hadn't someone said they were divorced?

Charles – Mr Mornay – said, 'Ellie was enquiring about our friend Gordon, and how we all got together, all those years ago.' He was enthusiastic in his friend's defence. 'Gordon's quite something, isn't he, Marge? What he's had to put up with, so much pain, and never complaining! A lesser man would have given up and become a complete invalid before now, but, did I tell you, Ellie, that on the days he feels all right, he works at a local day centre for the disabled, which is held in the church over the road? He's an example to us all, isn't he, Marge?'

Marge sipped her drink and said, 'Mm'hm.'

Charles went on, 'Look, Mrs Quicke, I know you're prejudiced against him for some reason. I suspect you've been listening to

Clemmie, right? Well, there's two sides to every story. Gordon has tried to love Clemmie even though, well, it's obvious, isn't it, that he's not her natural father? But she's a little witch; she throws all his care and good advice back in his face. I'm sorry to say this, but she is an ungrateful little girl. It's all of a piece, as he says. He was always afraid she'd end up doing something terrible, and look what's happened!'

Ellie absorbed that. She understood that if, like Charles, you had known Gordon for ever, and trusted his word, then you might only see Gordon's point of view. 'You've never had a serious, in-depth talk with Clemmie yourself?'

'Me? No. Why should I?'

Marge put her hand on her husband's arm. 'Darling, we're being remiss. Can you get Mrs Quicke a coffee? And another gin for me.'

'Of course.' A flustered retreat.

Marge produced a wide, confiding smile. 'Charles gets the oddest of ideas, sometimes. For a start, he thought he could persuade the family into letting me manage the sale of Poppy's houses . . .'

Ellie got it! Poppy and Juno already gave whatever business they had to Marge.

'But that was before he realized that Juno gets the lot . . .'

Which wouldn't make any difference to Marge.

'He's a determined little so-and-so when he gets an idea into his head.' Marge smiled, warmly, genuinely, inviting Ellie to join her in a warm appreciation of her husband.

Ellie began to like Marge.

Ellie said, 'It's nothing to do with me.' She, too, smiled, letting Marge know that they understood one another. 'Nothing can happen till probate is granted, anyway.'

'You and I both know that. Juno knows that, too.'

'You and Juno are good friends?'

Marge scrutinized the nail polish on brightly pink fingernails. And nodded.

Ellie went a step further. 'May I ask why you weren't at the funeral?'

A sigh. Half-closed eyes looking into the distance. 'When Juno phoned to tell me about Poppy, I'd just arrived on one of the Greek islands for a very much overdue holiday. I was supposed to have gone away a couple of months ago, but my elderly mother had had a fall and I had to get her settled in sheltered accommodation before I took time off. It was a stressful time for both of us. My mother is a right old battle-axe. I only hope I'm as contrary and as fighting fit when I'm eighty-five. I was over at the knees when I crawled off the plane and heard the news. I told Juno I'd fly back straight away. She said not to, that I couldn't do anything and that I needed the rest. She said Ray was arranging a pauper's funeral and that I'd hate it.' She winced. 'She said we could talk every day, which we did, sometimes for an hour at a time. I was worried about her. I've noticed that in grief people often go down with some kind of virus or infection and neglect to do anything about it. But she did tell me, the last time I rang her, that she'd been to the doctor and was feeling a bit better.'

Ellie guessed, 'You know she's gone missing? She rang and told you?'

A nod, but no comment.

Ellie said, 'I'm beginning to understand what went on in that marriage, and I'm not surprised she's gone missing, either. Do you know where she is? Or, do you think you can find out?'

'I'm not even going to try.'

Another guess. 'She asked you not to tell Gordon?'

'Why would she do that?' Arched eyebrows. Mock astonishment.

Ellie relaxed. 'You don't like Gordon, either?'

'Gordon is,' Marge considered her words with care, 'a slimy, treacherous, hypocritical toad with a wicked tongue. Oh, and he's a bully, too.'

Ellie nodded. 'My opinion, exactly. Who was driving the car when Gordon was injured?'

'My darling ex-husband, of course. Guilt, my dear. It's ruled his life ever since. I suppose he's fed you the line that he and I have had our troubles but that our marriage is sound? He's an old goat. I divorced him ten years ago, after the umpteenth betrayal. I live in the Docklands nowadays, but we do get together occasionally, for old times' sake. We might even go on a cruise this autumn if I don't get a better offer. I'm here now for Clemmie's sake. I hear she's in trouble. I don't know what Charles has told you, but to my mind she's a credit to her grandparents and to her mother. She's my goddaughter, incidentally.'

'Is she also a credit to her father?'

'Unknown,' said Marge with a bland smile.

Which might mean that he wasn't unknown to Marge. Would Marge lie? Yes, of course she would, if she thought it a good idea to do so.

Marge produced a business card. 'Call me any time if you think I can help.'

She wasn't missing a trick, was she! Marge must know that Ellie's trust fund had its own arrangement with a local estate agent. But where was the harm in trying? Ellie liked Marge all the better for it. Ellie took the card. 'I don't have any cards, I'm afraid. And I rather think I'm out of my depth in this case. Did your husband tell you I've been going around asking awkward questions, and that he doesn't know how to get rid of me?'

'Marika said you could help. I hope you can. I'm rather fond of Clemmie, you see.'

Marika's influence reached into surprising quarters, didn't it?

Charles returned, looking harried. 'You didn't say what sort of coffee you wanted, Mrs Quicke. Latte, cappuccino, filter, espresso, mocha? They've got the lot.'

'Don't worry about me,' said Ellie. 'I really must be getting back or Thomas will be sending out a search party. You stay and enjoy your supper. I'll get a taxi from outside the station.'

Anything to get away from these people and *think!*

She stepped into a taxi and gave her home address.

Every time she thought she'd got something straight in her mind, someone else contradicted it. Marika said this, and Charles said that. Marge refuted Charles's story, and Charles – though he'd probably been straight enough on the state of the garage finances – couldn't be relied on for a sound judgement on Gordon, and didn't seem to know all the family's secrets.

Back to basics. Gordon was going to go to the police on Monday morning to accuse Clemmie of murder and fraud, and this was Saturday evening.

What was for supper? Cheese and pâté?

She paid off the taxi, and let herself in to the house. 'I'm home!'

'About time, too!'

Diana, in a black and white rage. Black as to clothing, white of face, and livid of temper. 'Where have you been! Where on earth have you been! I've been ringing and ringing, trying to trace you, asking everyone I knew where you might have gone to ground!'

Thomas appeared in the doorway to the kitchen quarters, caught her eye, and shrugged. He mouthed, 'Are you all right?'

She grinned. While Thomas was around, she'd have back-up. She said, 'I'm OK if you're OK.'

He nodded, and disappeared again. Pleasant smells emanated from the kitchen quarters. Perhaps they were having something more than cheese for supper?

'I'm sorry, Diana,' said Ellie. Though she wasn't at all sorry, really. 'I got caught up in a difficult situation.'

'Tchah! Well, now you're here—'

Ellie started. 'Who's that with you?' A movement in the sitting room behind Diana had caught her eye. A pale-faced woman lay on the settee with a wet cloth over her eyes. Fair hair, rumpled white blouse, jeans. Ellie advanced and Diana gave way. Ellie could hardly believe her eyes. 'Lesley, is that you?' Her police friend? Looking as if she'd been in a car crash. Well, not a car crash, perhaps. But definitely in shock.

Diana said, 'Never mind her. She said she'd wait for you, and I told her you wouldn't have time for her today, but she insisted and—'

Lesley took the cloth off her eyes and gave Ellie a weak smile. Ellie's mind went into overdrive. Car crash? No. Broken engagement? Yes – there was no ring on her finger.

Lesley said, 'Sorry, Ellie. I just felt, well, as if I couldn't—'

Diana broke in. 'Yes, yes. That can wait. This is important. Mother, I've got in on the ground floor, it's an opportunity in a million. All I need from you is a loan of fifty thousand pounds, which you'll get back with interest, I promise you. But I need it tonight. The rest can wait till next week.'

Ellie said, 'If you've given him a cheque, try to get it stopped.'

'What!' A shriek.

Lesley put the cloth back over her eyes.

Diana said, 'Mother, I know you don't have a clue as to—'

Ellie tried not to roll her eyes. 'Try this. Ray Cocks came to see you. He wanted money. He told you he was about to inherit his wife's business and that he'll put the sale of it in your hands for a consideration. Perhaps he even offered to let you buy The Magpie's houses? You gave him money. I hope you didn't give him cash. I hope you were wise enough to give him a cheque. That's why I said, "Try to get it stopped."'

A blank stare. 'What on earth's got into you? It's a chance in a lifetime! He's willing to give us the right to sell the properties. The sole right, I'm no fool. I insisted on that.' She began to pace the room. 'Ten houses, he said. But he suspects there may be more. I rang round, trying to find out which estate agent they've been using. It's Marge Mornay. Marge Money, she calls herself. Got three or more offices, only one in Ealing, the rest somewhere up in town. I got back to him, asked why he wasn't giving her the right, and he said Marge had tried to cheat Poppy over the last house they'd bought, and he didn't feel right going back to her, so naturally I agreed.'

'Marge wouldn't cheat Poppy.'

'Mother, listen to me for once! I gave him a token amount for starters, and I'll borrow the rest from you till I can get a bank loan for the rest.'

'How much did you give him?'

'Ten thousand, cheap at the price. For the right to manage the sale of his wife's property. There's his house, too. A couple of million, that will go for. Maybe two and a half, possibly three. It's a big detached property in an excellent location. Now all I want from you to start with is the fifty thousand for which he'll grant us sole representation.'

Ellie sank into a chair. Midge the cat appeared from nowhere and jumped on to her lap. He started to tread money on her skirt, while keeping a wary eye on Diana. Midge didn't like Diana. And vice versa.

Ellie said, 'Look, Diana. I've had a long and tiring couple of days, trying to work out what's happening in the Cordover family. Almost the only thing I know for sure is that Ray hasn't inherited anything. It's all gone to Poppy's sister under a will made many years ago.'

'What? You're not listening! He's promised us—'

'He didn't know about the will until Friday morning. Didn't you ask around, find out what sort of name he has for business? He's a gambler who drove his wife to consider divorce. I repeat: under her will, he gets nothing. That includes the family's house, which was in her name at the time of her death.'

'You're wrong!' Diana reared up, fighting off the truth. 'He's a respected businessman. He owns a garage—'

'Did he tell you that in so many words? He handed the garage over to his wife some time ago in exchange for her paying off some of his debts. I got that from his accountant, whose opinion of Ray's business capabilities is about as low as you can get. After he lost the garage, Ray more or less abandoned the idea of working for a living, went back to the club and ran up yet more debts. What security did he give you?'

Diana sank into the nearest chair. The truth was gradually, oh so gradually, beginning to sink in. Oh, horror! 'I . . . he said, I assumed . . . everyone knows that . . . you've got it all wrong!'

'You have Internet banking, don't you? It may be after bank hours, but I should see if you can get that cheque stopped, if I were you.'

Diana breathed, 'My ten thousand pounds! I can have him for fraud!'

'It depends when you gave it to him. He didn't know the contents of the will till yesterday morning, after the funeral. If you gave him the cheque on Thursday, it wouldn't have been fraud because he didn't know the true position then – although, in my opinion, whatever guarantee he offered to give you would be poor value. As things stand, he will have no say whatever in what happens to Poppy's estate. Knowing him, if he's managed to cash that cheque, you won't see a penny in return. So my advice is to see if you can cancel it. It's worth a try. But I wouldn't waste any time.'

Diana's mouth went slack, and then firmed up. 'Can I use your computer?'

'No. Where's your iPad?'

'I left it at the office to recharge.'

'Try your phone.'

Diana rushed from the room, taking out her smartphone. A moment later they heard the front door slam.

Lesley hadn't moved a muscle during this. Ellie collected Midge from her lap, got to her feet and deposited him where she'd been sitting. She drew up a stool beside Lesley on the settee, and took her hand. Didn't say anything. Quiet descended. There really wasn't anything to say, was there?

Eventually Lesley took the cloth off her eyes and propped herself upright. 'You warned me. How come you know so much about men? More than I do.'

'Age, I suppose.'

'He tried to make out it was all my fault. He said I had no right to interfere in his family's arrangements for the wedding. I pointed out who was paying for the wedding, and he said I was accusing him of holding down a rubbish job, which isn't true, it really isn't!'

'Mm. Defence mechanism.'

'I told him to calm down. He said that if I wanted to drive a wedge between him and his family, it wasn't going to work. I said I couldn't care less about his family, and if he wanted to listen to them rather than me, then it wasn't a good start to our marriage. He shouted at me. I shouted back. I told him to leave. He refused.' She sounded incredulous. 'He actually told me that as I was in the wrong, I should leave. And it's *my* flat!'

Ellie sighed. Lesley knew, every policeman knew, that she could have got the police to throw him out of a flat which was in her name, but she hadn't done so. Was she protecting her own reputation? Couldn't she bear to be laughed at, a policewoman who had the might of the law on her side, but chose not to eject someone from her own flat?

Or did it mean that she thought she was in the wrong, somehow?

Lesley said, 'I threw a mug at him. Full of coffee. Hot. It smashed to pieces when he fended it off. And one of the shards cut his knee open.'

Ellie's lips twitched, but she managed not to smile. Clemmie had done much the same, hadn't she, with her first boyfriend?

'I had to take him to the hospital to be checked over and stitched up. He couldn't drive. He's sub-let his own flat. His parents live in Derby. He hasn't anywhere else to go.' A long, long sigh. 'So I took him back to the flat and left him there.'

'Because you knew you could come here.'

A nod. 'Because I knew you'd understand and back me up. You know I'm in the right.'

Ellie wasn't so sure about that. 'You may certainly stay here tonight. Have you told Susan? Is she making a bed up for you?' Speed-racing through Ellie's mind was the thought that wedding nerves are dreadful, and that Lesley could do with some tender loving care before the day. But how to bring bride and bridegroom together again?

Lesley said, 'Susan can fetch some things for me, can't she? Some clothes, my laptop. I'll make out a list.'

'How would it be if you moved in here till the wedding, to give yourself some space? You could be married from here. How does that sound?'

'The wedding's off.' She held up a ringless hand. 'I threw the ring out of the window.' Her tone was tragic.

Ellie subdued a grin. 'Out of which window? The one over-looking the street, or the one looking over the back garden?'

Lesley began to weep. 'The garden!'

'Did you toss it out, or throw it far away?'

'I don't know, do I? I tossed it. I couldn't have cared less. And now I suppose he'll want it back!' She wailed, sunk in misery.

Ellie moved on to the settee and held the girl in her arms. 'There, there. When you're feeling calmer, you can send him a text to say you're sorry. After supper, say. I don't suppose you've eaten much today, have you?'

A muffled, 'I couldn't eat.'

'You've got to keep your strength up. Has he tried to phone you yet?'

Lesley delved under the cushion and brought out her

smartphone. She looked to see if there were any messages. 'Up his!' She threw the phone across the room.

Ellie subdued the impulse to tell the girl to stop having a teenage tantrum, and rescued the phone. It was an up-to-date phone, the sort Ellie had no idea how to access. Did it open with a magic pass of your hand, or did you have to know the password?

She said, 'I'll just have a word with Thomas. I'll be right back.'

Once in the hall, she shut the sitting-room door, and dug out her own phone to ring Mikey.

The boy answered, sounding preoccupied. 'Yes?'

'Mikey, it's me. Mrs Quicke. Emergency. You're at your friend's house, right? Can you get hold of a magnet and go round to Lesley's flat? Yes, my policewoman friend's flat. Do you know where it is? The last house on . . . yes, that's right. She has the ground-floor flat. She threw her engagement ring out of the back window into the garden and is desperate to get it back. I'm not sure it's possible to find it, but do you think you could try, using a magnet or something?'

'What did she do that for?'

'She was upset. You'd better ring the bell at the flat before you go into the garden, and explain that she's sent you to find the ring. Her fiancé's laid up with a bad knee and can't look for it himself. Mind you, the odds on your finding it aren't good.'

Heavy breathing.

'Mikey?'

'Mm. Gold, is it? We could try a metal detector. Another of my friend's father's got one.'

'Mikey, you're a genius.'

'Twenty quid? For each of us?'

'Done.'

'I might have to give my friend's father a bit more, to borrow the detector.'

'Worth it. Thanks, Mikey. Ring back with a progress report, right?'

'Sure. It's way more real than playing war games. They're boring. How did you find the garage?'

'Financially? Dicey. The information you got was most helpful.'

'Right. See you.' Down went the phone.

Ellie looked up to find Thomas watching her, stroking his beard. She said, 'Oh, Thomas! The stupid mess some people get themselves into.'

He put his arm around her. 'Food helps.'

'Mm, yes. But first, here's Lesley's phone. Can you work out if her fiancé's been trying to contact her? They've had a quarrel over nothing much, but that sort of thing can escalate. She's broken her engagement off and I haven't a clue what to do next. She'll have to stay with us, I suppose. Has Susan gone out for the evening?'

'Susan has gone clubbing.'

Ellie's mouth fell open with shock. She repeated, '"Susan has . . ." Really? But Susan never . . .!'

'No, but she's got some new clothes and done something to herself. I'm not sure what, but she looks magnificent. She rang a friend and has gone clubbing.'

'Wow!' Ellie thought, what a difference a good bra makes! She said, 'Right, well, I'll make up a bed for Lesley after supper. Which reminds me: what are we having? Cheese and potato pie?'

'I can do better than that. Lamb chops with chips and salad; cheese for afters.'

'Wonderful. But, can you check Lesley's phone first? I feel so stupid, not being able to handle these new phones. You can do it. Everyone else can do it. I really ought to learn how to work them.'

'You,' said Thomas, 'have different skills, far more important skills than managing a smartphone.' He winced, looking at some recent messages. 'Mm. A couple of texts from someone who's forgotten how to spell. Or is it always this way with text-speak? The meaning is clear. Sent in a temper. Somewhat inflammatory. What do you want me to do?'

'Let's eat, and then we'll decide.'

TWELVE

Ellie licked her finger in order to collect the last crumb of cheese from her plate. She sighed with pleasure, then forced herself back to the problem in hand. She said, 'The thing is, that if Gordon isn't stopped, he's going to the police on Monday morning to accuse Clemmie of murder, rape, torture and treason.'

'What, all of those?'

'All right. I exaggerate. Murder and theft.'

'Has he any evidence? Do you want a cuppa? Shall I try Lesley again? See if she'll accept some food now?'

'Leave her be for the moment. Tea? No, I don't think so. Evidence? Pretty slim. For the theft: that can be disproved easily enough. It only requires someone in authority to look at the cancelled cheques with an unbiased mind, and perhaps ask Trixie a couple of questions. As for the murder; Gordon now says he saw Clemmie at the scene of the crime that night. He's kept that information to himself so far, which means either that he made the story up, or that he did see her but has refrained from telling the police in order to blackmail Juno into doing his bidding. On balance I think he'd lose more than he would gain by going to the police, because once they hear what he has to say, they'd have to investigate both the fraud and Clemmie's movements. Lesley did say the family had all got alibis, didn't she? Let's hope Clemmie's is a good one. The police certainly didn't look at hers in particular. But oh, dear. If Gordon goes through with his threat, I don't like to think what the resultant fuss would do to Clemmie, or the rest of the family.'

She thought some more about that. 'Well, I don't suppose Ray and Trixie would care, but the others would. Including a hunky great junior doctor who looks as if he played rugby and who used to be one of Trixie's boyfriends and is now after Clemmie with intent. Also, a fairy godmother, who has just popped up out of the bushes and is screaming for action.' She tried to laugh. 'All right, I'm exaggerating again.'

Thomas stowed dirty plates in the dishwasher and switched on the kettle.

She said, 'And Diana. Can you believe it? Ray Cocks spun her some sort of tale about putting the sale of his wife's property through her. He asked her for a fee to give her first refusal or some such nonsense, and she fell for it!'

Thomas smoothed out a grin. He didn't care for Diana. The feeling was mutual. 'You'll sort it out. You always do.'

Ellie clutched her head. 'This time, Thomas, I'm not so sure. I hear one story and accept it, and the next person I talk to gives me a different slant on events. The Cordover family is like an onion. Peel off one layer and you get another. Everyone's hiding something . . . except Trixie, I suppose. She's quite easy to read. She wants to be a film star and nothing is going to stand in her way. Today she invited a group of people to her house for a script conference. She's not interested in the fact that the house is falling to pieces around her. She'll not cook or clean. Somehow or other she'll get enough money together to make her film. Single-minded, that's Trixie.'

'Not bothered by her mother's death?'

'Not that I could see. Totally self-centred, that one.'

'Psychopathic?'

Ellie stared at him. Psychopaths were totally self-centred, weren't they? Was Trixie that far gone? Um, yes. Possibly. Far enough gone to murder her mother? Um. Not sure. 'What would she get out of killing her mother?'

'You said she thought she'd inherit some money?'

Ellie shook her head. 'She was the indulged daughter of a wealthy woman, and she didn't have to earn her living. When her allowance fell short of what she wanted, she stole – yes, stole – from her mother to make up the difference. But, no one's going to scream at her about it, are they? Maybe Poppy didn't want to believe her daughter could steal from her at first, but after Charles started his investigations, the suspicion that Trixie was involved must have jumped up out of the woodwork

and socked her on the jaw. Because Poppy knew her daughter
through and through. Poppy was a soft touch; she'd been
forgiving Ray all these years, and giving him just one more
chance, time and again. So of course she'd do the same for
Trixie. Why would Trixie kill such an indulgent mother? She
wouldn't. Yes, she wanted money to go into films, but if she
doesn't get it one way, she'll get it another. That one will never
run short of the readies.'

'Then who do you think did it?'

'Take your pick. I've been presented with a series of pretty
pictures. First the touching story of two orphaned children being
mothered by an aunt. Then comes the equally touching story
of two hard-working girls making their fortunes, while bravely
shouldering the burden of the no-good men in their lives. After
that we have the dashing Trixie, bound for stardom, and the
Cinderella Clemmie bound for the boardroom. Plus hangers-on
in the form of doting grandparents and friends of the family,
who polarize for and against. Now, I know that three people
seeing a car accident can each come up with different number
plates, makes and colour of car; but, in this case, where are the
verifiable facts? Nowhere.'

'Ask Lesley for them.'

Ellie stared at him. 'Yes, of course. I need dates and times
and the contents of the stomach of the deceased. Was the alarm
set or not? Was the inner door locked? Exactly when did Poppy
die and where was everybody at the time? All that stuff. Lesley
said everyone had an alibi. The senior Cordovers said Ray must
have done it, but then they went on to say that he had an alibi.'

'At the gaming tables?'

'If so, that can be confirmed with video footage, can't it?
Don't these gambling places have cameras to cover the tables?'

'Clemmie was placed at the scene?'

'It was Gordon who placed her there, and Gordon hates her.'

'Which also places Gordon at the scene.'

Ellie said, tiredly, 'I wish. But he can't climb the stairs and
has no motive. Oh dear.'

A stir in the doorway. Lesley, looking limp and holding
out a scrap of paper. 'I'll make up a bed for myself if you'll
show me where, but no, before you say it, I couldn't eat

anything. Where's Susan? I need her to get some of my things
from the flat.'

'She's out for the evening,' said Thomas. 'Give me your list,
and I'll get them for you while Ellie helps you make up a bed.'

'No, no,' said Ellie, interpreting Lesley's expression correctly.
'I'll go for Lesley's things, Thomas. She wouldn't want you
looking in her underwear drawer. You can drive me there and
bring me back in no time at all. Lesley, would you like to use
our old housekeeper's room, up the back stairs here? I'll get
out some linen for you and you can make the bed up yourself,
can't you? It's a nice bedsitter, en suite, and you can come and
go as you please. Remind me to give you a front door key.'
She got to her feet, her mind on bedclothes, airing the room,
towels and a fresh bar of soap.

'That's very good of you,' said Lesley, who was clearly
past caring whether it was good or not. 'I've lost my phone,
by the way. I don't suppose he'll ring. I switched it to silent
mode, so I couldn't hear it. If it does, which it probably won't,
and you come across it, well, I don't want to speak to him,
anyway.'

Which was probably a lie?

Thomas put his mug of tea down in front of Lesley's phone,
which lay in full sight on the table. And which was vibrating.

Lesley might think it was Thomas's? Yes. She ignored it.

Ellie said, 'Shall I show you where everything is?' And led
the way, saying, 'These rooms haven't been used for a while.'
She opened windows, fetched bed linen and made up the bed.
Towels, soap. Alarm clock and radio? Yes. Hot-water bottle?
Yes, even on this warm night. For comfort.

'Thank you,' Lesley said, looking around her with unfocused
eyes. 'You're very kind.'

'You'll feel better in the morning. I'll bring you up a cup of
soup in a minute. You need something to settle your tummy
before you go to sleep.'

Ellie left Lesley gazing into space and went back downstairs,
to find Thomas inspecting the latest message on Lesley's phone.
'He's calmed down a bit. Only two swear words this time.'

Ellie put some soup into the microwave. 'Do we give her
phone back to her?'

'It will only upset her further to read these messages. A couple of hours ago he was white hot with rage. Now he's calming down, but so far hasn't texted anything that she might enjoy reading. Let her have a good night's sleep, or as good as she can manage in her present state. We'll "find" the phone in the morning, shall we?'

'I'll take this soup up to her, and then we'd better fetch her things.'

Thomas picked up Lesley's list. 'She's not asking us to get much. Overnight stuff, basically. She'll need more than this if she plans to go into work on Monday . . . I assume she's not working tomorrow? She doesn't really mean to call off the wedding, does she?'

'I don't think she knows which day of the week it is, never mind what she should wear on Monday.'

'Do we mend fences, or keep out of it?'

She shrugged. 'I haven't the slightest idea. What's more, we've only got thirty hours or so to solve the murder before Gordon swings into action. We're going to need all the help we can get.'

'Then you'd better start praying.'

'You, too.'

'Yes; me, too.'

Sunday breakfast

Ellie moved around the kitchen, yawning. It was a bright, sunny morning, but she didn't feel either bright or sunny. Lesley's smartphone lay on the table, beside a plastic bag containing her engagement ring, which Mikey had triumphantly produced as Ellie and Thomas returned home with Lesley's night things.

Mikey had been well over the top with enthusiasm about metal-detecting, vowing to get a machine for himself. His friend – younger, monosyllabic – had nudged Mikey and pointed to his watch, meaning they were on a curfew. Ellie had paid them both off.

Thomas had said the ring would probably have to go back to Lesley's fiancé.

Ellie didn't know what to think about that. Or about what

had happened when they'd reached Lesley's flat and rung the front-door bell.

Oh well. Ellie made herself eat some cereal and have a slice of toast. Without enthusiasm. She wondered whether or not Diana had managed to stop the cheque she'd so foolishly given Ray Cocks. But then, would it ever have crossed Diana's mind to tell her mother she'd succeeded? Probably not.

Ellie thought, Coffee cures all. Well, not all. But it does help. She made some.

Thomas had gone out early. He was officiating at a communion service for a friend who'd gone on holiday, and planned to stay on to take a half past ten morning service. Ellie would normally have accompanied him, but she'd stayed at home to look after Lesley, who hadn't surfaced.

Ellie was feeling the effects of a lot of worry on top of a disturbed night. It had taken her ages to get to sleep and, at half past one, Susan had woken her up by crashing the front door open. Ellie had shot awake, though Thomas had continued to snore gently away beside her. She heard Susan apologize in a loud voice to the empty hall, and then had come the creak of stairs as the girl, with exaggerated care, crept up the stairs to her own quarters on the top floor.

It appeared that Susan had had an enjoyable evening as, in the morning, Ellie found the newel post at the bottom of the stairs adorned with a set of fairy wings, very pink, and a head-dress of glittering, wobbling, antennae.

Good for Susan.

Ellie took the Sunday papers and a cup of coffee through into the sitting room and opened the French windows on to the garden. Ah, peace and quiet.

The second flush of roses was good this year. The last of the winter-flowering pansies, which had done so well through the spring and early summer, ought now to be taken up. The dahlias were astonishing. One of them needed tying up to its stake. Midge the cat wandered into the room from the garden and curled round her legs. He'd been fed. He was not hungry, but acknowledging that his provider needed some gesture of affection now and then.

Lesley crept in, saying, 'Nice morning. Will we have rain later?'

Ellie was going to ask how Lesley was feeling, but decided not to do so. The girl had slept heavily – probably with the aid of a pill – and was looking heavy-eyed and languid.

Ellie put her cup of coffee down. 'Yes, the sky does look a bit too bright, doesn't it? What would you like for breakfast? Scrambled egg on toast?'

'I'm not bothered. Has that scumbag rung?'

'Your phone is in the kitchen with your ring.'

Lesley drifted along to the kitchen and sat at the table, waiting to be served. She ignored her ring, looked at the phone, picked it up, fidgeted with it, threw it back down on to the table. Had she actually looked at her messages or not?

Ellie put orange juice and cereal in front of Lesley and busied herself making scrambled egg on toast for both of them. Lesley seemed to be in a dream. Ellie didn't disturb her. 'Scrambled eggs coming up. And coffee.'

Probably because Ellie expected her to do so, Lesley started to eat. Finally, she pushed her empty plate aside and poured sugar into her cup of coffee. 'Thank you for getting my bits and pieces last night. Any trouble?'

'None. The bag was in the hall, waiting for us to pick it up. Angelica had packed it for you, and included everything you'll need when you go back on duty on Monday. Angelica said she intends to move in to look after her brother.'

A slow tide of red rose up Lesley's neck and suffused her face. 'What!'

Ellie hid a smile as she sipped her coffee. 'She says that since you had Susan to live with you for a while, she's moving in, instead. She plans to have lots of lovely parties in your flat.'

'Over my dead body!'

Ellie sipped more coffee, and nodded.

'How dare she! She's responsible for everything! The slut! The . . .!'

'Quite. You need to throw her out.'

Lesley seethed. 'I'll settle her hash for her!'

Ellie indicated Lesley's phone. 'You'd better ring him, tell him you're on the warpath. How dare Angelica try to take your place!'

'Indeed!' Lesley pressed buttons.

'You'll need this,' said Ellie, pushing Lesley's ring towards her.

A momentary hesitation on Lesley's part. Then she took the ring out of its bag and slid it back on to her finger. 'How did you find it?' She didn't really want to know. Her attention was all on her phone. 'No answer. He must have turned it off.'

'Leave a voice message.'

'What do I say?'

Ellie shrugged. 'Say you're sorry. That's a good start. You can qualify it later.'

'Like, "I'll have his guts for garters if he tries to do that to me again." Like, "If he ever puts his family before me again, I'll kill him."'

'Something like that. Something to show him you care.'

Lesley whirled round. He'd answered the phone. 'Where have you been? Where. Have. You. Been? I've been half out of my mind with worry. Are you all right? How's your knee? I can't think what got into you – into us – last night. I couldn't sleep . . .' She got up and moved out of the kitchen, gesticulating, restless, suddenly brought back to life. Still talking on the phone, she walked through the hall and out into the garden.

Ellie opened the kitchen window and set about clearing up the breakfast things. Fragments of conversation drifted back to her as Lesley walked to and fro. Ellie wasn't eavesdropping. It was a warm day and she needed some air.

'. . . yes, of course I love you, silly! You want me to do what . . .? Really? Delete all your previous . . . Oh, come on! Did you really say . . . No, I know you were angry, but so was I. Yes, of course Angelica's always been indulged, I do realize that but, be realistic . . . no, we really can't take her in while . . . Yes, your job is stressful, too and . . . suppose . . .?' A genuine laugh. 'Well, you can tell her that if she gets to destroy our future, she can pay for her own bridesmaid's dress! And I don't think she'll go for that . . . No, Susan's no problem nowadays. She's very snug where . . . What! You're going where this afternoon? But . . . No, I hadn't forgotten. At least, I remember that you . . . Are you sure? I mean, your knee won't . . .? All right, we'll go out to supper tonight. There's more wedding presents to . . . Yes, I'll cope. Of course I will . . .'

Then there were loving murmurs, too low for Ellie to distinguish the words.

Lesley returned, with a little colour in her cheeks, smiling. 'Storm in a teacup. He's playing cricket today, would you believe? In spite of his knee. Someone else makes the runs for him. He's got a lift there and back, and he's telling Angelica to make other plans. So all is well.' She regarded her engagement ring with a puzzled look. 'You know, I thought I'd thrown it out of the window, but . . .' She shook her head at herself. 'A bad dream.'

'No. You did. Mikey got it back for you, with a metal detector. It cost me sixty pounds. Think of it as an extra wedding present.' Ellie and Thomas had already given Lesley a new microwave.

'Why, thank you, Ellie. That was nice of you.' Lesley wasn't really listening, was she?

Ellie said, 'Lesley, I don't know what you'd think of this, but would you like to stay here till the wedding? You can see your fiancé all day and every day, but have a little pre-wedding respite. You're rather on top of one another in that tiny flat of yours . . .'

No, it had been the wrong thing to say. Ellie could see Lesley thinking how sweet and old-fashioned the suggestion had been. So last century, practically antediluvian, my dear!

'But not,' said Ellie, 'if you're happier being together all the time.'

Lesley looked amused, but tried to appear grateful. 'What a lovely person you are, dear Ellie. So thoughtful, but really, we're so used to one another now that . . . and he's going to tell Angelica to stop meddling, which is a great relief. The girl's aiming to be a model and is desperate to get away from home, for which, in all honesty, I can't blame her. But it was bad enough having Susan living with us for a while and now . . . No, he's agreed it just wouldn't work.'

'So you're at a loose end this morning?'

'Sort of. Not really. I ought to do this and that, but I must say I feel like taking some time out.'

'Thomas is out till lunchtime, which you're welcome to share with us. If I make some more coffee, could you bear to fill me in on some facts regarding the Cordovers? I think your police notebook is in the bag Angelina packed for you . . .?'

'I suppose. You want me to get it? I'd sooner talk about work than write thank-you notes. I didn't think people bothered doing that nowadays, but some of the aunts . . .' A giant yawn. 'Yes, why not? I'll pop up and get it.'

Ellie settled them both at the kitchen table, with a pad of paper and a pen in front of herself. 'What day did Poppy die?'

'Um, Thursday night? Late. She was discovered on Friday morning.'

'Who reported it?'

Lesley leaned back, and closed her eyes. 'I didn't sleep well last night, even though I took . . .' She rubbed eyes. Sipped coffee. Opened her police notebook. 'The accountant. Charles Mornay. Stiff sort of bloke. In shock. He was working on the books, didn't have a key, was waiting for the office manageress to arrive, or someone to open up from The Magpie next door. The manageress arrived, he said she was a bit late, he went on about that, compulsive something-or-other. He said she ought to have been there dead on half past nine or something and the shop ought to have been open by then, too.'

Charles had a key now. He'd locked up yesterday when he'd taken Ellie off to meet Marge. When had he been given it? Must check. 'I suppose he was blaming everyone else because he'd had a shock?'

'Sounded like it. Anyway, when one of them arrived and turned the key in the door, it wouldn't open. They pushed and shoved . . .'

Ellie winced.

'. . . and finally got the door open enough to see that Poppy's body was preventing them from getting in.'

'Was she cold? How long did the pathologist say she'd been dead?'

'She'd died between half past ten and half past eleven the previous night. Probably nearer half ten than half eleven.'

'Anything else from the pathologist?'

'You mean, poison, or an injection, or blunt-force trauma? No. Last meal was a ham sandwich, plus some coffee, some hours previously. There'd been some family rumpus or other and she hadn't bothered to eat. She'd fallen from top to bottom of the stairs, sustaining multiple injuries and breaking her neck. She died as a result of the fall.'

'She couldn't have fallen, survived and then someone broke her neck?'

'Her injuries were consistent with the fall.'

'How do you know she fell from top to bottom? Did she hit the walls on either side in her fall?'

'There was no blood on the walls. She was lying like a broken doll. No blood. But yes, a trail of destruction on the way down. The glass was broken in one picture, another had been dragged off the wall completely, and one had been tipped sideways.'

Ellie nodded. 'Easy enough to put right.'

Lesley nodded. 'No blood. Some glass splinters – they used a Hoover to clean up, I suppose. Oh, there was an extra mat at the bottom of the stairs which had absorbed the bodily fluids. You know what happens when people die?'

Ellie knew. The mat had been easily removed, afterwards. 'Was the alarm on?'

'No. We queried that. If she'd been working late by herself, she would normally have switched it on. But her sister had been there with her and, after she'd left, Poppy hadn't bothered to switch it on.'

'Or, she was expecting someone else? Ray, the accountant, or her daughter?'

Lesley shook her head. 'They'd all got alibis.'

'Even Aidan?'

'Who's Aidan?'

'Clemmie's boyfriend.'

'Oh, him. He was with her all night, if I remember correctly.'

'Was the overhead light on at the top of the stairs?'

'No. It's on a time switch, remember? If she'd switched it on to come down the stairs, it would have gone off again after sixty seconds or so. We checked.'

'When you found her, were the lights still on in the office?'

'Yes.'

'How was Poppy dressed?'

'A big white sweater, black trousers, a red silk scarf, shoes with a medium heel.'

'Had she left a jacket upstairs? There was a pretty pink cardigan left in her office.'

'Not big enough to go over the top she was wearing. It was a warm night. She wouldn't have needed a jacket.'

'She'd a handbag with her?'

'We found that on her desk upstairs. It contained keys, iPod, smartphone, cards, make-up. The usual.'

'You say she'd gone into the office to work for some reason. With her sister. Rather late at night for that, wasn't it? What was she working on?'

'There was nothing in particular on her desk. A petty cash book, that sort of thing.'

'A chequebook? A big one? A company one, not one for private use?'

A puzzled stare. 'Yes, I think . . . perhaps. I'd have to check. We took photos.'

'Were you aware that a member of the family had been accused of taking some of The Magpie's business cheques and forging a signature to pay off their bills?'

'What! Are you serious?'

'Very.'

'Why didn't anyone tell us that? This is crazy. How could they withhold such important information?'

'Yes, that indeed is the question.'

It certainly was. Why had Gordon held off for so long, if he was convinced that Clemmie had stolen the money? It can only be because it gave him a hold over Juno.

Lesley was hot on the trail. 'You think that Poppy and Juno were on to the fraud and were at the office trying to track down who the culprit might be?'

'I think,' weighing her words, 'that the family were having meetings about various problems that week. Ray's finances for one, and the missing cheques for another.'

'We know Ray couldn't have killed her. Are you suggesting that the fraudster might have killed Poppy to stop his or her wrongdoing being made public?'

'I think it's a possibility . . .' Would Trixie have heard that her sleight of hand had been rumbled? Would she have cared?

Not much, no. Ellie said, 'But most unlikely, given the character of the person concerned—'

'Who is it? Tell me!'

'—unless, perhaps, it was an accident.'

Lesley lifted both hands in the air. 'Now we're singing the same tune. It was an accident.'

'Only, you don't really believe that it was, and neither do I.'

Lesley sighed. No, she didn't.

Ellie looked at the clock. Time to put the lunch on. Thomas appreciated a roast lunch after he'd been taking services all Sunday morning. Ellie went to the fridge, got out the joint of lamb which she proposed to cook, and put it into the oven on a low light. What else? Roast potatoes, onions . . . and what vegetables did they have? A cauliflower and some carrots, perhaps? She took the potatoes to the sink to peel them.

She said, 'Poppy and Juno were working late, possibly on the fraud, possibly on something else.'

Lesley consulted her notebook. 'Juno went home at – let me check – about ten; no, about a quarter past. Thereabouts. She took a cab. We checked. We know that Poppy was alive after that because she came downstairs to see Juno off. The taxi driver confirms this. Apparently Juno had gone down the stairs and opened the front door, realized she'd forgotten her handbag and called back up to Poppy to throw it down after her. Poppy actually came down the stairs with the handbag, the sisters spoke for a moment or two, then Poppy went back up the stairs, Juno closed the front door, and got into the cab and went home.'

'The taxi driver couldn't have been mistaken? It was Poppy?'

'The sisters always used the same car firm. The driver knows both women by sight.'

'How did Poppy get to The Magpie that evening?'

'She'd brought Juno in her own car, which was parked round the corner.'

'Right. So after Juno left, Poppy stayed on. She wasn't ready to go home, or she'd have picked up her own handbag from the desk and turned out the office lights. No. She was still working at that point in time and she hadn't finished. As I see it, there are two ways of looking at what happened next. The first is that she had another visitor—'

'The fraudster?'

'Possibly. Let's suppose it was. What might have happened next?'

'An argument, leading to a tussle. Perhaps Poppy asked the person to leave and they refused? Perhaps she pushed them, and they pushed back, causing her to fall down the stairs and die.' Ellie shook her head. 'I can see that there might have been some sort of argument ending in her falling down the stairs without intent to murder. But then what happens? Does the visitor rush down the stairs to check whether Poppy is still alive or not? Did he or she then panic, step over her to heave the front door open, pull it to behind them and make a getaway undetected? The body would at that point still be easy to move, as rigor mortis wouldn't have had time to set in. I'm half a mind to settle for accident and panic.'

'Only half a mind?'

'Yes, because, with a little common sense, a convincing accident could have been staged. Once the visitor had ascertained that Poppy was dead, he or she ought to have gone back up the stairs to shut off the lights in the office and thrown her handbag down beside her. Consider the picture if he'd done that. It was late at night. Poppy was tired. She turned off the lights, picked up her handbag and prepared to leave. At the top of the stairs, she tripped over herself and fell. End of story. Were there any fingerprints apart from Poppy's on the handbag?'

'No. It was sitting on her desk. There was no evidence of any visitor.'

'Not Juno?'

'No. I mean, she had every right to be there. We know she was there earlier. But she didn't leave any trace of herself which ought not to have been there, and we know Poppy was alive when she left.'

Ellie put the peeled potatoes into a pan of cold water, salted it and put it on to boil. She set about preparing some onions. 'Then let's suppose that Poppy went to the top of the stairs under her own steam for some reason. Someone used the intercom to ask Poppy to let them into the office. Poppy then went to the top of the stairs to operate the lock on the front door to let them in.'

Clemmie rang the bell, wanting to be let in. Just because you like the girl, it doesn't mean you shouldn't look at what she might have done. Let's talk it through.

She continued, 'Poppy goes to the head of the stairs to let them in. They climb the stairs to where she was standing, and throw her down?'

A pause while they both thought about that.

'No,' said Ellie. 'No sign of a struggle. It can't have happened that way.'

Lesley shook her head. 'No.'

Ellie said, 'There were no strange fingerprints anywhere?'

'None.'

Ellie noticed that the potatoes had come to the boil. She drained the water off, sieved flour and a spoonful of made mustard on to the potatoes in the pan and shook it, hard. 'Any phone calls to The Magpie landline making an appointment to see Poppy at the office that evening? Or to her mobile phone?'

'Nothing. We checked. Juno used her own mobile phone to call the cab which took her away. That checked out, too. As you so rightly say, if only we'd found the office lights off and Poppy's handbag at the bottom of the stairs, we'd have gone for an accident without a second thought.'

'And ignored the toxic state of affairs in the family.'

'That is so.'

'Therefore, it all comes down to alibis. How good are they?'

'Each and every one of them is properly accounted for.'

'Really?' said Ellie, popping the floured potatoes and the peeled onions around the joint. 'Tell me all.'

THIRTEEN

Lesley did not want to talk about alibis. She was restless, now rubbing her fingers and admiring her engagement ring, and now looking at the clock over the cooker. She went to the window to look up at the sky. 'It's clearing up. Should be a fine afternoon. What does he want to play cricket for, when we need to talk?'

Ellie held back a sigh. Lesley didn't know much about men, did she? 'Men need their space, just as we do.'

'I don't.'

This was untrue. Lesley had a difficult, stressful job and needed to relax and think about something else when she was off duty. Lesley was being difficult. Wedding nerves again?

Ellie said, 'Do you want to watch him play?'

A shoulder twitched. 'What, sit all afternoon on an uncomfortable chair while he prances around pretending to be a good batsman . . . which he is not? What's in it for me? I'm expected to commiserate with him when the umpire signals that he's out, and listen to the other women talk about their teenage children and how appalling it is that the police pick on them when they'd only been having a bit of fun? Oh, and then, to show how grateful I am to be included on such an important occasion, I'm expected to wash up after tea.'

Ellie had to laugh. 'Yes, I see what you mean. What would you rather be doing?'

'Dunno. I thought about joining a sailing club. Something physical. Something that would make me concentrate on anything rather than work.'

'Good idea.'

'He's not interested. So, I wonder, are my future weekends going to be spent watching him play cricket in the summer and football in the winter?'

'You can develop your own interests, surely. You often work at weekends, and police work fascinates you. You're a born hunter.'

Lesley slapped the table. '*He* isn't. I can't think why I didn't realize it before.'

'Does it matter? You wouldn't want to marry another hunter.'

Lesley accused her, 'You're a hunter, too. You look as if you couldn't say "boo" to a goose, but you're a hunter. How do you manage, being married to Thomas . . . who isn't?'

'Different skills. We are two halves of one. We balance one another.'

A frown. 'Does my fiancé balance my needs? No.'

'You threw the mug of coffee at him. You wounded him. He's forgiven you. He's invited you back into his life.'

Lesley indicated her smartphone. 'Not until he'd said a lot of things that hurt.'

So Lesley had accessed the messages he'd asked her to delete? Well, it was good to know what your partner was capable of. Wasn't it?

Ellie said, 'It's important to know when to have a fight about something, and when to give way. You might let him have a green settee when you'd rather have blue, but if it's a question of running up bills for things you can't afford, you put your foot down.'

'That's not very romantic.'

'It's practical.'

'I'm supposed to be a blushing bride, adoring my husband-to-be, thinking his every word is the Law—'

'I bet you know the Law better than he does.'

Lesley was forced into a laugh. 'That's true. Yes, he's kind and hard-working, generous and thoughtful. He'll never make headmaster, but he'll always remember my birthday and to put the rubbish out on Thursdays. He's a semi-detached-house sort of man. I suppose he ought to be good enough for someone like me, who's never going to darn his socks or remember to pick up his dry cleaning.'

Was that enough? Ellie thought of the deep connection between herself and Thomas. She remembered the moment in which she'd realized that he was her best friend, and that he'd become so necessary to her that she couldn't bear to think of his moving away. And – she suppressed a grin – we won't talk about the fun we have with rumpy-pumpy! There were moments when she did feel left behind by his wholehearted service to the Lord, when she realized that she'd never be able to match him there . . . even as he seemed to think, which was nonsense, that she had a special, if different, talent for serving Him.

Would Lesley's marriage turn out so well?

Ellie told herself that every couple had a different dynamic, and what suited one, might not work for another.

The meat was cooking nicely in the oven. What should they have for afters? They'd plenty of cheese. That would do.

Lesley stared out of the window. 'Cricket is so boring.'

'Men don't think so. What about those alibis? The Cordover parents – Gerald and Marika – what were they doing the night their daughter died?'

Lesley pushed her fingers back through her hair, picked up her notebook, riffled through the pages. 'There'd been a meeting at their house, family stuff. Marika served sandwiches and cake. All the usual suspects were there except Ray. Present were Gerald and Marika, plus Poppy and Juno and Gordon. I think the accountant, as well? Yes. Him, too.'

'Not the next generation? Not Trixie or Clemmie?'

'Adults only.'

'What about Ray?'

'At the club. The staff agree he was there. CCTV confirms it. He was there, losing, of course. He stayed till after one, and then went home.'

'There were a number of things the family needed to discuss,' said Ellie, thinking that it wasn't only Ray's debts which were a problem. What about Poppy wanting a divorce? What about Clemmie's debts and Trixie's ambitions?

Ellie had learned a lot about the family since the Cordovers had called her in to help them. Some of it Lesley seemed to know, but not all. So, how many of the family's secrets ought Ellie to pass on to the police? If Poppy's death really had been an accident, then Lesley really did not need to know anything more than she did already.

Ought Ellie to keep quiet about Gordon's accusations re Clemmie, for a start? It might help Lesley to hear what he intended to do, but not if they were groundless – which Ellie was pretty sure they were. 'Did Trixie have an alibi?'

'She was in a restaurant with her manager and some friends, discussing how to raise money for her film project. The Indian restaurant in the Avenue. They were thrown out about half eleven.'

'Some time after Poppy died?'

'Considerably. Four or five of them went on clubbing, including Trixie. That checked out.'

'When did Poppy and Juno leave their parents' house?'

'About nine. They went off by themselves to talk over how to deal with Ray, and how they could pay him off in the event of a divorce.'

Lesley didn't know that Ray had signed over the garage to Poppy? Should Ellie tell her? No. Or not yet, anyway. 'Gordon's a non-starter—'

'Exactly. He couldn't have got up those stairs.'

'Which leaves Clemmie.'

'She had a driving lesson earlier that evening and then had some more driving practice with a friend. She lives in a small terraced house not far away. The friend was with her until late, long after Poppy died.'

No mention of Gordon's seeing Clemmie knocking on the door of The Magpie? Ah, but precisely when had that happened?

Had Aidan really given Clemmie an alibi? He was supposed to be on nights at the hospital, wasn't he? But even junior doctors didn't work nights all the time, did they? 'Clemmie's friend; that's Aidan?'

'I interviewed him. He confirmed he was with Clemmie all evening. Nice lad. Straightforward.'

'Mm.' Ellie wasn't so sure about that. 'What about Juno, then? You say she took a cab back home, after she'd been with Poppy for . . . how long? Not that I think she killed her sister. Well, she couldn't have done, since Poppy was alive when Juno left The Magpie.'

'Agreed. Juno left about ten fifteen, just missing Gordon, who'd gone round to The Magpie to pick her up after he left the senior Cordovers. She'd already called a cab and gone by then.'

Yes, that fitted. Juno had gone to her parents' house in Gordon's car, but left with Poppy in Poppy's car to go to The

Magpie. She hadn't had her own car with her that night, so she'd called a cab when she wanted to leave The Magpie.

Lesley said, 'We found the cab driver. He remembered the fare because both sisters were standing outside when he arrived at The Magpie, and he didn't know which was his fare till one got into the cab and the other went back inside. He dropped Juno off back at her house at ten thirty, ten thirty-five. Some neighbours were at that very moment returning home from a function, and saw her arrive. She was exchanging a few words with them when Gordon returned. She helped him indoors and garaged his car for him.'

'Timing?'

'A quarter to eleven or thereabouts.'

'Wait a minute. Have I got this right? Juno and Poppy left their parents' house to go off and confer. Gordon was also at the meeting, but he didn't go with them because he couldn't get up the stairs at The Magpie. Were the twins deliberately excluding him from their meeting?'

'He said he'd stayed on at the Cordovers' to continue discussions with the accountant and his parents-in-law.'

'Why didn't Juno wait for Gordon to pick her up from The Magpie?'

'She said she didn't know how long he'd be.'

'And Poppy's car?'

'We found it parked round the corner.'

That would belong to Juno now, too. Ray would have co-opted it, wouldn't he? Even if he'd lost the Lexus to the club, he still had Poppy's car. It was unlikely that Juno would insist on his handing it over to her, wasn't it? Or was it?

Ellie probed a bit more. 'Gordon went round to The Magpie to collect Juno. We know Poppy was alive when Juno left, but Gordon must have been there about the time that Poppy died?'

'He thinks, just after. He's got a specially adapted car which he can drive anywhere he likes. But once he steps out of that, he has to get into his wheelchair or use two sticks. Clearly, he could never have got up the stairs to tussle with Poppy. And, he's no motive.'

'That's true.' And, no means. Ellie had seen for herself that in his wheelchair he couldn't even get over the step into The

Magpie shop without help. What a pity! Of all that family, Ellie would have liked Gordon to be the villain, whereas he was the only one who couldn't physically have done it.

'What about the accountant?'

'Stayed on at the Cordovers' till they threw him and Gordon out, which would be about a quarter past ten. The accountant went straight home. He lives five minutes away in one of those expensive flats overlooking the Green. As soon as he got in, he switched his computer on to check Facebook. He's having a long-distance flirtation with someone in Hull. We checked.'

Ellie subdued a need to giggle. Did Marge Money know about that? Mm, Ellie would bet that she did. Would Marge care? No, she wouldn't.

'So that's the lot? The senior Cordovers didn't go out again that evening?'

'No. After everyone had gone, they had a hot drink and then went to bed.' Lesley looked at her watch, looked out of the window. Fidgeted. 'You know, I usually clean the flat on my day off. I wonder . . .'

Lesley was going to cry off lunch and return to the flat, not necessarily to clean it, but to make sure Angelica had vacated the place and to re-establish her position as its mistress. Ellie thought of the large quantities of food she was cooking for lunch. Well, Thomas would be very happy to have seconds, and any leftover vegetables could go into soup.

'Do you know,' said Lesley, 'I think I might as well make a move. It's been lovely of you to have me, especially when I was feeling so "down". I'm grateful.' Lesley's mind was already all on what she planned to do next. She was smiling to herself. 'I'll just pop upstairs and gather my things together. Shall I strip the bed?'

'No need.' Perhaps Lesley would need it again before the wedding.

As Lesley went up the back stairs, Ellie got out her phone and rang Diana, who wouldn't be at work on a Sunday, but who probably wasn't cooking a roast dinner, either.

Ellie's grandson, little Evan, picked up the landline phone. 'Hello, who is it, Mummy's busy. Shall I fetch Daddy?'

'It's me, Evan. Granny. Could you ask Mummy to come to the phone for a minute?'

He shouted, 'Mummy! It's Gran!'

Ellie could hear Diana's voice in the background. 'Tell her it's all right!'

Heavy breathing into the phone. Evan said, 'Mummy says it's all right. Are you coming over now? We could go to the park.'

'Not today, my love. Thanks for being so helpful.'

'What about tomorrow? Can we go to the park tomorrow?'

'I'll ring you as soon as I'm free.'

Ellie could hear Diana in the background. 'Evan! Come and get your lunch!' And the phone went down.

Well, good. Probably. Diana wouldn't have said it was all right if she hadn't managed to stop Ray's cheque, would she?

Ellie looked at her watch. With a bit of luck, she could manage twenty minutes or so in the garden before lunch. Now, where had she put her secateurs?

She was happily dead-heading the roses when she heard her landline phone ring. Bother! Perhaps Thomas would answer it. No, he wasn't back yet. Perhaps Susan . . .? No, of course not. Why should she? It wasn't her phone.

Ellie stumbled indoors and reached the hall just as the phone stopped. Someone was leaving a message. Well, good. She could leave it till later. Oh, better not. She pressed Play.

It took her a moment to realize who was speaking. It was Ray Cocks. Containing rage, just. 'Mrs Quicke, I believe you were so kind as to put my wife's valuables and money back in the safe for me. That was,' gnashing of teeth, 'very helpful of you. Unfortunately I think you must have misdialled when you closed the safe, as our combination doesn't work any longer. Do you think you could remember exactly what you did? This is rather urgent. Please, ring me.'

Ellie pressed the Delete button. Grinning to herself. It was Aidan who'd suggested she made up a new combination, and she had done so. She had no intention of giving the new combination to Ray. The money, the jewellery, the safe and the house now belonged to Juno, and Juno would be given the combination when she surfaced again.

Ray could ask till he was blue in the face, but she would refuse to give it to him. And, if he did happen to threaten her – oh dear, he might, might he not? – then she could always play the doddering old lady and pretend to have forgotten it.

What a delightful morning it was turning out to be! Back to the garden . . .

Thomas returned home just as Lesley was leaving. They exchanged pleasantries in the hall and then Thomas came into the kitchen, rubbing his hands, to find Ellie dishing up lunch.

'Parky for the time of the year.' He kissed Ellie's ear, and gave her a hug. She could tell that his morning had gone well and that he was at peace with himself.

As usual, he said, 'I'll lay the table, shall I?' And proceeded to do it.

Susan stumbled into the kitchen when they had almost finished their first course. Susan was tousle-haired and yawning, but looked pleased with herself and the world in general. She was wearing a sleeveless T-shirt with a very low neckline and shorts. She had quite some cleavage! And, she had a love-bite on the side of her neck.

The meat dropped off Thomas's fork, halfway to his mouth.

Susan's eyes glistened. 'Oh, proper food. Is there enough for me?'

'Masses,' said Ellie, trying to be pleased that Thomas still had enough testosterone to react to a well-filled bra, but slightly annoyed that it was Susan's which had attracted his notice instead of Ellie's own – not inconsiderable – affairs of interest. She got up to serve Susan who, still yawning, had seated herself. Ellie said, 'You went clubbing?'

'Mm. My friend Maya, she's on the same course as me, she's been on at me for ages to go, and when I texted to tell her about the dress and the bra, she met me in Marks and made me buy some new clothes and she stood over me till I stopped hiding my "assets", as she calls them. She made me throw back my shoulders and, well, display them. A bit like a peacock, only the wrong sex, if you see what I mean.'

Ellie saw. So did Thomas. Thomas met Ellie's eye and said he could do with a second helping, if she wasn't keeping it for later. Ellie obliged, phasing out Susan's monologue until she heard a name she was familiar with. 'What was that? You met Angelica in the queue for the club?'

'She was with a coupla men. Giggling to them about me being an overweight fatty, like she always does. She asked if I'd managed to find a bridesmaid's dress big enough for me, and Maya nudged me the ribs and said, "Show!" so I chucked off my jacket, and made myself tall and, well, Maya was quite right. The new bra does have an effect on men. Angelica is very flat, poor thing.'

Ellie noticed that Thomas was wide-eyed. Also, he'd suspended operations on his food. She wanted to kick him, but was too far away.

Susan hoovered up the food on her plate, then sat back, patting her tummy. 'That's better. I was hungry. Maya says I don't need to go on a diet, and that if a man asks me out I am not to make an excuse, but accept. So I did. At least,' she frowned, 'he offered to bring me home and I said yes, but when he got too fresh I gave him the old one-two and that was that. What's for afters?'

Sunday afternoon

Thomas wanted a snooze with the newspapers after lunch. Ellie could have done with a snooze herself, but felt she couldn't rest until she'd done something to help Clemmie who, if Gordon fulfilled his promise, was going to be accused of murder and fraud the following morning.

Where to start? Well, she could see if Clemmie were available for a chat, and ask her if she really had been banging on The Magpie's door the night Poppy died.

Ellie tried Clemmie's mobile phone number, only to be told it was not available. Ellie had thought everyone younger than her kept their phones permanently switched on because they couldn't bear to be out of touch with their peer group, yet Clemmie had switched hers off. Ah, a thought. The girl was probably having a last-minute driving lesson. Wasn't her test due tomorrow?

Perhaps Ellie could call on Gerald and Marika? Ellie was convinced they knew more than they were telling. When they'd asked her to help them on Thursday afternoon they'd been wracked with anxiety, yet by Saturday afternoon Marika had been calmly knitting and willing to let Ellie deal with the problem. Had something happened between Thursday afternoon and Saturday afternoon to alter the situation for the better? And if so, what?

At a guess this meant Juno had been in touch with them and was well on the way to sorting things out in the family. But, if Juno had been in touch with her parents and her daughter – and possibly Celine as well? – she had failed, judging by their continuing anxiety, to reassure Ray or Gordon.

Ellie supposed this was why she'd imagined that Juno had left Gordon. Looked at in a cold and clinical manner, Ellie really had no basis for thinking this. She couldn't recall anything being said or done which would lead her to that conclusion, except that – wheelchair or no wheelchair – if she'd been married to Gordon, she'd have taken an axe to him by now. Or poisoned him. Or, arranged a fatal accident. Or something. She sighed. No, it wasn't worth going to prison for such a scumbag.

Walking along to the Cordovers' house, Ellie tried to think clearly. Charles Mornay had known Gordon for ever, and thought him a saint. Humph! But if Charles had been responsible for the accident which had left Gordon in a wheelchair, it was natural that he should feel guilt and overcompensate for his friend's failings. It did not follow that a person had the patience of a saint if they were confined to a wheelchair.

'By your works you shall know them.' Ellie had seen Gordon in action and his actions were not that of a kindly or patient man. In fact, the reverse. 'Malice' and 'spite' were the words that trickled into Ellie's head when she considered Gordon.

Clemmie's experience of Gordon had been somewhat different from that of Charles. Ellie believed Clemmie's version of events one hundred per cent. Clemmie hadn't pretended she was a saint. She acknowledged she'd been a difficult child, but Gordon's lashing out with a cane came under the heading of abuse, didn't it?

Marge Mornay's opinion of Gordon chimed with Ellie's.

Marge didn't have any axe to grind, did she? She was a successful businesswoman who didn't need anyone's approval for what she said or did. She'd known the twins for years and she disliked Gordon. Ellie liked and trusted Marge.

Only, if Gordon really had seen Clemmie trying to get into The Magpie about the time that Poppy died . . .? No, Clemmie wouldn't have killed her aunt. Definitely not.

Come on, now! You know perfectly well that the most innocent and gentle of people will kill if pressed too hard. Supposing it had been an accident . . .?

Very well. Let's suppose it was an accident. Clemmie, in distress, discovered she'd killed her aunt and asked Aidan to alibi her. He had done so. Neither of them realized that Clemmie had been spotted and that tomorrow the false alibi was going to blow up in their faces.

Ellie rang the doorbell at the Cordover house, and waited for a response. It was a pleasant Sunday afternoon. A jet scoured the sky on its way to Heathrow airport. Two gardens away, a child on a scooter quarrelled with another child who was slightly older and on a tricycle. Something about taking turns.

The Cordovers were probably having an afternoon nap. Ellie wished she were, too.

Marika opened the door. For a moment Ellie thought she was not going to be allowed into the house but, if there was a hesitation, Marika quickly overcame it. She even managed a smile, but put her finger to her lips. In a soft voice, she said, 'If you don't mind . . .? He's having a nap, watching the football or the cycling. It always sends him to sleep. His way of recovering from the stress of the week. Do come in. We were talking about you at lunchtime, wondering how you were getting on. Would you mind sitting in the kitchen? I can make us some tea.'

Marika led the way. She must have been sitting at the kitchen table before Ellie rang the bell, because a small television on the central unit was relaying the news; some knitting – not the same garment as before – lay beside it. An extractor fan had removed all cooking smells, the surfaces were clean and the dishwasher was happily chugging away.

Marika put the kettle on, and gestured to Ellie to take a seat. 'Would you prefer a herbal tea?'

'Thank you. Yes.'

Marika made two peppermint teas in china mugs and handed one to Ellie, before taking a seat herself and resuming her knitting. The wool this time was of a finer ply, and she was using larger needles.

Ellie was intrigued. 'Is that a shawl you're knitting? Do you always use the same patterns?'

'I've used this pattern – let me see – three times. I make one jacket, one shawl, two pairs of mittens each time. I look at new patterns sometimes, but I like to stay with those I know.' She inclined her head to Ellie. 'And now . . . yes?'

Marika was wearing a wedding ring on her right hand. Lesley had told Ellie that Polish women did that. An interesting fact which Ellie hadn't known.

Ellie said, 'I've talked to a number of people. I can't say I've come to a firm conclusion about whether Poppy's death was accident or murder.'

'Sixteen, eighteen . . .' Nimble fingers, downcast eyes.

'I've talked to the police, trying to get an idea of the timetable of events.'

The clever fingers stilled.

Ellie smiled. 'I didn't disclose any secrets, but it may not be possible to keep it that way. What influence do you have over Gordon?'

A hard look from narrowed eyes. The knitting was laid down. 'What is he up to now?'

'Revenge, I think. He's announced his intention of going to the police tomorrow, Monday, to accuse Clemmie of murder and fraud.'

Marika ran her tongue over her lips. She made as if to rise from her chair, but then sat back. Her eyes went out to the garden, where the parasol flapped idly in the breeze. A wasp buzzed past the window.

Marika said, 'Revenge, you say?'

'I think it's because he's never liked her. And, because Juno has left him.'

Marika picked up her knitting again. 'Can you not stop him?'

'It's easy enough to disprove the fraud. The paper trail leads to Trixie and not to Clemmie, but it wouldn't be pleasant for Clemmie to be arrested and interrogated while the matter was sorted out.'

Marika nodded, her eyes on her work. 'Not good.'

'There's more. Gordon says he saw Clemmie hammering on the door at The Magpie and ringing the bell at about the time Poppy died.'

Marika frowned into space, but didn't comment.

Ellie continued, 'Clemmie has an alibi for her whereabouts that evening which depends upon the word of her boyfriend. I think – and the police will probably agree – that he'd lie his socks off for her. I am sure she is innocent of her aunt's death, but I can't prove it. The police have decided not to take any further action unless someone comes forward with fresh evidence, and that's exactly what Gordon plans to do. Can't *you* stop him?'

'Whatever could we say or do?' Marika pulled another length of wool from the ball. 'Clemmie is not in any danger. The boy will stand by her.'

Almost, Ellie despaired. Why wouldn't Marika take the threat to Clemmie seriously? She decided to take another tack. 'Could you bear to tell me exactly what went on that night? I know there was a family conference here. The twins, Gordon and Charles Mornay came here to talk about . . . what?'

'Gordon said Clemmie had stolen cheques from The Magpie and used them to pay her bills. Charles backed him up. Charles is very clever in his way, but he is always "yes" man to Gordon, and we are sure he has made a mistake. We say we have confidence in Clemmie, but Gordon goes on and on till Poppy agrees to look into it. Gordon wants Poppy to say she will sack Clemmie, but we tell him not to be so silly. Gerald makes us laugh. He says, if Clemmie is sacked from The Magpie, he will take her on in his own business. Gordon is so cross! He says we are not taking him seriously. And, in truth, we have more important things to talk about.'

'Ray and his debts. Ray and Poppy's marriage.'

A decisive nod. 'Poppy says she is ready to talk about a divorce. All those years, never a bad word does she say about him. She and Juno, most alike. Faithful wives. Every year, Poppy says, "One day his luck will change." But at the last she understands he cannot change. Charles says that if she lets Ray carry on gambling, he will strip her of everything she has. Gerald says that if you don't try to stop an addict, you are agreeing with what they do. We can all see that is true.'

'Very difficult.'

'Poppy is worried about Trixie, too. That funny man who hangs around the girl. What sort of agent is he, anyway? Is he interested because there is money in the family? Has she any talent? Mrs Quicke, have you any opinion about that?'

'She is not as strong a personality as Clemmie, but there doesn't seem to be any harm in her. Yes, I think there might be some talent there. Can't you get someone in the trade to give her an audition? You were prepared to put some money into her film, weren't you?'

'We are thinking that way, yes. Get her a camera test. Gerald and I are thinking to let the grandchildren have the money now, when it will help in their careers, rather than after we die. What we do for Trixie, we will do the same for Clemmie.'

Ellie liked the sound of that. 'At some point the discussion here ground to a halt. First the women left, and then the men. Can you remember roughly what time that would have been?'

Marika pulled up some wool, thinking. 'The girls? About nine, I suppose. The men stay on to talk more to Gerald about Clemmie's supposed fraud.'

'Why didn't the girls stay here?'

'Gordon . . .' A shrug. 'He refuses to talk about anything but the fraud. The girls want to talk about divorce and how it might affect The Magpie, so they went there to be quiet and to get away from him. Juno says the stairs to The Magpie office keep her sane.' A tiny smile.

Ellie also smiled. Yes, she could see how that could be. Gordon couldn't get up those stairs. Sanctuary! Ellie said, testing her theory, 'The girls had each come in their own cars?'

'No. Gordon brought Juno. Poppy came in her own car, yes.'

'Poppy took Juno off in her car when they went to The Magpie? And then what?'

Marika stood up and stretched. Was she trying to change the subject? Was there something she was not telling? What on earth could it be? 'You're going to see Gordon now? I'll give you the address.'

FOURTEEN

Ellie felt as if she'd been thrown out. Surplus to requirements. Made use of, and dumped in the trashcan.

She knew perfectly well that Marika wanted her to go to see Gordon but, perversely, it was the last thing Ellie wanted to do. She couldn't think what she could say to him. There wasn't anything she *could* say, was there?

She got to the end of the road and her phone rang. She didn't realize it was her phone at first, but looked around for someone close by who might have their phone out. And then realized it was hers. She was surprised, because she didn't usually leave it switched on.

'I'm bored.' A boy's voice, half-broken: Mikey. 'Can't you find something for me to do?'

'I thought you were playing games with a friend.' She looked around for a place to sit and spotted a low wall. She perched on that, hoping the householder wouldn't shoo her off.

'We were. I beat him. As usual. And yes, I have done my homework. Mum's having a rest on her bed and Dad's under the car. Not that he knows a gasket from a gastronome. He told me to go away and play. So, where are you, and have you any ideas?'

'I've been visiting someone on the other side of the Avenue.' Ellie fished in her pockets and then delved into her handbag. 'Yes, I could do with some help, and you'd be much quicker at it than I. There's an estate agent called Mornay. Marge Money or Marge Mornay. She has several offices, only one of which is local. I want you to look up for me any recent sales of property in this area. I'm thinking maybe a penthouse suite, or a flat in a new, luxury block, with garage parking. Two bedrooms . . . no, perhaps only one. No, make it two. There must be a speakerphone entry system.'

'You're not thinking of moving?'

'Certainly not. You know about the Cordover affair, and the

woman who died from falling down the stairs? I think that one of the family might recently have been looking for a bolthole while she considers divorcing her husband. She'd want somewhere safe, quiet and local. Money's no object.'

'Why two bedrooms?'

'She might need to keep a room for her daughter to sleep over.'

'You think Poppy was buying a hidey-hole?'

'No, I think it was Juno. Now I don't want you ringing people up and entering into chit-chat about this. I don't want Gordon or anyone else following our trail.'

'You think Juno's in danger? Whoopee!'

'Oh, Mikey! You're such a child, sometimes.'

'I'm better than you with a computer.' Boasting.

'I'll grant you that. I think Marge Money has been handling all The Magpie transactions. They've known one another for ever and Marge is no friend of Gordon's, so it makes sense that Juno would ask her to find her somewhere safe to hide. Can you do it by going on their website, and seeing what they've offered for sale recently?'

'How recent?'

'I'm not sure. Juno used to go away every now and then to spend time at a spa hotel. Her family checked, and that is exactly what she did. After the reading of the will on Friday, she stepped out of her parents' car and disappeared. At first I thought she might have gone to Poland to stay with relatives, but now I think she might – just might – have been planning to leave Gordon for some time. If so, she will either have bought or rented somewhere local, perhaps within walking distance of The Magpie. Only, she's not given anyone her address.'

'What's she afraid of? Being pushed down the stairs like Poppy?'

'You've got it.'

'You don't want flats that have stairs, then. Or they can have stairs, but only for fire exit purposes. You want luxury and lifts, right? There's quite a few flats around here like that. But, she might have bought one that's never been advertised.'

'I know. The problem is that if you can find her through the Internet, then so can Gordon.'

'And then what?' Joking. 'Why would he try to kill her?'

'I'm not sure. Out of revenge because she's leaving him? That's a guess and probably wrong. But, if you feel like doing a bit of digging around on the computer, it might turn up three or four places which . . . oh, I don't know, Mikey. Now I'm talking it through with you, it sounds like a wild-goose chase.'

'Dunno about that. Thomas says you've an extra sense about people that ordinary mortals don't have. Can I use your computer? Thomas will let me, won't he? Are you going to be home later? Where are you? Shall I come and get you? It won't take me a minute on my bike.'

Ellie had a vision of herself sitting pillion on the back of Mikey's bicycle. She closed her eyes. No, no, *no!* 'You're not giving me a lift unless you've aged to eighteen overnight, passed your driving test and are able to provide me with a comfortable seat in a modern car.'

He thought that was funny. 'All right. You can always ring for a cab, can't you?'

'I'm going to Gordon's house next.' She rummaged in her bag to produce the piece of paper Marika had given her. 'It's not far. One of those big detached houses at the top of Kent Avenue.'

'Nice houses. What number?'

'Can't quite read it. It's got a name. Gateway House? Something like that. I'm only going to drop in for a minute or two, and I can't think what I'm supposed to say. Marika wants me to go there, and so I'm going. I'll be back by teatime.'

'Has Susan been baking?' Mikey was always hungry.

'I've no idea. Now, don't you go bothering her if she hasn't.'

He laughed and switched off. Ellie looked to see if she'd got any voicemail messages. She hadn't, so she put her phone away and set off again.

Kent Avenue was a road of expensive buildings. There was a run of early nineteenth-century terraced housing, and two blocks of four-storey flats. Between these were a few modern, detached houses with brick-laid forecourts behind electronically operated gates. The ones for Gordon's house stood open. Also open were the doors to a double garage. Ellie could see into the garage. One car had extra roof space; that would be

Gordon's adapted car. Next to it was a sleek Lexus. That would be Juno's?

There were two other cars parked in the forecourt. One was another Lexus, a twin to the one in the garage. The number plates were consecutive. Those two cars had been bought and registered at the same time. So, the one on the forecourt would be Poppy's car, which she'd driven to The Magpie and which the police had located later in a side street. Presumably Ray had taken that over and was now driving it around.

Oh. Did she want to meet Ray at the moment?

She felt slightly guilty about withholding the new combination she'd put into the safe at his house . . . which reminded her that she ought to have written it down somewhere as soon as she'd done it. It wouldn't do to forget it altogether, would it?

Now, the fourth car. Whose would that be? Ellie wasn't good at recognizing makes of cars or remembering number plates, but she'd seen this particular car the evening before. She couldn't remember the registration number. She told herself that there must be dozens of similar family cars in the neighbourhood. It was a middle-aged car. A car for a man who earned a considerable salary but didn't care to run a sports car.

'By your cars you shall know them.' Who did she know who fitted that middle-aged car? And the answer was . . . Charles Mornay.

If she were right, then Gordon was at home and his visitors were Charles and Ray. A toxic mix. Three men who had married women who were successful in their own right. Three men whose marriages either had failed, or were failing. Two of those three men bore no love for Clemmie and were plotting to bring her down.

Ellie could see why Gordon and Charles had met to talk, but what about the third man? Did Ray want to join in the persecution of Clemmie, or was he after money for his own kitty?

He was after money.

A ramp led up over the step to the glazed front door. On either side of the ramp stood some bright blue pots planted with variegated ivy . . . the only greenery in sight.

Ellie rang the bell, and the speakerphone squawked at her. She said, 'Mrs Quicke to see you.' The door clicked open and she entered a square hall with stripped wooden flooring, suitable for wheelchair use. Ahead lay a staircase with a stairlift at the bottom. Looking up to the landing, she spotted an empty wheelchair. So Gordon could get around the ground floor as much as he liked, could take the chair upstairs and transfer to another wheelchair there.

The house had been expensively adapted for his use. All the electrics were at hip height and doorways had been widened. In other words, Gordon had complete freedom of movement in his own house. When he wanted to go out, he could take his wheelchair to his adapted car and transfer to that. He could, in fact, go anywhere and everywhere, except up and down stairs.

A mellow, mocking voice. 'Hey, look what the cat brought in!' Ray was standing in the doorway to a room on the left. He was holding a glass of what looked like whisky. Half seas over, and it was only three in the afternoon. His speech was slightly slurred. 'Why haven't you returned my phone calls?'

'Have you been phoning me?' A bland smile. It might work.

'I need the combination of the safe.'

'Oh, that. I wrote it down as soon as I got home. Remind me to give it to Juno when she returns.'

'I need it now!'

Ellie acted helpless. 'I'm so sorry. I'm hopeless at numbers. That's why I wrote it down when I got home. It's on the back of the calendar in the hall. I think. If I can't find it, I suppose Juno will have to employ a locksmith to open the safe for her.'

'Tcha!' said Ray. Yet he didn't seem as desperate as Ellie had thought he might be. Had he located some other source of income?

'Who?' Charles appeared behind Ray. 'Ah, the interfering busybody.' He was also the worse for alcohol. Charles swept her an elaborate bow, nearly spilling his drink as he did so. 'Come into the spider's den.'

Ellie obeyed and entered a large, sunny living room, which stretched from front to back of the house. More stripped wood flooring. Sliding glass doors at the back gave on to a patio adorned with a gas barbecue and all the trimmings. Beyond that was another low-maintenance garden, all shrubs and lawn, probably attended to by a contractor.

Centre stage was Gordon, ensconced in his wheelchair, also with a glass in his hand. There was a pervasive scent of whisky and something else. Something rotten? Food that had gone off? A dividing wall had been removed at the back of the room to give access to an up-to-date kitchen. Presumably the smell came from there.

The room had been furnished in pleasantly neutral colours, save for three rather-too-bright abstract pictures on the wall, which someone had recently attacked with malice aforethought. Glass fragments clung to the frames and twinkled on the floor below. A cut-glass vase on a glass-topped coffee table had been knocked over, and the roses which it had contained were now strewn, dying, on the floor. The water which had been in the vase had stained the wooden floor.

Gordon is destroying the things which Juno had cared about. I wish I hadn't come.

Ellie tried to ignore the evidence of violence, and managed a social smile. 'Marika asked me to drop in on you this afternoon.'

'Hah!' Ray threw himself down into a capacious armchair, spilling some of his drink. He swore, and licked his hand. 'The mother-in-law from hell.'

Ellie took a seat, unasked. 'Ray; she was worried about you. And Gordon. She wanted me to find out how you were both coping.'

Gordon drained his glass and held it out to Charles. 'Get me another, will you?'

Charles was still on his feet. He had been drinking, but was not as far gone as the other two. Charles was uncomfortable, though still willing to play along with the boys. Charles took Gordon's glass but said, 'Are you sure?'

'Course I'm sure. Who's master here, eh?'

Ray grinned. 'You are, me old mate. I knew I could rely on you.' He patted his coat pocket.

Ah-ha. Problem solved. Gordon had advanced Ray some money? More fool Gordon. What precisely were the financial arrangements in this household? Did Juno pay for everything? Probably. Did she have a joint account with Gordon? Mm, possibly not. Juno was the breadwinner. She would keep separate

accounts for work and home. She probably paid a certain amount
into a separate account for Gordon's personal use every month.
So what collateral had Ray advanced to persuade Gordon to
give him some money? Ah, he'd used Poppy's car, which she'd
left round the corner from The Magpie . . . a car which must
now belong to Juno?

Gordon took his glass back from Charles. 'So, Miss Prunes
and Prism, what did you really come for? You're not really here
to see how we're getting on, are you? We're doing brilliantly,
aren't we, Ray?'

'I am now,' said Ray, fatly grinning. 'I knew I could rely on
you to see me through. I'm off to the club tonight and feeling
lucky. "Luck be a lady tonight!" Payback on Tuesday when her
cheque clears.'

Oh. The collateral was not Poppy's car, but Diana's cheque?
Ellie said, in a small voice, 'A cheque my daughter gave you?
You'd better make sure she hasn't stopped it.'

'What!' He spilled his drink again, but this time didn't
bother to lick his hand. A stain spread out on the arm of his
chair. That was going to take some cleaning, wasn't it? 'Your
daughter? Who . . .? No, you can't mean . . .! The estate agent
in the Avenue?'

Charles leaned against the wall. He was still on the side of
good nature. Just. 'What estate agent? Not Marge. She's no
friend of yours, Ray. She wouldn't lend you any money.'

'Advance, not loan,' said Ray. 'The woman advanced it
to me if I promised to put the sale of The Magpie houses
through her.'

'But they don't belong to you.' Charles, frowning.

Ray giggled. '*I* know that. *You* know that, *Gordon* knows
that. But the itsy-bitsy girl at the estate agency doesn't
know that, and you're not to tell her. Promise?'

Gordon rapped the arm of his wheelchair. 'The Quicke woman
says you should make sure the cheque hasn't been stopped.'

'Mrs Diana wouldn't do that.' He tried to flick his nose in a
secretive way, and failed. 'She trusts me, silly bitch.'

'More fool she,' said Charles; his eyes were on Ellie. 'Mrs
Quicke, what do you know about Ray's cheque?'

'My daughter made enquiries and discovered that Ray didn't

own the properties concerned, so she cancelled the cheque she'd made out to him.'

Gordon started to laugh, started to say something, swallowed some more whisky, got the hiccups. Flailed his arm about, trying to get the words out. 'Hic! You mean you haven't any money coming in? You bastard, Ray! Give me back my dosh! Hic! What did you think . . .? Hic! I'll flay you alive!'

'Honest!' Ray was still giggling. 'This one don't know nothing. Your money's safe with me. Twenty thou. Life-saver. You can have it against Poppy's car, if you like.'

'What do I . . . Hic! . . . want with Poppy's car? If you've tried to scam . . . Hic! . . . me, it will be the worse . . . Hic! For you!'

'Don't get in a fratch. Your money's safe with me.'

'You'd better be right . . . Hic! Or I'll sue the pants off you.' Gordon waved his hand at Charles. 'Get me . . . Hic! . . . water!'

Charles went off into the adjoining kitchen, only to call out, 'There's a heck of a stink in here, Gordon! The freezer door's open. Oh, my God! Everything's . . .! Fish and . . .? I'd better open some windows. Where's the back door key?' Banging sounds, off. 'There's one hell of a mess. And the fridge . . . why is there a towel over the fridge door? Everything in it is spoiled!'

Gordon was back to sipping his whisky, having got his hiccups under control. 'Leave it be, Charles. Juno will have to clear it up when she returns tonight. Think of it as a Welcome Home present for her.'

'But,' Charles returned, looking worried, 'how can you be so sure that she is coming back?'

'I told her, no more Mister Nice Guy. I said, "You've got to knuckle under, my girl!" I said, "No more of your nonsense, or your precious Clemmie will be in jail for life!"'

Ray laughed. 'You put her right. Silly cow!'

Gordon's mouth took an unpleasant twist. 'The bitch will be back this evening, just you wait and see. I know how to keep order in my own household, don't I?'

Ray dreamily sank some more whisky. 'You sure do, mate. I wish I hadn't been so soft with Poppy. She could always twist me round her little finger. She could do anything with me, she could.' Two fat tears appeared on his cheeks, and he slipped down in his chair.

Charles kept sending sharp looks in Ellie's direction. 'You can report back that all is well, Mrs Quicke. Ray's got a loan to tide him over and Juno will be back home tonight. Gordon, that kitchen: you'll have to get someone in to clear it up. All that spoiled food!'

'Juno can do it. In fact, I'm going to sit here and watch her. I'll make her lick the floor clean. I'm going to tell her to take off her clothes and use them to mop up with.'

Ray tried to pull himself up in his chair. 'I shoulda done that with Poppy. What a bitch! Leaving me in the lurch like that.'

Charles looked sick.

Ellie felt sick. She had a feeling that she ought to get up and go while the going was good, but if she stayed, she might get them talking. They were all drinking, and with any luck might say something to help her understand better what had happened. She tried for a diversion. 'Marika thinks Juno is safely with her relatives in Poland.'

Gordon nodded. 'I thought of that and looked, after the funeral. It's true her passport isn't here. She keeps her business papers in the safe at the office. That's where it'll be. She'll be back. Trust me, she won't let her precious Clemmie be arrested.'

Ray stirred in his chair. He was weeping gently. 'My lovely Poppy. No one but you, ever. What did you have to go and leave me for? We'd have worked it out. My luck would have changed . . .' He slid further down into his chair. The glass slipped from his hand on to the floor. His head rested on his shoulder. He snored.

Ellie asked, 'Gordon, did you ever really love Juno?'

'Of course I did! And she adored me!'

'Or were you enamoured of the wealth she represented?'

'She was the most beautiful thing I have ever seen! I was crazy about her.'

'She wasn't sure she loved you, was she? Something happened on the night of her eighteenth birthday party. Did you force her to have sex with you?'

'Don't be ridiculous. We'd been having it off for ages. She

always made a fuss about it, stupid bitch, but that was all show. She was gagging for it. And I gave it to her, didn't I?'

'She didn't enjoy it?'

'Poppy loved it,' said Ray, waking up, struggling to sit upright. 'Couldn't get enough of it.'

'Some girls give themselves gladly and without pain. Juno wasn't an easy conquest, was she?'

'She was a cock-teaser!'

'You left her in the wood, in tears, perhaps?'

'Crocodile tears! She could turn it on like a tap. Every time! Pretending she didn't want to, pretending it hurt her. She knew how much it turned me on, her making out she didn't want it. Some women are like that, you know. She recovered quickly enough after, didn't she? Dancing with that chocolate soldier. Just as well he disappeared into the woodwork, or I'd have had to warn him off.'

Chocolate soldier. Does he mean the colour of his skin, or was he really a soldier?

Charles lifted his glass to his lips. 'Marge, too. Though she wasn't exactly backward in coming forward. That was a night to remember!'

'You say the man disappeared?'

'Rejoined his regiment. Went overseas. Good riddance.'

'Did you try to find him, after?'

'No one knew who he was,' said Gordon. Smiling. Lying? 'He'd come with a friend of a friend, gatecrashing the party, as these lowlifes do.'

Ellie said, 'When Poppy and Juno discovered they were pregnant, Gordon and Ray offered to marry them. Poppy was happy enough to marry Ray. Juno, I suspect, was not so happy to marry Gordon. Did she try to contact the soldier? And fail? So I suppose she made the best of a bad job as so many girls have done before her. I'm sure she tried to be a good wife.'

'She loved me to distraction.'

'I think she did her best.' Ellie contemplated the wreck of a man before her. 'You say you really loved her—'

'I did. Of course I did. Why else would I have offered to marry her?'

Why, indeed? For money, because she was the most beautiful and most unattainable girl? Because she'd liked dancing with someone else?

She said, 'Then Clemmie was born. That must have been a shock.'

'I stood by her. I suggested that she give the baby up for adoption so that we could go on as if nothing had happened. She wouldn't hear of it. She put the baby before me! That shows you what a fine wife she was! She betrayed me, but I was prepared to forgive her on one condition. I said I would love and cherish Clemmie as if she were my own, provided Juno gave me another child straight away. She agreed, but—'

'You discovered you were infertile.'

Anger sharpened his voice. 'No need to go on about it!'

'And then came the accident.'

'No need to go on about that, either!'

Ellie almost felt sorry for the man. He'd had a run of really bad luck. Some men would have grown to meet the double challenge, would have become more instead of less loving to their family. Gordon said he'd loved Juno to distraction, but Ellie doubted that. The sight of his wife nursing Clemmie must have reminded him of everything he'd lost. He hadn't treated Clemmie well. Ellie was beginning to wonder how it had been for Juno. Had he taken out his frustration on her, too?

She said, 'Juno lost out, too. She was young and beautiful but her husband had dwindled into a wheelchair.'

Gordon shouted, 'She'd promised to love me till death do us part, and what happened? She foisted a bastard on me!'

'You promised to love her, too. Did you fulfil your promise? Juno tried to, didn't she? She did her best to love and serve you in every way she could. But it wasn't enough, was it? You knew she was a good woman and she had said she would never leave you, but you didn't believe her. You set out to break her spirit in many mean little ways. I think she's been drifting away from you for a long, long time, but her vows, her compassion, kept her tied to your wheelchair.'

Gordon's face twisted into a grimace.

Ellie sighed. 'It seems to me that both sisters began to think of divorce about the same time. Poppy had been driven to acknowledge that Ray's gambling had got way out of hand. And Juno—'

'What's that? What!' Ray had heard his name and struggled to fight off sleep.

Gordon ground out, 'You're off your trolley, woman! She'll never leave me.'

Ellie said, 'The trigger that precipitated the final act of the drama was that someone stole some of The Magpie cheques and the twins asked Charles to do an audit. He uncovered the problem but thought it was Clemmie, rather than Trixie, who'd been responsible for it. He made his suspicions known to you, Gordon, which was like setting a match to a rocket. You saw a way to reinforce your hold on Juno, believing that she would never let Clemmie be prosecuted for theft.'

Gordon laughed. 'I told her that I'd keep the evidence locked up for future use in case she ever thought of leaving me.'

'Juno didn't believe Clemmie had stolen anything, so this threat didn't disturb her, causing you to widen the scope of your plan. You organized a family meeting and got Charles to repeat his accusations against Clemmie to her grandparents and to Poppy. That didn't work too well, did it? Clemmie's grandparents rejected the idea out of hand. Juno kept her mouth shut. But you worked on Poppy. You thought that if only you could persuade Poppy to prosecute, what fun that would be!'

'Clemmie was guilty as sin,' said Gordon.

Ellie shook her head. 'I disproved that yesterday. Charles knows.'

'Leave me out of this,' said Charles, unsteadily replenishing his glass.

'I wish I could,' said Ellie, 'but you're all in it, to some extent. Poppy died, and this altered the balance of power. Juno was grief-stricken. She was sleepwalking. You didn't like that. You'd tried to make her pay you attention by getting Charles to accuse Clemmie of fraud, and that hadn't worked too well. So you tried something else. You told Charles that you'd seen Clemmie trying to get into The Magpie at about the time Poppy fell down the stairs. Charles was very ready to believe you. How delicious was that! You had no notion of actually going to the police with that story. Oh, no! Because if you did, you would lose your hold on Juno.

'It was at this point I got drawn into the affair by Gerald and

Marika, who asked me to look into Poppy's death. I went to the funeral and the reading of the will afterwards, which was a revelation. At the funeral, Clemmie and Juno attended to your every want, Gordon, as if they were your nurses doing their best for you, but not as if they loved you. In turn you ordered them around as if they were your servants. If I could see how distanced they felt from you, so could you, Gordon, and that's why you—'

'Showing me up like that, in front of everyone!'

'So you got Juno to yourself on the return from the crematorium by telling Clemmie to go in someone else's car—'

'She didn't want to travel with me, any more than I wanted her around. She was happy to go with Ray.'

'Um?' Ray, bleary-eyed. 'Yeah, that's right. She came back with me. Trixie was with her agent and Gordon told Clemmie to come with me. Clemmie's all right, you know. Not a bad kid. Always been fond of her Nunky.'

Gordon laughed. '"Nunky!" indeed. If you think she cares about any of us . . .!'

'Well, she does,' said Ray. 'She said she was worried about me. Asked if I'd eaten anything that day, and should she get me something when we got home. Which I didn't want, but it showed willing. I don't believe she stole from the firm, either.'

Gordon laughed again. 'So Clemmie's pulled the wool over your eyes, eh? I wasn't going to make a scene in public, but I could see Juno didn't even want to touch me at the funeral. So I got her on her own, and I told her I'd seen Clemmie going into The Magpie just before Poppy died. I said I didn't want to go to the police about it, unless she forced me to do so. She understood exactly what I meant. She was devastated.'

'I'll bet she was. Especially since it wasn't exactly the truth, was it? You told Charles you'd seen Clemmie hammering on the door and ringing the bell, but you didn't say anything about Clemmie actually going inside because she didn't. Right?'

'Near enough.' Gordon's face transformed into a grinning death's head. 'I told my dear wife that she was going to have to change her ways in future. No more giving me the cold shoulder, and leaving me out of family discussions. I told her that when we got home, she was going to have to go down on her knees to me and beg me to take her back into my bed.'

So that was how it had been. Ellie sighed. 'Juno had sacrificed a great deal to keep her marriage going, but once you had laid out your terms for the future, she could see it meant nothing but misery. Also, perhaps you hadn't noticed? She was unwell.'

Gordon frowned. 'Nonsense. It was all in her mind.'

'She looked ill to me,' said Ellie. 'Celine thought so, too. After the reading of the will, Juno almost passed out. Clemmie and Celine were both worried about her. She was not only grieving for Poppy. But also, on the way over from the crematorium, she had received your ultimatum. That's when she decided to run away.'

Gordon waved his cane in triumph. 'She'll be back this evening. She knows I'll fulfil my promise to go to the police tomorrow if she doesn't.'

'Perhaps she's betting that you won't do it. Because once you've been to the police, you will have lost your power over Clemmie, and thus, over Juno. And now, I'll be on my way.'

Gordon smiled. Not nicely. 'But you haven't had a drink yet, Mrs Interfering, Prying Old Woman. Charles, get her a drink. Make it a big one. No ice, no water.'

'Thank you, but I really don't drink,' said Ellie.

'I insist,' said Gordon. 'I want to see you falling over drunk. I want to take piccies of you disgracing yourself in public. I shall put them on Facebook and send them to the newspapers. Everyone is going to see that the High and Mighty Mrs Quicke is nothing but a broken-down old sot. A drunk and a has-been.'

FIFTEEN

'Really? You want to get her drunk?' Charles wasn't sure whether Gordon was joking or not.

'Snap out of it, Charles!' said Gordon. 'Give the lady a drink. After she's had one drink, she'll have another and then another till she's totally out of it, and she won't be so keen to pry into other people's lives then, will she? The way I see it, Charles, is that we can't let these women walk all over us. We've got to make an effort. We've got to show them what a man expects of his women, right?'

Charles grinned. He liked the sound of that. Though, if Ellie were any judge of the matter, Charles had never worn the trousers when he was married to Marge, and still less did he have the upper hand of his ex-wife now.

Ellie said, 'My husband will be expecting me home any minute now, so—'

'So what are you doing here, on a Sunday afternoon, when you should be looking after him, baking him buns for tea, ironing his shirts, making a proper home for him to return to after his day's work?'

'Well, he's supposedly retired but he still fills in for—'

'And he lets you go out, poking and prying into other people's lives? Shame on him. Isn't it shame on him, Charles?'

'Yes, it is.' Charles was beginning to enjoy this. He fetched a tumbler from the kitchen and poured a hefty measure of whisky into it. 'Would this be enough?'

'For starters,' said Gordon, also enjoying himself.

Charles hesitated. 'It seems a little extreme.'

'Do it. You owe me! Women should understand their place,' said Gordon, reaching behind his chair for something, and producing a cane. 'That's the problem with the world today. We're not educating girls to know their place. I think you need to go back to school, Mrs Quicke.'

Charles, uneasy, began to laugh. 'Gordon, I'm not sure that—'

'I'm sure. Very sure.' He whipped the cane up and down. Slash, slash. It cut the air.

Ellie shivered. 'Did you use that on Clemmie?'

'Of course. The only way to tame her.'

'And on Juno?'

'It was never necessary.' A silky tone. 'I only had to threaten her little darling, for Juno to do whatever I wished.'

Ellie's phone rang in her handbag. 'Excuse me,' she said, and rummaged for it. At the same time, the front door bell rang.

Charles dithered. 'Shall I answer that?'

Gordon shouted. 'Get that drink down her! Ignore her phone! I want to see her crawl around the floor, puking like a baby. Do it, I say!'

The phone went on ringing. Charles took a step towards Ellie and stopped. Indecisive.

Ellie tried to keep calm and carry on. Her hands shaking, she extracted her phone and pressed the right button. She hoped. 'Mikey, is that you?'

Ray stirred, managed to get his eyes open. 'Is that the front door? Or the phone? Whose phone is it?'

Charles said, 'Look, Gordon, I don't think—'

'You never did think. Give me that glass. I'll do it myself!'

It was Mikey on the phone. 'Is this the right house? We're at the front door, ringing the bell, but nobody's answering. Are you there?'

We are outside. Who was '*we*'?

Gordon dropped his cane and launched his wheelchair at Ellie, preventing her from rising by pushing his bony knees up against her legs.

Ellie raised her voice. 'Yes, I'm here, Mikey. I'm being held against my will.'

'Permission to break a window?'

'Now!' Gordon wrested the phone from Ellie and tossed it to the floor. He was a lot stronger than he looked.

Ellie yelled, 'Permission granted!' and hoped Mikey would hear it.

'Give it here!' Gordon gestured to Charles to hand over the full glass of whisky, while keeping Ellie pinned to her seat with his wheelchair.

Ellie struck his hand away and might as well have tried to deflect an iron bar. His eyes were wide open, staring. A drop of saliva formed at the corner of his mouth. His hand cupped her chin, pushing her head back and back and . . .

Bang!

Ray started upright in his chair. 'What was that!'

'What the . . .!' Gordon swung round in his chair, spilling the whisky.

Crash, *crash!* BANG!

Tinkle of falling glass.

A draught blew into the room from a broken window, the one which overlooked the street.

Mikey was using one of the plant pots which stood outside the front door to smash glass out of the window. His head appeared in the centre of the hole he'd made. Tinkle, tinkle. 'Hello there! Didn't you hear us ring the doorbell?'

Ellie managed to push Gordon's chair away from her long enough to stand. First things first. She scrambled to rescue her phone, shouting, 'Thank you, Mikey. Good work!'

'WHAT!' A shriek from Gordon. 'What have you done?'

Mikey was grinning. 'Rescuing a damsel in distress. You OK, Mrs Quicke? Thomas is working his way round to the back to let you out, but I wanted to be sure you were all right.'

Charles leaned back against the wall, and put his hands to his head. 'Oh, my God!'

Ellie said, 'Well, yes, Charles. You could do with some help from Him, couldn't you? Don't you think you ought to start thinking for yourself, instead of acting as enforcer for Gordon?'

'WHAT!' Another shriek from Gordon. 'You can't do this! Breaking and entering! Damaging property! Trespass! I'll have the Law on you! Charles, get me my phone. Ring the police!'

Charles slid down till he was sitting on the floor, legs stretched out before him. Charles was in shock. Charles was re-evaluating his position.

Ray had his phone out, staring at it. 'This is Poppy's phone, isn't it? I'm not sure how to . . .!'

'Give it here!' Gordon snatched it from Ray, and fumbled with the settings. 'I'm calling the police! How do I get—'

Thomas arrived from the kitchen, looking larger and more

formidable than usual . . . and he was a big, burly man by
nature. 'Ellie? You all right? The back door was open.'

'I'm fine, thank you,' said Ellie. 'I suppose Mikey told you I
was coming here. Did you bring the car? I really don't think
I can ride on the back of Mikey's bike to get home.'

She was trembling, although she really didn't know why.
Gordon was just a vain, stupid man who had tried to become
a Big Time Villain, and been defeated by a teenaged boy and a
pacifist in a dog collar. Although, to be fair, Thomas's beard
did conceal the dog collar rather well.

'What about the damage you've done!' Gordon, unable to
find his way into Poppy's phone, flung it from him in a rage.

'What about the damage *you've* done, Gordon?'

He was past listening to reason. 'Tell Juno, remind her!
If she's not back this evening, I'm going to the police tomorrow
morning, to tell them Clemmie killed her aunt.' He meant
it, too.

Thomas put his arm around Ellie and would have shepherded
her to the front door, but she made him stop in front of Charles.
She said, 'Charles, why don't you come with us? Get in touch
with Marge, talk it over with her.'

'I . . .' He didn't meet her eye. There was a flush high on
his cheeks. He was ashamed and confused. He didn't know
what to do next.

'Charles!' Gordon, screeching.

'Let's go,' said Thomas, and guided Ellie out of the house.

She took a deep breath of fresh air. Oh, that was so good.
That house – apart from the rotten food smells from the kitchen
and the spilled whisky – stank of misery. She looked back at
it, broken window and all. 'I don't suppose Juno will ever return.
Perhaps Marge will fetch her clothes and other belongings
sometime.'

'I had to park the car outside in the road, on a double yellow
line. I hope we don't get a ticket.' Thomas was using his terse
voice, the one which told her he was angry but holding on to
his temper.

She pressed his arm. 'Thank you. I was getting worried.
Actually, I think you might have done more good in there than
I did. So much distress, so many tangled relationships.'

He said, 'Look, the sun is shining! It was so dark in that house. I could smell evil. I'm glad Mikey called me. Let's go home.'

Mikey was waiting for them at the kerb, licking at a tiny cut on one hand. 'I'll ride back and be there before you. I think Susan's baking. I hope.'

'Never on Sunday,' said Ellie, trying to make a joke. Trying to lighten the mood. Wondering what on earth she could do to stop Gordon going to the police.

Ellie updated Mikey and Thomas once they'd all got back. Neither had had anything to say about what had happened, except that it was a good thing she'd told them where she'd planned to be.

Home again. The house lay quiet about them. Susan had not been baking. She was probably having an afternoon nap, after having been out clubbing the night before. There was no message from Lesley on the landline; perhaps she'd gone to watch her fiancé play cricket, after all.

There was a message on the landline from Diana enquiring when Ellie would be able to take little Evan to the park. He'd been asking, she said. Diana didn't say anything about stopping the cheque she'd given Ray. Ellie hoped that meant it had been stopped.

The garden was looking bright in the sunshine. She stood in the window and thought that she ought to get out there and do some more titivating.

Thomas and Mikey had retired to the library-cum-study at the end of the corridor. No doubt they were on their computers.

'I'm stuck,' thought Ellie. 'Dear Lord, I'm stuck. What do you want me to do next?'

She waited, trying to make her mind go blank, to stop thinking, to receive instead of battering away asking for help. He couldn't get through to her if she was shouting at Him all the time.

She was worried about Charles. Gordon had a hold over Charles. Perhaps not just because Charles had been driving in the accident which had left Gordon in a wheelchair? Gordon was a past master at manipulation. He relied on his weakness to get other people to do what he wanted. And he was good at it. Oh, yes.

Charles was not a bad man. Or, not very bad. If Marge were being truthful – and Ellie rather thought she was – then he'd been the one whose adventures had caused Marge to divorce him. He'd broken the marriage. But, they were still talking to one another. Perhaps Marge could drag Charles out from under Gordon's shadow. Charles seemed to have a good reputation as an accountant. Gerald Cordover wouldn't have used him, otherwise.

Charles had had no reason whatever to kill Poppy.

Ray? Ellie sighed. Would he ever be able to curb his gambling? If not, he'd probably end up on the streets. Oh dear. Yet what he'd said about his wife indicated that he deeply regretted her loss. Some of the family had thought him responsible for Poppy's death because he had expected to inherit her wealth, but Ellie had seen no signs of guilt in him. Lots of other signs – desperation, mostly. The curse of the addict. Nothing can be of any importance to an addict, compared to their need for drink, or drugs, or gambling.

If Ray's alibi at the club could be broken, could he have killed his wife? Well, it was possible, perhaps. In a moment of madness, a confrontation gone wrong?

Gordon couldn't climb stairs, so he couldn't have killed Poppy. And why would he want to, anyway?

Ellie rubbed her eyes. Of all the people in the Cordover family whom she'd got to know, Gordon was the only one with the urge to control others. If she didn't do anything to help, tomorrow he'd do his best to destroy Clemmie . . . which raised the question of what exactly it was that Marika thought Ellie could do to keep her granddaughter safe?

Let's recap.

Juno cared deeply about Clemmie. Juno had run away. Quite right, too. She'd kept in touch with her parents, with Clemmie and with Marge. Probably also with Celine. So, what had she asked them to do to protect Clemmie?

The only thing Ellie could think of, was asking Ellie herself to interfere . . . which was not, pardon me, but really, not enough!

Thomas came in. Didn't speak. Hovered.

She said, 'I know. You think I ought to be up and about, doing something to help Clemmie. I quite agree, but I don't know what.'

'It might be good to have Clemmie's version of events? Suppose Gordon has invented that story about seeing her going into the office that night?'

'The thing is, I believe that he did see Clemmie there.' She thought about it. 'No, that's not quite right. Charles told me Gordon had seen Clemmie hammering on the door and ringing the bell. And I said, "Didn't she have a key?" And Charles said that she must have had one, but had forgotten it or something. So he didn't actually see her go in. Or, did he?'

He put his arm around her. 'Are you fed up with the lot of them? Ready to throw in the towel?'

'Certainly not. All right, I'd better go and ask her, I suppose. What's Mikey doing?'

'Muttering to himself. Accessing websites. Making notes. Twirling pencils around as if he were a conjuror.'

'He's a good lad.'

'Yes. Do you want him to come, too?'

Thomas's offer of help touched her so much that it caused her to reach for a hanky, which she failed to find. She sniffed. 'You want to take a hand? That would be good. Gordon scares me. I'm really afraid of what he might try to do.'

He took her seriously. 'You aren't easily scared.'

'Gordon has changed since the funeral. I think perhaps he was always a bully to Juno and Clemmie but to others he represented himself as a victim. Since last Friday, he's gone from querulous complaint to fury. I think if he knew where to find Juno, he'd attack her physically.' She back-tracked. 'Oh, I can't think why I said that. Surely he wouldn't . . .? Would he?'

'From what you've told me, from what I've seen for myself, yes; he would. Let's go and see Clemmie. Warn her what's about to happen.'

'I keep thinking about Juno. She's a brave woman who has managed to cope with Gordon all these years. I cannot think she'd disappear and leave Clemmie undefended. She must

somehow have managed to put some sort of protection in place
for her . . . but what? Is she relying on Marika and Marge?
Or on me? But, what can any of us do?'

'One step at a time. Why don't you ring Clemmie, see
if she's in?'

'She's probably out having a last-minute lesson in the
car. Didn't Aidan say he's been giving her lessons? You
should see his funny little two-stroke. He's a big lad, and
when he gets in, it sinks down. You can almost hear it groan.
I suppose it's good in traffic.'

She rang Clemmie's mobile.

Clemmie was in a hurry. 'Sure, drop in later, if you like.
I'm just about to go out and have one last driving practice,
and after that I'll have to cook something for Aidan's supper.
He's on nights. Do you know where I live?' She gave the
address. It wasn't far from the shop.

Ellie switched off. 'Now let's find out what Mikey's doing.'

Mikey was still on the computer. He looked frustrated. 'I've
got a list of half a dozen places which were advertised this
last week. All central, within walking distance of the shops.
Modern, with lifts and speakerphone entry. Two have security
cameras. One has a balcony. Nearly all have two bedrooms,
three with wet rooms. All have some kind of arrangement for
car parking or have a garage in the basement.'

'Are any of them rented furnished? Juno might have gone
for that.'

Mikey ran his fingers down a pencilled list he'd been making.
'Two. On six-monthly leases.'

'Are you sure you're on the right track?' said Thomas. 'Juno
might have been preparing a bolthole for months. She could
have taken her time, leased an unfurnished flat and chosen
furniture and furnishings for it over a period of time.'

'Somehow, I don't think so. I don't think she decided to cut
her losses until after Gordon threatened to go to the police about
Clemmie. I think she acted on the spur of the moment. First
she went off with her parents and, when she was safely away
from Gordon, she left their car to go . . . where? Possibly, to
a hotel? From there I think she phoned Marge and asked her
to find her some place into which she could move straight away.'

'That makes sense. Can the police get hold of her telephone records? If we had proof she'd phoned Marge at that point, we could confront her, get her to tell us where Juno is staying.'

Ellie shook her head. 'The police won't act unless we can give them good reason to do so. And that, we don't have.'

Mikey was restless, fiddling with a pen. 'Did they find her laptop at work? That would show whether or not she'd been planning her escape through Marge, wouldn't it?'

Ellie clapped her hands together. 'Ah, let me think! Yes, that's it! That's the missing piece of the puzzle. There was no laptop on Juno's desk or anywhere near it at The Magpie, only a PC. Juno vanished after the reading of the will with just the clothes she stood up in and, I assume, a handbag. Credit cards, smartphone, even an iPad . . . yes, all those could have been in her handbag and she could order whatever else she needed with them online, with delivery the following day or earlier. She didn't have a laptop with her, because she wasn't expecting to have to disappear . . . and who takes a laptop to a funeral?'

'So where is it?'

'I don't know. Let's think. Like Poppy, she'd have kept all her private business separate from her home accounts on a personal laptop, wouldn't she? Or maybe an iPad? Oh dear, what do I know about iPads? Would a businesswoman keep everything on an iPad, or would she need a laptop as well?'

Thomas shrugged. 'An iPad is too fiddly for me.' He had a smartphone and a computer but no iPad.

Mikey agreed. 'An iPad's all right for small stuff but I'd want a laptop as well, if I were paying the bills for the house as well as running a business. She'd have done her online banking on the laptop, wouldn't she? She wouldn't have used her office computer for that. You say Poppy had an iPad, a laptop and a computer, so wouldn't Juno have had the same?'

Ellie held on to her head. 'That's right. They'd both have wanted to keep their personal information separate from work. A sensible precaution to take in view of what their husbands were like. When I visited The Magpie office, Poppy's laptop was still there and Lesley says that Poppy's handbag contained an iPad. That accounts for Poppy's stuff. There was no laptop beside or on Juno's desk. I'd swear to it. So, where on earth is it?'

Thomas frowned. 'Perhaps Juno took it home with her in the week after Poppy died, after the police said they were not investigating the death any further?'

'No, no. She liked to keep the two sides of her life separate. She ran that household on silken rails. I don't think Gordon ever lifted a finger for himself. If he saw that laptop, he'd be reminded she had a life outside his, and he'd have wanted to know what secrets she was keeping from him.'

'The laptop would be password-protected,' said Mikey.

'He was perfectly capable of making a scene or even smashing the laptop if she refused to let him see what she was doing. No, she wouldn't have taken it home. Poppy kept her laptop at the office, and surely Juno did the same. She had no reason to believe that she was going to have to disappear straight away, so I think she left it in her office as usual. She'd think it would be safe from Gordon there.'

'He didn't retrieve it somehow, after Juno disappeared?'

'How could he? He can't climb stairs, and he wouldn't have the keys, would he?' She tried to think straight. 'Poppy dies, the police are called in and seal the office. While the office is closed, Juno arranges for all business calls to be rerouted to Laura, the office manageress. This keeps the business going. The police decide not to take their enquiries into Poppy's death any further, and they withdraw. The office and the shop remain closed until the day after the funeral on Saturday, when both reopen.

'Celine and Clemmie open the shop that morning. Celine keeps the shop open all day, with the help of Clemmie in the morning and a teenager in the afternoon. Laura and Ruth open the office on the Saturday morning, with Charles. Clemmie joins them in the afternoon, which is when I visit the office and note that Juno's laptop is gone. I don't think Juno removed her laptop during that week, because she didn't anticipate the need to disappear. So it's reasonable to assume it was taken after the reading of the will on Friday and before the office was opened on Saturday morning. What it comes down to is: who had keys to the office and knew the code to shut off the alarm? That's supposing, of course, that the alarm had been set when the police turned the premises back to the family. I think either Clemmie or, possibly, Celine, took it.'

She rubbed her forehead. 'I'm getting confused. Why do I think that Clemmie didn't have any keys? Surely they trusted her with keys, didn't they? But if either Celine or Clemmie took it, how did they get it to Juno? I would take my oath that neither of them knows exactly where she is.'

Mikey and Thomas were following her reasoning with deep concentration. Mikey said, 'They gave it to Marge to hand over to Juno. Didn't you say Marge was Clemmie's godmother?'

'Yes, but Marge was away on holiday, and didn't get back to this country till the Friday night after the funeral.'

Mikey said, 'You said Juno was ill, hardly able to walk.'

Ellie nodded. 'Yes, she was. I think she pulled herself together after she got away. Perhaps she even went back for the laptop herself, which means she can't be far away. Oh, I give up!'

Let the whole boiling lot of them stew in their own juice. They'd brought their problems on themselves. None of them was anything to do with her. She remembered the watchful eyes of Clemmie . . . and Marika . . . and Marge. Withholding knowledge, but asking for her help.

Thomas and Mikey were looking at her in much the same way. Speculatively.

'What?' she said, exasperated.

'Waiting for you to tell us what to do,' said Mikey. He struck a jaunty pose. 'I've been praying about it. A bit. Well, I did when I thought about it.'

Thomas smiled. He'd been praying, too.

Mikey added, 'I've not got to be back till supper time.'

Ellie glanced at her watch, which as usual was going slow. 'I suppose I could warn Lesley that Gordon is going to denounce Clemmie as a thief and a murderer tomorrow morning.'

'Before you bring the police into it,' said Thomas, 'let's check Clemmie's story. Has she – or has she not – got keys to the office? We really need to hear her version of what happened on the night of the murder.'

'All right, let's go.' Where had she put her handbag? She'd seen it a moment ago. 'But first we have to rescue Charles.'

Ellie hadn't meant to say that. It was the last thing she wanted to do. The words had shot out of her mouth without her thinking through what they meant. She sighed. Well, all right! She found her handbag and rummaged through it till she found the card he'd given her ages ago, when she'd first bearded him in his den – or rather, in the office at The Magpie.

'I'd better ring him. He's probably perfectly all right, but I'll just check.' She rang the mobile number Charles had given her. The phone rang and rang . . . and rang.

Finally, 'Hello . . .?' A voice that quavered.

'Charles? Ellie Quicke here. Where are you?'

'I'm not sure. I'm on the pavement . . . somewhere. Not sure where. I drove away from Gordon's, but I nearly . . . the other driver shouted at me so I . . . I'm shaking! I didn't think I'd had too much to drink but . . . Stupid! I got out of the car in case they do me for being drunk in charge. I'm not drunk. At least, I don't think I am.'

Patiently, 'Where are you? We'll come and fetch you.'

'Um. Dunno. Oh, there's the school opposite. I'm by the roundabout.'

'You're out of the car, aren't you? Walk up and down. Have you any water to drink?'

'Yes, I think. I'll look. Sometimes I do keep some in . . .' He shut off his phone.

'Let's go,' said Ellie.

'You don't really want to rescue him, do you?' Mikey, in distaste.

'Not particularly,' said Ellie, 'but Thomas thinks we should and he's driving.'

Thomas got out his keys. 'Yes, you're right.'

Mikey said, 'Can I put my bike in the back? Or on the roof? Do I have to ride it?'

SIXTEEN

Sunday late afternoon

They found Charles walking up and down beside his car. He'd glugged down a bottle of water and didn't look too bad. Slightly dishevelled, not as precise as before but reasonably sober. And, worried.

Ellie opened the back door of the car and he stumbled in next to Mikey saying, 'Well, er, thanks. Good of you to bother. Especially since . . . I don't know what's come over Gordon. I suppose, in the circumstances . . . understandable, but I told him . . . he can't really expect me to . . . I'll fetch the car in the morning. Can you give me a lift home?'

Mikey said, 'You don't think we're doing this out of the kindness of our hearts, do you? We're off to see the Wizard . . .' And he started singing the theme from the *Wizard of Oz*. His voice had broken and he enjoyed letting rip.

Charles shuddered and reached for the door handle to let himself out of the car.

Thomas said, 'Shut up, Mikey.' He signalled right and joined in the stream of traffic going up the hill.

Charles settled back in his seat. 'Where are we going?'

Ellie said, 'To undo some of the wrong that's been done.'

Charles's mouth twisted. 'What wrong?'

'Do you have keys to The Magpie office, and if so, how long have you had them?'

'Why do you need to know?' Not amused. Not inclined to give any information.

'It would help us to work out what happened.' Coaxing him, babying him. 'Surely it can't do any harm for you to admit that you didn't have any keys when you started work on the books at The Magpie, but acquired some later on?'

'No, I suppose not. You're right, I didn't have any when I first started. That didn't matter because Laura always arrived early. Then Poppy died and both the office and the shop were closed till after the funeral so I didn't need to get in.'

'After you picked Ray's books up from the garage on the day of the funeral, you kept them at your place overnight because you still hadn't any keys to the office?'

'Correct. I arrived there early on Saturday, even before Laura, and couldn't get in. Celine was just opening the shop, so I asked her if she had keys for the office. She had a spare set which she kept at the back of the shop for emergencies, problems with the drains, or the meter readers when the office was shut.'

'She gave you the code to shut off the alarm?'

'Yes. They use the same code for office and shop.'

'You were the first to go into the office that morning. Was the alarm on?'

'Of course it was. Annoying, that. You have to climb the stairs to shut it off at the top and, unless you're quick, it makes a hellish noise.'

'Did you tell Gordon you had keys and the code for the alarm?'

'For heaven's sake! Why would I do that?' Angry, and uncomfortable.

Was that the truth? Yes.

'Charles, you know that Gordon wants to accuse Clemmie of fraud. We'd like you to review the evidence.'

'I told you already. She did it.' Truculent. He belched.

Thomas opened the windows a crack and slowed down. 'Charles, we want to clear Clemmie's name, so we're now going to ask Trixie about those cheques. Do you want to come with us while we do that, or would you like us to drop you off on the corner so that you can walk home?'

'Ridiculous! Why should she . . .?' But he sank back in his seat and made no further effort to get out of the car.

Mikey, with his chin on his shoulder, said, 'This is a busy road. I wouldn't like to have to ride my bike along here. I'd have to go on the pavement.'

Charles turned to stare at Mikey with raised eyebrows, but Ellie and Thomas refused to react.

Thomas turned into the forecourt of Ray's house and parked. There was an expensive car already there: one that Ellie had seen before; one with tinted windows and personalized number plates. The businessman-cum-club-owner?

The Lexus which Ray was using was not here. He was probably still back at Gordon's.

Trixie's sports car was there, piled high with luggage. As they watched, the businessman came out of the house with two large suitcases, which he put in the boot of his car. He glanced at Ellie and Thomas without interest and returned to the house.

Charles exclaimed, 'What's going on?'

Ellie got out of the car. 'Is Trixie leaving home?'

Charles followed her, stiffly. 'Does Ray know?'

'She's old enough to make her own choices.'

Mikey slid out, with a glinting smile. 'She's sold herself for stardom, hasn't she?'

Thomas switched off the engine, and got out, too. 'Or to pay off her father's debts?'

The businessman emerged from the house, carrying an armful of expensive-looking dresses wrapped in plastic. He ignored the newcomers to lay the precious garments flat on the back seat of his car.

Ellie led the way inside.

Trixie descended the stairs, carrying a couple of hat boxes and a leather-bound jewellery box. She wore a scarlet and white polka-dotted dress with a matching red bandeau round her hair. She looked stunning.

At the foot of the stairs was the middle-aged leather-jacketed man who'd been hanging around Trixie at the funeral and the reading of the will. He was not a happy bunny. 'You don't have to do this, girl!'

'I read the small print in your so-called contract, and it told me all I needed to know about you and your schemes. Now get lost!'

'You'll regret this one day!' A bluff? Trixie disdained to reply. Leather jacket scurried out, passing the businessman with averted eyes.

Trixie spotted Ellie and Co, and her beautifully shaped eyebrows snapped together. 'Now, don't you start. If you've come from my father, you can tell him he's no right to lecture me after the mess he's made of things. I'm not staying here to be dragged down to his level. He'll be on the streets before long, and I'm on my way up.'

'We're not here to stop you,' said Ellie, 'but before you go, would you answer one question? Have you got the receipts for the bills you paid with The Magpie's cheques?'

'I suppose so, somewhere. I've been clearing paperwork out all morning. They might be in the bin in the kitchen, if you're lucky. I did do some shredding, but I didn't have time to do the lot.'

Ellie lifted an eyebrow at Mikey, who slid from her side to find the kitchen.

Charles squeezed his eyes shut and opened them again. 'You mean that it was you who took the money from your mother's business account?'

A pretty shrug. 'It isn't important, is it? If I'd asked Mum, she'd have said it was OK, but with Dad making such a song and dance over his debts, well . . . I took a short cut.'

Ellie repressed rage. 'Did you know that your mother thought it was Clemmie who'd taken the cheques?'

'Really?' Arched eyebrows. 'That was a bit stupid, wasn't it? It would never have crossed straight-laced Clemmie's mind to do that. Anyway, so what? Water under the bridge.'

She looked around her. How long had she lived in this house? Not all that long? Three or four years, the solicitor had said. She was saying goodbye not to the house, but to her past life. She turned to the businessman. 'I think that's the lot. Let's go, shall we?'

The man put his arm around her, shepherding her to the door, looking down on his latest possession with pride. She threw back her head and smiled up at him. A smile full of promise. A smile for a day without a cloud in the sky.

That smile probably wouldn't last through the next wintry storm, but it pleased them both, for the moment.

Charles didn't know what to do with himself. He took two hasty steps after them, then stopped, swaying. He glared around, picked up a plastic bag which had strayed into the hall, looked it over as if it were of major interest, and dropped it again.

Thomas followed Mikey into the kitchen.

Ellie wondered if the dishwasher still contained the dishes from the coffee and sandwiches which had been dished out on Friday. Had the businessman spotted Trixie before that day or had he met her before? Had he made a point of attending the reading of the will in order to discover how she was fixed? How soon had she realized that his interest in her might translate into a starry future?

Would he put money into a film for her? Possibly, possibly not.

Would her grandparents help her out when the businessman tired of her, or she of him? Very probably.

'Got 'em,' said Mikey, popping out of the kitchen with a handful of papers.

Thomas was also holding some papers. And frowning. 'Ellie, there's a lot of unpaid household bills here as well: council tax, electricity, gas, and so on. It's all very well for Trixie to shove them in the bin, but someone's going to have to deal with them.'

'Clearly not Trixie,' said Ellie, feeling bleak. 'Give them to Charles. He'll sort them out with Juno when she gets back.'

Charles started on hearing his name. When Thomas handed him the bills, he looked at them as if he'd never seen any paperwork before. 'What . . .?'

Mikey flourished some more papers under his nose. 'Madam Trixie's bank statements, credit-card statements, and bills from the period when she stole the money. Happy now?'

Charles mouthed the words 'Happy now?' They didn't seem to mean anything to him.

Mikey couldn't be doing with Charles. Mikey picked up the stray plastic bag, emptied all the papers into it, and handed them to Charles. 'I suppose you'll make more sense in the morning.'

'Or perhaps,' suggested Ellie, 'after he's had a good long talk with Marge.'

'Marge,' said Charles. His eyes glistened with tears. 'She's angry with me.'

'Give her a ring now. See if she'll let you go round to have a chat with her.' She signalled to Thomas and Mikey. 'Before we go, I have to check . . .' She went into the sitting room at the back. And yes, someone – Ray or Trixie? – had taken the picture off the wall and, judging by the scratches on the wall around it, had tried to open the safe. Ellie concentrated, recalled the code, opened the safe and checked that the contents looked exactly as they had when she had put them there. She closed the safe up again, reset the dial and replaced the picture. 'That's for Juno to deal with. Now . . .'

When she got back to the hall she found Charles still standing there, looking limp. He said, 'She won't answer the phone.'

Ellie took his arm and steered him out to the car, following in the footsteps of Thomas and Mikey. She said, 'Never mind, Charles. Try again later. She won't be angry if you can marry up these receipts with the cheques stolen from The Magpie. She'll be very happy that you've managed to clear Clemmie of fraud. Now, sit in the back of the car and we'll drop you home, right?'

Thomas said, 'Have we got any keys to lock the house up?'

'Drop the latch and shut the door. I'm assuming Ray has keys to get back in with.'

Not that he'd be able to stay there much longer. Even if Juno allowed him to rent it, how would he cope with such a big place on his own?

Ellie got Mikey and Charles into the car and then, and only then, it hit her. Charles was so . . . She didn't know what he was, but . . . Was he? Could he be? Oh!

Thomas enquired where Charles lived, and drove them neatly to the block of flats in which he lived on Haven Green. Ellie looked up at the ranks of windows. 'Which is your flat, Charles? Do you have a good view over the Green?'

Charles got out and, without a backward look or word of thanks, disappeared into the nearest doorway.

Mikey was disgusted. 'What's wrong with him?'

Thomas sighed. 'Think, Mikey.' He signalled and drove off.

Ellie said, 'I'm so angry with myself. Why didn't I see it before? When Marge said she'd divorced him after multiple betrayals, I thought it was odd because I hadn't got him down as a man who chased young girls. It wasn't girls, was it?'

Silence. Mikey grimaced. 'Oh, you mean . . . that. It's no big deal nowadays, is it?'

Ellie said, 'A loves B. B loves C. But who does C love?'

Mikey could follow that. 'Charles loves Gordon? Is that right?'

'Yes. It explains a lot.'

'Gordon loves Juno. That's easy. And Juno loves Clemmie? Right?'

Yes. Or, was there someone else lurking in the background? Someone pulling strings? Someone whom Marge and Marika knew about but didn't want to mention?

Ellie rubbed her forehead. 'Why didn't someone warn me about Charles? Why didn't I see it until it was almost too late?'

Thomas said, 'Light of my life, your innocence serves to keep me aware that God loves everyone.' He slowed down, drew into the kerb and parked.

Mikey shuddered. 'Maybe. But Gordon is evil. Why have we stopped?'

Thomas said, 'I'll have to go back. Did he give you his card? It might have his flat number on it. I'm sorry, Ellie. Can you and Mikey find your own way home?'

Mikey didn't move. 'Why?'

Ellie said, 'Because, Mikey, Thomas is afraid that Charles might do something silly.'

'What sort of silly?' Silence. Mikey thought about it. He shifted in his seat. 'Oh. You mean, he might top himself? Well, I could drive your car, couldn't I? You could give me a quick lesson, and I could drive.'

Thomas sighed, but didn't reply.

Ellie got out of the car, and held the door open for Mikey to do so, too. He got out, sulkily. Together they watched Thomas execute a quick U-turn and disappear.

Mikey said, '*Why* does Thomas think that Charles might do something silly?'

'Instinct and training,' said Ellie, trying to orientate herself. 'No need for a taxi. I think if we walk up here we'll come to the Avenue.'

'I wouldn't like Thomas's job.'

Ellie slowed down as she spotted a bus stop in the street, not far off. 'Mikey, can you make your own way back from here? I have just one quick call to make which won't take long, but I know you're due back home at suppertime.'

'Who? I don't see why I shouldn't come, too.'

'Not this time. I promise I'm not going to beard any more dragons in their dens.'

Narrowed eyes. 'Will you tell me where you're going, and
ring me in an hour's time to say you're all right?'

'Promise.'

Clemmie lived in a terrace of two-up and two-down houses,
which had originally been built for factory workers but which
was undergoing gentrification. There were no front gardens
and the front doors led straight into the main room, but fresh
paint was everywhere and window boxes sprouted here and
there. Almost all of the houses had had a loft conversion, which
added another storey to the original building and moved them
up several council tax bands. There were no garages but there
was adequate parking in the street. Ellie looked for Aidan's
two-stroke and failed to see it.

Clemmie opened the door, looking flushed and wearing an
apron with pictures of cats on it. She beckoned Ellie inside.
T-shirt, jeans and trainers today. 'I'm a bit behind. I got stuck
behind a lorry on the A40 and almost lost my nerve. The driving
test's tomorrow morning. Do you mind waiting a mo? I'm
cooking, you see.'

She shot off to the back of a light and airy living room,
which had been created by throwing the original two small
ground-floor rooms into one. An extension at the back housed
a small but well-fitted kitchen area. A modern staircase climbed
the left-hand wall, with a cupboard beneath it. The furniture
was simple, all pastel shades. A couple of abstract prints hung
on the walls – Juno's taste? A Sunday newspaper was strewn
half over a small settee and half on the floor . . . which was
uncarpeted but had a couple of good rugs on it. Central heating.
Blinds at the windows. All fresh and clean.

Through the open kitchen door Ellie could see a square patch
of garden surrounded by high walls. There was an outhouse
which had probably once contained a privy. Aidan was there,
wrestling with a lawn mower. As Ellie watched, he picked the
lawn mower up and shoved it into the outhouse. There was a
lot to be said for brute strength when objects needed to be
hauled about.

Clemmie skittered around, dishing up and talking at the same
time. 'Hope you don't mind, I've got to get some food into

Aidan before he goes off. Nights, you know. He mustn't be late. I'll eat later. In fact, I'm so nervous about tomorrow that I might just have a sandwich.' She laughed. 'Do have a seat, Mrs Quicke.' She pulled open the back door to shout, 'Come and get it!'

Aidan came. Also in T-shirt, trainers and jeans. 'Hi, Mrs Quicke. Forgive the mess. Complete domesticity.' He washed his hands under the tap. 'I'm thinking she'll pass the test first time.' Smiling. Relaxed.

As was Clemmie, apart from a certain nervous excitement. 'You told me you had two goes at the test before you passed.'

'Well, I wasn't taught by someone as good as me!' He ambled into a chair and held his hands up for the piled plate of food she brought to the table for him. He smiled. 'One of the first things I said to her was that a man needs quantity, as well as quality. In food, anyway.'

Ellie said, 'She's not taking the test on your mother's little runabout?'

'No, no.' Round a mouthful. 'No, no. I got my own car back, at last. It's been in the garage following an encounter with an ambulance which backed into me when I was properly parked in the hospital car park, would you believe?'

Clemmie said, 'Aidan's mum's nice. She said that if teaching me to drive kept Aidan off the rugby field, it was a good thing. His dad's given me a couple of lessons, too. And his brother. So I've driven . . .' she counted on her fingers '. . . a total of five different cars, some automatic and some not.' She busied herself slicing two bananas and adding a whole carton of yoghurt. 'Was there something special, Mrs Quicke?'

'Yes, my dear, there was. I'm sorry to say that your stepfather has worked himself up into a right old paddy. He's threatening to go to the police tomorrow, to accuse you of this and that?'

If Ellie had hoped for a guilty reaction, she didn't get it.

'Oh, what now!' And to Aidan, 'Do you want redcurrant jelly on it as well?'

'Mmphm!' Meaning, yes, please.

Tut! Didn't his mum ever tell him not to speak with his mouth full?

Ellie said, 'Someone stole some cheques from The Magpie and used them to pay off their own bills.'

A slight frown. 'Was that why you asked me which bank I'm with?'

'You're in the clear and Charles knows it. We have proof that it was someone else who did it.'

Clemmie and Aidan exchanged looks.

'Trixie?' A frown from both of them.

Ellie jumped on that. 'She's done it before?'

'Not exactly,' said Aidan, 'but she's always short of the readies, and if you lend her a tenner, you don't get it back.'

Clemmie said, 'She's always been kind to me.'

Neither of them was worried about this.

Clemmie whisked Aidan's empty plate away. 'Something else, Mrs Quicke?'

'Yes. Your mother's laptop seems to have gone missing. Have you seen it?'

A slight frown. 'That's odd. When it's not in use on the big table, she keeps it beside her desk. Are you sure it's not there?'

Ellie was. She was equally sure that it wasn't Clemmie who had taken it. 'Gordon says that on the night your aunt died, he saw you hammering on the door at The Magpie, trying to get in.'

'Yes, that's true.' No anxiety. 'There was a light on upstairs and I thought Mum or Aunt Poppy must be working late. I'd been trying and trying to tell them my good news about paying off my debt and taking my driving test, but they'd been so preoccupied with stuff – I think it was to do with Uncle Ray – that they kept putting me off. Anyway, when I saw there was a light on upstairs in the office, I thought it would be a good time to talk to them. I tried to make them hear me. But they didn't.'

'Didn't you have your key with you? Why didn't you let yourself in?'

'No, I don't have a key at the moment. Laura lost hers and she's using mine because she always arrives first. Mum was going to get another one cut, but she didn't have time to do so before . . . before. I'm only working there in the afternoons when the office is already open, so it doesn't matter that I don't have a key.'

'Was Aidan with you that night?' Hoping against hope.

'Of course. It was his last free evening before he went on nights. He'd arranged to take me out for a practice and had borrowed his dad's car, so we went up by the North Circular and into the back roads for some three-point turns, and four times he made me park on a busy road. When we passed The Magpie and I saw the light on upstairs, he let me out and waited to see if anyone responded. But they didn't. I looked through the letterbox and couldn't see anything. It was all dark inside, so I went back to the car and he brought me home.'

Aidan said, 'I didn't want to leave her there in the street at that time of night. I parked opposite and waited for her. She was never out of my sight.'

'You spent the night here?'

'On that widgy settee of hers? Don't make me laugh. It's far too short.' Aidan reached out one huge arm to catch Clemmie's hand and hold it, while continuing to eat his pudding. 'She chucked me out at eleven. She thinks I'll give up and go away if she keeps saying "No", but I'm the persistent sort and I'll get there sooner or later, won't I, Half Pint?'

'Man Mountain!' She bent over to kiss the top of his head. And smiled.

Good genes. Well educated. Satisfactory work ethic. A tender, jokey relationship plus a strong physical attraction. Clemmie could do a lot worse.

Aidan said, 'When we heard about Clemmie's aunt dying on the stairs, we wondered if she were already lying behind the door while Clemmie was trying to get in. It must have been about that time that she fell. I'm glad Clemmie didn't have a key to try to open the door. I'm glad someone else found her.'

'Did you see Gordon's car outside while you were trying to get in?'

'Didn't look. Was he there?'

He must have been, or he wouldn't have seen Clemmie ringing the bell.

Clemmie looked out at the garden. 'Oh, Aidan! You've missed a patch of grass, see? Right in the middle!'

'Who's a perfectionist, then? Never look a gift horse in the mouth. Now, give me a kiss, and I'll be off!' He picked her up bodily, and held her close.

She put her arms around his neck and pressed her head against his.

He set her down on her feet with tender care. 'See you tomorrow? Text me the result when you've taken the test?'

She nodded, trying to smile. Succeeding, almost.

He left. For a big man, he could move quickly when he chose.

Clemmie began to clear the table. 'Aidan's a bit of all right, don't you think?' She tried to sound as if she didn't care about Ellie's answer.

'I do. I gather his family approve, too. You'll have to watch his weight in middle age, though.'

Clemmie started to laugh and it turned into tears. 'Oh, how can I think about the future, with everything else that's going on?'

SEVENTEEN

Sunday evening

Ellie left Clemmie's house and backtracked to the nearest bus stop. She didn't want to hang around and wait for a cab to collect her. She didn't want to ring Thomas because he would be busy with Charles. She didn't know what she wanted.

Yes, she did. She wanted to kick somebody or something.

She had cleared up a number of mysteries and still didn't know whether or not Poppy's death had been an accident.

Everyone was properly accounted for on the night in question, except for Gordon, who couldn't have done it. Unfortunately. Apart from the fact that he couldn't have got up those stairs, he hadn't a motive to kill Poppy. Urrrgh!

Ellie used her leisure pass to get on the next bus which came, and sat down to grump away to herself. Eeeny, meeny, miney, mo. Which of them dunnit? Or had it been an accident? It might have been an accident. Wrong, wrong, wrong! Every feeling revolts. It was not an accident. It was planned.

No, not planned. It was an off-the-cuff thingy. Poppy was there, Gordon was there. He was angry. He threw her down the stairs? But, he couldn't. *She* threw herself down the stairs.

A spot of prayer is the answer. When stuck, pray. That's what Thomas always said. Of course, he was a lot better at it than she was. But oh well, here goes.

Please. It's up to you. I know Gordon did it but . . . No, I can't possibly know! Well, if you want me to do something about it, you'll have to give me a clue.

She looked up and to her dismay found she was not on the usual bus route. She hadn't intended to go this way. She was getting near Gordon's house, which was the last place on earth that she wanted to be. The bus was stopping. Good, she'd get off and phone for a cab. Phew!

There was a church on the brow of the hill, wasn't there? Was this where Gordon was supposed to go to a day centre for the disabled? What time was it? It was still quite light up to ten at night. She might walk that way, out of curiosity. There wouldn't be anyone there, anyway.

Lights. People going in? Some kind of youth club, perhaps? Yes, ripped jeans and long hair, huge earrings and stilettos. Shruggy shoulders for the boys and bare shoulders for the girls. Mikey would have a ball here, or would he say it was juvenile? Yes, probably. He wasn't a joiner, was he?

'Can I help you?' Middle aged, paunchy, shaved head. Man in charge.

Ellie tried to think what she needed to know. 'Sorry, wrong night to come. I was told there was a day centre here for disabled people.'

'Sure, we use the same rooms. You want a look?'

'That would be kind. I represent a local charity, and someone said . . . but I like to see these things for myself.'

'Bless you, yes.' He raised his voice. 'Not that door!'

'Sorry!' floated back. A door slammed.

'Kids!' he said. 'A baker's dozen tonight, and every one a challenge. Three adults between thirteen kids ought not to be a problem, but . . .' He shrugged.

Ellie nodded. Kids, indeed. Mikey times twelve. No, thirteen. This man had his work cut out.

He showed her around. She saw a hall, currently occupied by youths of both sexes scrimmaging in a soft-ball game; a servery leading out of a kitchen; a couple of smaller rooms. Scuff marks on cream paint, a cracked windowpane. The man indicated locked cupboards. 'Equipment for the day centre, for the uniformed organizations and for the nursery. There's afternoon and evening lectures, slots for the uniformed organizations, committee meetings and so on. If you come during the week they can give you more information.'

'I was told about it by – now, what's his name? – in a wheelchair. Gordon. You know him?'

'Him?' A frown. A shrug. A cool tone of voice. 'He's generous with his time and money.' Ellie got the impression that Gordon wasn't Mr Popular with this man.

She said, 'I can see the building is well-used.'

He grimaced. 'A bit run-down, you mean? We're always looking for funding. The budget cuts, you know. Yes, we could do with some decorating. It's ongoing, because the building's in use all the time. I don't mind getting up a work party to redecorate, but the cost . . .' He raised his voice, 'I can see you!'

Muffled laughter. A trace of cigarette smoke drifted down the corridor. 'I need eyes in the back of my head.'

'I'm full of admiration.' And she was.

They turned back into the hall, where the ball game had ended and, under supervision, a couple of youths were setting up a projector while a girl fiddled with some sort of sound system.

'Ahha,' said Ellie. 'Is that one of those state-of-the-art projector things that throws pictures on the wall? I remember the days when we had slide shows and portable screens which toppled over in the slightest draught.' To her great pleasure, a cartoon figure appeared on the wall.

'On Sunday evenings we have a video. They use the equipment during the week, too. Lectures, educational, that sort of thing.'

'Yes,' said Ellie, staring as two youths backed into the hall, fighting with . . . lasers? No, pens which shot out a beam of light.

The man in charge lifted the lasers from the boys with effortless ease. 'Now, now. These aren't toys, you know.'

Ellie was interested. 'Are those the pointers that lecturers use to highlight different things on a screen? They have quite a range, don't they?'

'These aren't true lasers. These are telescopic pen-pointers, see?' He extended and then collapsed them again. 'You can get all sorts on the Internet. I believe military lasers can inter-fere with planes coming into Heathrow by throwing a beam into the pilot's eyes. Dangerous.'

'Indeed.' Ellie felt as if she were sleepwalking. 'Thank you so much. My name is Ellie Quicke, by the way. I have a trust fund for local charitable purposes. I'll get someone to come round and have a look at what you're doing. They'll contact you beforehand. Would you mind not mentioning my visit to anyone for the time being? We have so many requests for funds, I don't want to raise false hopes.'

'You got it. I'm zipped.'

And, probably, he was.

She walked outside into the evening air and sat down on a nearby bench. So now she knew how Gordon had done it. With a pocket pointer of the type used in the day centre as a lecturer's aid. A military laser would have been unnecessarily powerful at such short range, but a pocket pointer, shooting straight into someone's eyes as they started down the stairs . . .?

With malice aforethought.

Not caring how much damage was done.

Not even particularly aiming to kill.

To hurt, yes. Lashing out because he'd been hurt.

And, he'd got the wrong girl.

Ellie felt limp. She got out her phone and tried Lesley's number.

'What!' Lesley was not amused at being interrupted.

'I know who killed Poppy, why and how. Interested?'

'Can't it wait till morning?' Languorous, sated. In bed?

'I suppose so. I haven't any proof, but perhaps you can get some.'

A groan. 'All right. I'll come round first thing tomorrow morning and you can tell me all about it. Till then . . . goodnight!'

Monday, mid-morning

Thomas rolled into the house, looking drained.

Ellie said, 'Breakfast or bed?'

'Breakfast and then bed. I got through to Marge a couple of hours ago, and she came straight over. She'll see he comes to no harm.'

'Confession was good for the soul?' Putting a large glass of orange juice in front of him and reaching for the frying pan. 'Two eggs, bacon, and anything else I can find?'

'Wonderful.' A deep sigh. 'Poor man.'

'I know you can't tell me . . .?'

'Marge told me, and it wasn't in confidence. She says that Charles had a thing about Gordon when they were all at school together. Gordon was half flattered and half annoyed by it. Even in those days he was fixated on Juno, who wasn't interested but did go out with him now and then. Juno wanted a career. Ray was playing the field, and so was Poppy.'

'And Marge?' Throwing tomatoes and mushrooms into the pan, Ellie switched on the toaster.

'Like Juno she wanted a career, but on the night of the party everyone got drunk and paired off. Ray with Poppy, Gordon with Juno, et cetera. To her surprise, Marge found Charles pursuing her, and . . . well, she enjoyed it. He swore he'd long got over Gordon, that it was nobody but Marge for him in future. They got married the following year and—'

'She found that he hadn't really got over Gordon after all?' Ellie switched the kettle on and flipped the bacon over.

'It was all right for a while. They had a couple of children, who are now grown up and flown the nest. Over the years, Marge kept up with Juno and Poppy. They acted as godmothers for each other's children, used to babysit for one another.'

'Marge was Clemmie's godmother. How did she feel about Clemmie's birth?'

A shrug. 'She understood how it had been. She said she wouldn't have minded a tumble in the hay with the man concerned herself. She loves Clemmie, wishes the girl would let her do more for her. Marge is no fan of Gordon's, said he was a master of mental abuse and it was a wonder that Juno had stayed sane. She knew all about Juno and Gordon trying for another child, and failing. It was Charles who volunteered to take Gordon to get the result of his fertility tests, because Gordon's car was having its MOT and the girls were both working. Gordon told Charles the bad news that he was infertile, Charles tried to console him, and they ended up in hospital.'

Ellie eased a spoonful of baked beans on to an overflowing plateful. 'Guilt. Which explains why Charles will do anything for Gordon nowadays. Marge kept the marriage going for a while?'

'She did, but Charles was never the same to her after that, and after a while he began experimenting with other men, so she cut her losses. She hasn't been interested enough to try matrimony again, but she still has some fondness for him.'

'Poor Marge. Poor Charles.'

'Not poor Gordon?'

'He may have been warped by what happened to him, but he didn't need to treat Clemmie and Juno so badly, and he certainly didn't need to kill Poppy, even if it was manslaughter and not murder.'

Thomas temporarily suspended operations on his food. 'Light of my life, explain!'

'He meant to get Juno, of course.' Two rounds of toast were whizzed on to Thomas's side plate and she depressed the plunger on the cafetiere. 'Would you like some fruit for afters? I've told Lesley all about it, and she's getting a warrant to search Gordon's house, hoping to find the lecturer's torch which he used to dazzle whoever came to the top of the stairs at The Magpie. Gordon was in a terrible temper. He was obsessed with the idea of getting Clemmie convicted for fraud, but no one except Charles would take him seriously. He was furious that Juno had gone off with Poppy to consult behind his back. He was also afraid that she was seeing someone else.'

'Someone else? Any cream for my coffee?'

He wasn't usually allowed cream in his coffee, but perhaps she could make an exception today. She fished a carton of double cream out of the fridge and handed it over. She said, 'The god in the machine. The shadow who protected Clemmie. The man who Gordon called the chocolate soldier. And, above all, the knitting.'

'You've lost me.' His eyelids drooped. He sipped coffee and relaxed. Thomas could neck down a pint of strong coffee and go to sleep straight away. Ellie couldn't so much as look at a cup of weak coffee after teatime. Everyone's different.

'Up to bed with you,' she said. 'You go and sleep it off. I'm expecting a couple of phone calls. If I have to go out, I'll leave you a note to say where I've gone.'

* * *

The first phone call came at lunchtime.

Lesley, on her mobile. 'Phew, Ellie! Talk about mad, bad and dangerous to know! Although I can't say I saw any charm, whereas Byron was supposed to be charming, wasn't he?'

'Gordon didn't attack you?'

'Not me, no. I had taken someone with me when I asked him to come down to the station. Someone large and capable. I don't think he'd have taken any notice of a woman by herself.'

'Did you find any evidence?'

'Evidence of hate. He's scrawled her name all over the bedroom walls, calling her every name under the sun. He's pulled all her clothes out of the cupboards and sprayed them with chemicals. Smashed all her toiletries.'

'No pointer-pen lights?'

'Two, on a ledge in the kitchen, which was a pigsty, by the way. He says they're for lecturing and that's what he uses them for. They don't leave any trace when you throw the beam in someone's eyes. We can't get him for that.'

Ellie sank into a chair. 'You can't get him for anything?'

'Oh, yes. Nice and tight. He asked for a solicitor. We got him one. He started quiet and crescendoed to fury. His solicitor tried to stop him, but he was unstoppable. Out it all came. It's all Juno's fault, by the way. She ought to have been at the office. She'd said that was where she was going. He knew, he just knew, that she was meeting her lover there. He'd smelled the man on her, he was justified in teaching her a lesson, and that's what he did. He drove himself to The Magpie, got out of the car and manoeuvred himself across the pavement with two sticks. He wanted to surprise her so he didn't ring the bell. He took the spare key she'd had cut recently but had forgotten to take into work. He opened the door and called out to her to come down and, when she came to the top of the stairs, he used the torch and got her in the eyes. She lost her balance and tumbled down. And it was all her fault that it wasn't the right woman. Juno was responsible for her sister's death, not him.'

'You got it on tape?'

'You bet. He said he had every right to discipline his own

wife and that it was only a matter of time till she came home and he was going to give her the hiding of her life when she did. As for her daughter, well, that was another story, and when we'd heard what he had to say about her, she'd be locked up for life!'

'Irrational, would you say?'

'Very. We charged him with manslaughter and he went berserk and tried to ram his way out of the interview room. He threw his solicitor a punch because the man had tried to stop Gordon incriminating himself. He's been remanded in custody and there'll be tests and hearings and the Lord only knows what.'

'They won't let him out straight away, will they? Not without warning us?'

'One moment he was threatening to sue everyone in sight, plus the Man in the Moon, and the next he went all cold and wouldn't speak. Except to discharge his solicitor, who seemed very happy to escape. I was relieved to leave the room, too. I deal with all sorts, Ellie; you know how it is. Fraud, drink, drugs; stabbings and brutal beatings; domestics which leave the victim scarred for life. But it's rare for me to feel as if I'm being taken over by . . . well, you'll laugh . . . evil.' Lesley tried on a laugh for size. It didn't fit very well. A sigh. 'Well, that's another case tidied up, thanks to you.'

'Thank Gerald and Marika. Thank your instincts, which refused to let you accept the verdict of accident.'

'And, well, just "thanks", Ellie. You know? In general terms. For this and that.' A change of tone. 'You say Susan found herself a suitable bridesmaid's dress? I should have asked you to be matron of honour.'

Lesley didn't really mean it. It was just a compliment. Ellie was pleased, though. It was good to be appreciated. 'See you at the church. Don't be late.'

'As if!' Lesley rang off.

Ellie rang Marge and told her the good news. Gordon had been charged with manslaughter and remanded in custody.

'Thank God for that,' said Marge. 'I think we can all breathe more easily now. Even Charles.'

'He's asleep now?'

'Sound. Your husband is something else. Charles says he was suicidal when Thomas arrived on the doorstep and talked him down off the proverbial window ledge. I understand it took all night. Your man called me at eight and I came straight over. Charles was calm enough by then. Poor old soul. There's no great harm in him, you know. We'll always be friends, no matter what. He's going to take some time off, and we'll go on that cruise we'd talked about.'

Ellie said, 'That's good news. So, on to the multi-million-dollar question. I need to see Juno. I have a list of various properties on your books in this area which might have interested her. Would you like to point me in the right direction, or get me an invitation to visit her in her new home?'

A gurgle of laughter. 'There are no flies on you, Mrs Quicke, but you're way out on that one.'

'Ah. The soldier made his own arrangements?'

'Precisely.'

'Was it he who collected Juno's laptop from The Magpie office?'

'I believe so. I'll get her to phone you. Anything else?'

'Do you know if Clemmie passed her driving test?'

'She doesn't take it till one, does she? I'm sure we'll hear as soon as she's done.'

Within the hour there was another phone call for Ellie. Would she like to call round at teatime, address supplied?

'Yes, please. Have you heard about Clemmie's—'

The phone clicked off. Oh well, she'd find out soon enough.

It was a large house, almost as large as Ellie's, and much nearer to Ealing Broadway. It was also a secure residence, with remote-controlled access via wrought-iron gates. It sparkled with loving care and attention to detail. There was a double garage at one side, whose doors were closed. The forecourt was paved with bricks, the paintwork and windows gleamed, there were hanging baskets spilling over with colour and ditto in wooden planters here and there. Dust was not allowed to settle here. There was a car which Ellie recognized in the forecourt. What was the Cordovers' solicitor doing here? Ah, perhaps Juno was at last beginning to make decisions about the future. Or to draft a new will?

As Ellie reached for the entryphone button on the gates, the solicitor emerged from the house and entered his car. The gates opened and he drove out, as she walked in.

Someone was standing in the porch, holding the front door open. Waiting for her.

The chocolate soldier, as Gordon had insisted on calling him? Well, he had the coffee-and-cream skin and handsome features that characterized Clemmie. His bearing was that of a soldier, but he was in mufti, wearing fawn chinos and a roll-neck jumper. He had quite a presence. Strong, patient, reserved and intelligent. Like Clemmie.

'Mrs Quicke?' He held out his hand to Ellie, assessing her with Clemmie's eyes. 'Hugh Major. My surname is Major, which is confusing, since I retired from the army with the rank of major. Juno is expecting you.'

He led the way through a tiled-floor hall to a sunny sitting room with French windows open on to a riotously colourful, south-facing garden. Major (retired) Hugh might impose order on the house, but in the garden he'd allowed his love of beauty to run rampant, with a close-cut lawn overhung with climbing roses, mounds of lavender and box, and beds full of herbaceous plants. There was even a fishpond. What, no gazebo? Yes, there was, at the back.

Coming from the shadowy hall into the light, Ellie blinked. The sitting room was furnished in quiet good taste, with a mixture of antiques and modern pieces. There were flowers everywhere, but the most beautiful thing in it was the woman lying on a chaise longue with a light rug over her knees. Her fair hair was loose around her shoulders, and she was wearing something light and lacy in blue.

She held out her hand to Ellie, saying, 'Thank you. Thank you a thousand times.' A sapphire and diamond ring glinted on her left hand. An engagement ring?

Hugh moved behind the chaise longue to put his hand on her shoulder. Juno gave him such a fond, tender look in return that tears came to Ellie's eyes.

'Do take a seat. You'll have some tea?' Juno swung her legs round.

Hugh said, 'You stop there. You promised you'd rest.'

'I will, I will.' Juno was laughing, almost mischievous. And to Ellie, 'He's a dreadful bully. Won't let me do anything.'

Hugh's face relaxed into a smile. 'As if anyone could make you do something you didn't want to do!'

Juno grimaced. 'There's lots I've done that I didn't want to do.'

Ellie said, 'Duty is a hard taskmaster, isn't it?'

'Oh, you understand, too!' Eagerly. Juno looked back up at Hugh. 'Hugh understood, even when it almost tore him apart. I know most people would say I was stupid to stay with Gordon, but I'm glad I did, in a way. I couldn't have broken my marriage vows easily, but I'm sad, too, because Hugh and I have missed so much.'

A stir in the doorway and there was Marika with the tea tray. Of course, she would be there, and Gerald would drop in on his way home from work that evening. 'We owe you a debt of gratitude, Mrs Quicke. You'll take some tea with us?'

'I will. But only on condition that you tell me the whole story from the very beginning. I've got most of it, I think, but there's still bits missing.'

'The very beginning? I suppose you mean the night of our eighteenth birthday . . .'

EIGHTEEN

Juno said, 'Poppy was the party girl; me not so much. Poppy had been sleeping with Ray for some months. I'd paired off with Gordon by default, really. Why did I let him make love to me? I really don't know. Because everyone else was doing it? He told me I was frigid because I didn't enjoy it, and I accepted his judgement because I knew no better.

'Then came the party. We lived in a big house with a garden which stretched down to a coppice at the end. It was wonderful for parties, with fairy lights in the trees. Poppy and I invited all our friends and of course there were one or two gatecrashers.'

Hugh said, 'I was one of the gatecrashers. I'd come down from the Midlands to stay with a friend before going overseas the next day. We'd heard that a girl called Poppy was having a birthday bash in a posh place, so we bought some beer and turned up. We introduced ourselves to Poppy and she said "the more, the merrier"!'

'Poppy loved parties,' said Juno, 'but I'm a fish out of water on such occasions, partly because I don't drink. Someone spiked the fruit punch which my mother had prepared. Gordon said I was being a party-pooper, that I ought to loosen up, so I had a glass. Before I knew what was happening, Gordon was leading me up – or rather down – the garden path. No, no excuses. Poppy had been down there that evening with Ray. Marge with Charles. I should have said "no", but I didn't.

'Gordon was quick and brutal as always. He was always so pleased with himself afterwards, while I felt violated. He said he didn't understand why I always made such a fuss about it because we were going to be married, weren't we? He told me to pull myself together and went straight back to the party. I wept, and I don't often cry.

'Which is where I came in,' said Hugh. 'My mate was dancing on the patio with a girl so I took a stroll down into the wood, and found this beautiful creature curled up under a tree, weeping her heart out. I knew she was one of the birthday girls, and I'd noticed she hadn't been throwing herself into the spotlight like her sister. I asked her if I could fetch someone for her—'

'And I said – stupid me – was it always so quick, and what was wrong with me that I never enjoyed it? I was such an innocent. I looked up at Hugh and saw kindness and compassion and strength. If Hugh had asked me then and there to leave the party and fly round the world with him, I'd have gone. He held me, so gently . . . and he kissed me and it was oh, so sweet.'

Juno smiled up at Hugh. 'He showed me what real loving could be. I had never known anything like it. He took such care of me, such tenderness.' She held his hand against her cheek, saying to Ellie, 'Eventually we went back up to the party. Hugh made me eat something and have a soft drink. We danced on the patio and I didn't want the evening ever to end.'

Hugh said, 'Then people started to leave. Suddenly Juno was surrounded by her guests, saying goodbye. One of them had lost a shoe and needed a taxi to get back home. Juno had to see to them. I watched from a distance as she spoke to each one, being kind and loving to them all. I was in a haze of love.

'Then my friend caught me by the arm and said we had to go. I suddenly remembered that I was due to go off to Germany the next day. We'd come on my friend's motorbike and, if I didn't leave with him then and there, I'd be stranded with my kit miles away and wouldn't be able to report for duty in time. So I asked one of the other guests for Juno's surname. He told me it was Smithson. I wrote down my own home address and gave it to him and made him promise he'd give it to Juno. He said he would . . .'

Juno said, 'By ill fortune Hugh had given his address to Ray, who passed it on to Gordon, because everyone knew that Gordon was my boyfriend and what did a gatecrasher want with Gordon's girlfriend? Can you believe our bad luck? Gordon put Hugh's address in his pocket and never told me. I didn't find it for over a year, when I was turning out Gordon's pockets to take his jacket to the cleaners.'

Hugh said, 'The following day I sent some poor householder crazy, ringing up asking for a girl he'd never heard of. I was distraught. But then I had to put her out of my mind – or try to – because I was off on my next posting.'

Juno said, 'I waited and waited for him to ring. And he didn't. I was terribly hurt because I'd fallen for him, big time. Life looked grey. I was being sick all the time. I thought I'd picked up a bug. Then Marika took me down to the doctor's, and I discovered I was pregnant.

'I told Gordon, thinking he'd turn tail and run, but he didn't. He assured me he was happy that I was pregnant and said that we must marry straight away. I told him I'd had an interlude with Hugh, and Gordon said I'd been conned as Hugh had left the party with his arms round another girl. I was devastated. I felt so ashamed that I'd taken Hugh seriously when he hadn't been serious about me. All the time Gordon knew that Hugh had tried to contact me after the party, and that he had Hugh's address in his pocket! Oh, when I discovered it . . .!

'But at the time, I couldn't think straight. Gordon said everything would be all right when we married, that he'd forgiven me my "little lapse" with Hugh and that we wouldn't talk about it any longer. Poppy turned up with a ring, too; only she was happy about it. So I let Gordon sweep me along into marriage. I ought to have gone on saying "no", but I didn't. Everything that happened after that was really my fault.'

Ellie said, 'Did Gordon ever really love you, or was he in love with what you represented: your money, your wealthy background?'

'I've asked myself that many a time. I think in the beginning he did love me, as much as he could love anyone but himself.'

'Was he a good husband?'

'Was he kind? No. It isn't in his nature. He was careful of my feelings at first, because my father had bought us a house each and set us up in the shop. Gordon liked it that I was bringing money to the marriage. He was training to be a solicitor, but that didn't go as well as he'd expected. He started to belittle me, I think because I was making a success of work and he wasn't. He made fun of me before our friends. But when my baby was born . . . oh boy! One look at Clemmie and I knew she was Hugh's child. She was mouth-wateringly gorgeous. I loved her to distraction.

'Gordon was shattered. Understandably. There were terrible scenes. He wanted me to give Clemmie up for adoption. I refused, and my parents backed me up. I offered to let Gordon divorce me, but Gordon didn't want that. In the end he said he'd accept the child as his own, if we could have another of our own straight away. Which we did try to do. And kept failing. Each month his temper got worse. I learned to keep Clemmie away from him. One day I turned out the pockets of Gordon's jacket before taking it to be dry-cleaned, and I found Hugh's home address in the Midlands. I thought he ought to know about the child, so I wrote to him, telling him about Clemmie and saying that all was well and I didn't want anything from him.

Hugh took up the tale. 'The letter wandered around the earth until it found me eventually, and on my next leave I arranged to see Juno and meet my daughter. Juno insisted it be in secret because Gordon was so touchy. So we met in the flat above The Magpie, and I fell in love all over again, this time with both mother and daughter. I begged Juno to leave Gordon. I'd never stopped thinking of her, fantasizing what it might be like to see her again. She refused to leave him. She said that rightly or wrongly she had married Gordon before God, and that she'd done him a great wrong by doing so. She did agree that I could be an unofficial godfather to Clemmie and, though I was not allowed to see her, I could send her gifts at birthdays and at Christmas and Juno would send me photos of her every now and again. I promised that if ever Clemmie was in need, I would be there for her. I put money on one side for her every month and have continued to do so to this day.'

Juno said, 'Gordon did try to be kind to Clemmie until he found he couldn't sire a child, and then there was the accident, which didn't improve his temper. I think he began to hate her then. The best times were when he ignored her. He refused to pay her nursery fees, or for her private school.'

'I paid them,' said Hugh, 'for about four and half years, until The Magpie was doing so well that Juno said she could afford them from that time on, and that I should save for my future instead. Which I did.'

Marika was at her knitting again. 'You've missed a bit, Juno.'

'We . . . ll,' said Juno, blushing slightly, 'Gordon was never very easy to live with, and after the accident he couldn't perform his usual duties, so I started to go away for the odd weekend—'

Hugh grinned. 'What she means is that we met at intervals whenever I was stationed in this country. We didn't think anyone would find out.'

'I guessed,' said Marika, pulling wool out of the ball. 'And so did your father, of course. Also I think Clemmie suspected there was something going on between her mother and her godfather.'

'But she didn't *know*,' said Juno, 'and neither did Gordon, though he did suspect. He accused me of breaking my marriage vows, asked if I didn't feel guilty. And of course I did. I knew it was wrong but I couldn't seem to help myself. I told Gordon I'd never walk out on him and I meant it, but he couldn't leave it alone. He has a bitter tongue. Every now and then he'd bring it up and go on and on about it till he'd reduced me to tears and, as I said, I don't cry easily.

'When Clemmie got into that spot of trouble abroad, Gordon threw her out. Hugh was with me when Clemmie eventually reached me on the phone and told me what had happened. Hugh immediately said that he'd pay off her loan, but by that time Clemmie had been to see my parents and got refinanced. We were so proud of her!'

Hugh said, 'I sent her a couple of hundred pounds, which was as much as Juno thought Clemmie would accept from her unofficial "godfather". I wanted to pay the rent of the house she moved into, but Juno wouldn't let me do that. She said it was good for Clemmie to stand on her own two feet.'

Juno said, 'Strangely, things were a little easier after Clemmie left home because Gordon didn't see her every day. I honestly thought we might jog along for the rest of our lives . . . until Ray found out how many buy-to-let houses there are now and told Gordon, who was livid. He couldn't bear to think that I, the whore, was doing so well in business, while he, the injured party, was living on the allowance I made him. He demanded that I sell my share of the business and devote my life to him . . . and there I struck. I couldn't bear the thought of becoming a full-time carer. I like getting the right clothes on people so that they feel good. I love taking run-down houses and doing them up and letting them out to people who appreciate them.'

Hugh said, 'Again, I begged her to leave him. By this time I'd been retired from the army for nigh on three years, and I've built up a nice little business for myself in security. Not guard dogs and bouncers, but in the IT world. My offices are upstairs here and, unless interrupted by beautiful women in distress, I work twenty-four/seven.'

Ellie said, 'I think I know what happened on the night of Poppy's death, but can you confirm it?'

'Gordon called a meeting at our parents' house and threatened to put Clemmie in jail for fraud. Charles backed him up. Poppy was distraught, what with one thing and another, so she and I decided to go over to The Magpie office to get away from the men, using the excuse that we wanted to look at the evidence against Clemmie. Frankly, neither of us was thinking straight that night. I wasn't feeling too good, either, so after we'd talked things over for a while without coming to any definite conclusions, I called a cab and went home. Poppy stayed on to check her bank balance, worrying about how to pay Ray off. And that was the last I saw of her.' Tears stood out in her eyes, but she refused to cry.

Marika lifted her head. 'You're missing a bit out again.'

Juno smiled, looking back up at Hugh. 'Yes. Six weeks earlier, Hugh and I had had a weekend together. We'd always been so careful, I can't think how it happened, I thought I was starting the menopause but—'

'It was another baby on the way? Which was why you went to the doctor early on the morning of the funeral? Did you tell Hugh?'

'I didn't have a chance to tell anyone. I was in shock. I just about managed to get home, get changed and go off to the funeral. I couldn't think straight, couldn't decide what to do. I had to tell Gordon and Hugh, I knew that, but . . . how? And when? Then, in the car going on to Ray's house for the reading of the will, Gordon boasted that he'd killed my sister, but that nobody would ever be able to prove it. He said he was going to denounce Clemmie as the murderer. That was the moment my marriage ended. So, when my parents wanted to take me home, I decided to disappear, to give myself time to think, to get away from Gordon and finally to be with Hugh. So I got out of my parents' car, rang Hugh, and he brought me here. And here I plan to stay.'

Ellie said, 'You sent Hugh to fetch your laptop so you could continue to access your finances?'

'Indeed.' They smiled, happiness lightening their serious expressions. 'We're a little worried about how Clemmie's going to take it, Mrs Quicke. How did you know, by the way?'

'Your mother's knitting, and you looked so ill on the day of the funeral.'

They all laughed, relaxing. Marika offered another cup of tea.

'And now,' said Ellie, 'how do you see the future?'

Juno sighed and moved into a more comfortable position. 'You've all been very patient, waiting for me to feel better and take hold of life again. And yes, Mrs Quicke, we were also waiting for you to sort Gordon and Charles out. I know things won't be easy for any of us for a while, and there's a horrid cloud hanging over Gordon and his future, but there's one or two things I can do straight away. I've had my solicitor here today, made a new will and started divorce proceedings. Once I get back to work, I shall reorganize The Magpie, setting up a limited company and making Celine and Clemmie directors. Neither Laura nor Ruth want any more responsibility, but they will get a hike in salary to make up for my taking some time out.'

She flashed a smile at Hugh. 'Yes, he knows I intend to go on working. We're both workaholics, but we've made a pact to spend as much time with one another as we do at work. And, if he doesn't stick to it, I can always walk away because I'm my own woman.'

'And, my wife-to-be,' said Hugh.

Juno laughed. 'Twenty years later than anticipated.' She turned back to Ellie, her smile fading. 'I've instructed the solicitor to write to Ray and to Gordon saying that I will make over to them the houses they lived in and their cars, in quittance of all claims on me. Since they both signed pre-nups, and in view of their present circumstances, I think they should agree.'

'That's generous,' said Ellie. 'I suppose they will sell up. Both need money: Gordon for his defence in court, and Ray to gamble. I'm sorry to break some bad news, but before you officially hand the houses over to Ray and Gordon, I suspect they'll need some attention. Gordon was in a destructive mood. I suggest you get someone to rescue any bits and pieces you would like to keep and get a cleaning team to go through the place. Oh, and to mend at least one window. The same at Ray's.'

'I'll do that,' said Marika. 'I've got a stronger stomach than Juno at the moment.'

Ellie nodded. Yes, that would be best. 'Did you know that Trixie has moved out?'

'She phoned us,' said Marika, counting stitches. 'Wanted our blessing, if you please. I asked her if she would like any of her mother's bits and pieces, and she said she wouldn't mind her mother's jewellery, but she wants it put into a safety deposit box till she asks for it. She showed more common sense than I expected.'

Ellie delved into her handbag. 'Which reminds me. I put a new combination on Poppy's safe, and wrote it down. Yes, here it is. Juno, you'd better keep that somewhere safe.'

Juno smiled. 'Mother said from the start that we could trust you. Now, I can't help Ray any more than Poppy could, but I suppose if Trixie's latest initiative fails we'll help her to start again.' She looked at her watch. 'We've invited Clemmie to join us this evening. She's out looking for a car to buy at the moment.'

'She's passed her test first go?' Ellie was pleased.

'Of course,' said Hugh. 'Isn't she my daughter? I can't wait to meet her properly. I'm torn between "Will she like me?" and "If she's as stroppy as her mother, will I ever get a word in edgeways?"'

Tuesday morning

A late breakfast. Both Ellie and Thomas were feeling languid.

Thomas said, 'Shall we take the day off? Fly to the Scilly Isles and watch the puffins . . . except I'm not sure which islands the puffins live on.'

Ellie put the last of the breakfast things in the dishwasher. 'It would be good to go out for the day. No phones, mind. No emails, no texts. Just the two of us. Shall I make sandwiches?'

'Let's splash out on lunch at a restaurant.'

The phone rang.

So did the doorbell.

Ellie hesitated. 'We could pretend we're out.'

The doorbell was pressed again, with even more force.

'Diana,' said Ellie. 'Wanting me to babysit?'

Neither of them moved. They heard someone leave a message on the phone.

Thomas's conscience kicked in and he got to his feet. 'I'd better answer it, I suppose.'

Someone leaned on the doorbell. Diana intended to be heard, didn't she?

Ellie groaned, but followed Thomas into the hall. He was already on the phone, saying, 'Yes, I agree. It is an emergency. Do you want me to come round to you straight away, or shall I meet you somewhere?'

So much for their day off.

Ellie opened the door and found not one, not two, but three people in the porch.

Little Evan launched himself at her, immobilizing her by the simple expedient of hugging her knees. 'Go to park! Now!'

Diana, all black and white and barely concealed impatience said, 'My nanny's off sick and I've got appointments double-booked, so you can look after him for a bit, can't you?'

But it was the sight of the other woman which caused Ellie's mind to go into a whirl.

Well, not really a woman. More of a grown-up girl. Long blonde hair, big blue eyes, a slender figure and a will of iron.

Angelica: the pretty, pushy sister of Lesley Milburn's fiancé; the one who had tried to rot up Susan by picking an unsuitable bridesmaid's dress for her. The one who'd tried to move into Lesley's flat when the wedding had been called off. The one who aimed to have a good time in London with lots of parties.

Angelica, surrounded by luggage. Innocence shining from every long, false eyelash. With pathos in her voice, a teardrop ready to fall and a sob at the ready, Angelica said, 'I've nowhere to go. Susan said you might have a room you'd let me stay in, just till I can get something more suitable? I'm in such trouble!'

Ellie wondered what would happen if she slammed the door in their faces and took off on a flight to the moon . . .